Just a Boy Friend

Just a Boy Friend

Lucy Keeling

Book 1 – Friends

Where heroes are like chocolate – irresistible!

Published 2021 by Choc Lit Limited
Penrose House, Crawley Drive, Camberley, Surrey GU15 2AB, UK
www.choc-lit.com

ISBN 978-1-78189-462-0

Printed and bound in Great Britain
by Clays Ltd, Elcograf S.p.A.

To my gorgeous boys,
please don't read this book.

Acknowledgements

A big thank you to my early readers, Brenda, Charlie, Abby, Gwen, Kim, Helen, Michelle & Clare. Thank you also to the people that propped me up with cake and beer and allowed me to go on and on about it, I'm looking at you Terri, Emma, Nic Nic, Nic, Michelle and Sarah. All of you gave me so much support and I will be forever grateful.

Thank you to my wonderful family you have all helped me in so many ways whether you know it or not. Thank you as well to my amazing Twitter & Facebook families especially Lucy, Lucy, Emily, Jeanna, Eilidh, Sandy and Rebecca. You guys have inspired me and kept me going every step of the way, this story would not exist without all of your encouragement.

To Heather and the lovely lot at Rescue Kitties who gave me quite the insight when it comes to fostering kittens, please go and check them out if you can.

To my gorgeous husband, thank you for your unceasing support and continued belief in my success and for getting my MacBook fixed, in a very literal sense this story would not exist without you.

To the wonderful people at Choc Lit and also my amazing editor, who turned my story into something extra special. Thank you as well to the rest of the Choc Lit family for your support and best wishes.

A big thank you to the actual star we were searching for Christine Penhall. I am so glad we got to do this together.

The biggest thank you to the wonderful people at *Your Cat Magazine* and especially the Choc Lit tasting panel: Dimi E, Lauren Mc, Donna M, Lucie W, Sharon W, Carol D, Joy B, Allie L, Anne E, Cordy S and Heather P. Whilst searching for a star they found me instead, and if I ever meet any of you in real life, the chocolate, the brews, the wine, the cocktails, the hugs are on me. Thank you.

Finally, thank you to you dear reader, I'm so very grateful that you bought my book I don't have the words to describe it x

Chapter One

'Erm, Soph did you mean to upload this video?' Polly's brow wrinkled, her eyes concentrating on her phone as she sat on the floor, her back to the sofa, a tiny black ball of a kitten curled quietly in her lap. Mya reached over, moving Polly's red hair out of the way to look at her screen.

'Have you just poked yourself in the eye with the mascara wand?' Mya started to laugh. 'Soph, this is internet gold!'

Sophie carefully scooted across to them as fast as she could from her position sat on the floor with another kitten – all white except for a black patch on its face – pawing at her leggings.

'What are you talking about? Show me.' Reaching over, one hand carefully cradling the kitten on her legs, Sophie shuffled until she could see the screen as well.

'Wait, no that's not right, that can't be right.' Sophie snatched the phone from Polly's hand. 'No, no, no. How has this happened?' Sophie asked no one in particular as she scanned the video.

Polly looked nervously towards Mya. Mya grinned and shrugged, returning her attention to the third tuxedo-marked kitten who was playing with the gold bangles that hung on her wrist, alternately trying to swipe at them and bite them.

'Right, I've sorted everybody out downstairs, how are my foster kids and babysitters?' Paige asked as she strolled into her front room, her hoody on back to front as the fourth and final kitten poked it's head out of her hood, surveying the scene in front of it. 'Aww they're having a great time playing on the floor with you guys. So time for a catch-up. Wait, what's the problem?'

Sophie hadn't moved. The phone was still clutched in her hand, and she was leaning slightly towards Polly. But when she did finally look up from the phone, her face was pale behind the foundation she had expertly applied and her brown eyes were wide in shock.

'I've uploaded the wrong bloody video,' she whispered. 'I can't believe it. I must have checked a million times. I've always been so paranoid. What have I done? How could I have been so careless?'

There was a moment or two of silence.

'Well, it's done now. What's the worst thing on it?' Paige asked with a smirk, as she too sat on the floor that was partially covered in newspaper so that the kittens could play and pee freely.

'It's not funny. It's completely unprofessional. It must be the non-edited video, the one where I poke myself in the eye with the mascara wand and run around for five minutes swearing like my dad when he's arguing with the sat nav!' Sophie groaned.

'Yeah but so what? It's just a video on social media. Nobody was naked, nobody was injured, apart from you. Is there the slightest chance you're overreacting?' Mya asked. There was a sucking of teeth sound as Polly winced, already anticipating Sophie's reaction.

'How can you even say that? You know how important this is to me. I have to be professional. I have a brand. And this... wrong video could seriously set my career back. I spent ages editing it as well, and yet somehow, this is what I've uploaded. It's just what I don't need at the moment.'

Her number of followers had at one point been increasing steadily, but lately, not so much. Sophie was scared to admit that they had become sort of stuck. That was bad news. If her numbers didn't increase then what was the point? She was delivering make-up advice to around thirty thousand dedicated followers. That was fine, and to a lot of people that would be successful, but it wasn't enough for what she wanted. For what she had planned. For what she deserved. But considering her latest video it might be a moot point.

What make-up company would want her reviewing their products after this?

'By now I'm supposed to have over one hundred thousand followers across my platforms, companies are supposed to be begging me to use their products and they're nowhere to be seen. I gave up so much for this. I've taken so much flack. So yeah, this wrong video is *massive*. Now I'm going to have to re-write my business plan. I'll never not be a barmaid.'

Paige coughed before muttering, 'You're welcome, by the way.'

'You know I didn't mean it like that. Thank you again for letting me come back and be your barmaid. I really am grateful.'

'Sorry, Soph. I get the importance, I just don't think it will matter as it shows a more human side to you. Your fans might love it. You might even get new subscribers,' Mya said as she held her kitten up to her face to give it a quick nuzzle before picking up her own phone.

Polly reached over and placed her hand on Sophie's arm. 'What can you do?'

Sophie took a deep breath. 'I could probably delete the video, if it's not gone very far. How many people have seen it? How many comments are there?' Sophie looked down at Polly's Facebook page trying to analyse some of the statistics together in her head. It had been scheduled to upload an hour ago so maybe she could delete it if only a few people had seen it. But who was she kidding? An hour on social media was as good as forever. Just then a notification flashed up across the screen.

Your Friend Mya Chatterjee just shared this video.

Sophie's face shot up. 'Mya, what the hell?'

Mya looked up from her phone and grinned. 'What? It's hilarious. You should cut everything but the mascara bit. Then you'd at least be a decent GIF, if not completely viral!'

Mya was almost snorting she was laughing so hard, her

shiny brown hair falling over her face, the kitten in her lap instantly trying to bite at it. Polly gave her a dirty look, and Paige had a small smile on her face, but was otherwise quietly observing.

'Too many people have seen it already, and people are sharing it. It's too late.' Sophie sighed as she finally leaned back, getting herself into a more comfortable position on the floor before handing the phone back to Polly, Sophie's kitten leaping off her lap to play with Mya's.

Her friends might not understand, but this had the potential to set her back significantly. All the hard work, the thousands of followers that she had built up over the last six months didn't happen by magic. It happened with a carefully constructed and well thought out plan that was normally carefully executed. She knew she was on the cusp of breaking through as a social media influencer. If she was right, then companies would soon be sending her products to review, from there she would be invited to review even more products, her videos would be licensed and paid for and then even more options would be available, maybe even her own line of make-up and cosmetics. She had been so close and now all she was... was embarrassed, and frankly annoyed at herself.

Sophie felt defeated, and looked at Paige for support. Paige had been left an inheritance and created her dream bar. It had been difficult for her at times, and the whole thing nearly fell through, both literally and financially, but in the end she did it, just as she swore she would. She hadn't been fazed for a second. Sophie really wished she could have some of that quiet confidence; it would be so much easier if she had a crystal ball and could see into the future and know that her goal was achievable. It was incredibly hard to stay the course when the odds were stacked against her.

Paige smiled softly as if she had heard Sophie's plea for assistance. 'I don't think that this is going to be as bad as you think it is. Mya's right. It makes you appear more human.

People adore watching other people's mistakes.' She reached down and pulled the now sleeping kitten out of her hood, placing her onto one of the huge cushions decorating her flat. Standing up she walked through the open plan apartment towards the kitchen area and returned with her hands clinking. Before Sophie knew what was happening a very welcome, and a very large, shot of tequila had been placed in front of her.

'Drink this, and come up with a new plan,' Paige instructed.

'Thanks,' Sophie said. She downed the shot, hissing as she put the shot glass on the coffee table. To calm her thoughts, she looked around Paige's flat. A large sectional sofa in a number of primary colours was central to the open plan and wooden flooring. There was a large TV screen in front. But the real entertainment in the room was in the form of four fluffy little kittens. There were newspapers and litter trays scattered about, with cat toys, cat treats and toilet roll innards all around and on the usually clear coffee table.

The apartment was a decent size, which wasn't surprising considering it covered the entire floor space of the bar below, which Paige also owned. It was located in one of the quieter – and therefore cheaper when she purchased it – areas of Manchester, although it was quickly becoming the new stomping ground, and prices as well as eateries were going up everywhere. If Sophie was a betting person, she might have thought that Paige had predicted the areas success.

Sophie was lucky that Paige's business had succeeded, because it meant that she had been able to ask Paige for her old bartending job back when she had come back to Manchester. She'd tried to use her qualifications to become a freelance make-up artist, but the industry was so competitive, the money not all that great, and with all the travelling she couldn't put the time and energy into the dream career that she wanted.

Bartending meant she had more time to become a social media influencer. What she could do without, however, was uploading the wrong sodding video. She still hadn't taken her own phone out of her pocket. She couldn't bring herself to face it. The notifications that normally gave her such a thrill would now be indicative of her cock-up.

Sophie stroked the kitten that had returned to pawing her legs and felt rather than saw Polly and Mya both watching her, no doubt cautiously.

'It's OK, I'm not going to bite,' Sophie said, her tone suggesting otherwise.

'Top her up please, Mya,' Paige requested, nodding back to the tequila on the coffee table.

'Here you go, Soph.' Mya passed her the shot glass, the only sound in the apartment the loud but still developing mewls of the kittens.

Sophie downed the second shot and looked around at the faces of her friends. Polly was absent-mindedly stroking the kitten in her lap that was still fast asleep, her attention fixed on Sophie, her face tight with concern. Sophie had known Polly since school and knew that Polly cared deeply and worried about those around her.

Mya's face had more of a 'suck it up buttercup' kind of vibe about it, which was pretty standard Mya really. Sophie had met Mya at college where they were both studying make-up. Mya hadn't lasted longer than two months, but they had stayed in touch and she had introduced Sophie to Paige and here the four women were years later, friends through thick and thin and kittens and make-up.

'Well, am I boring? Is that what it is?' Sophie asked, her perfectly shaped eyebrows flying up to her head. She had done an hour long video about eyebrow shaping that she had yet to publish, she suspected it was too long and, if she was honest, just a little bit too technical, and by technical she meant boring.

'What rubbish are you spouting now?' Mya asked.

Sophie sighed. 'It's not just the mistake with the video. My numbers aren't great. Well, they're not bad, but they're just not increasing. They need to be a lot higher. They *have* to be a lot higher. So, is it me? Am I boring, because short of a personality transplant I'm not sure what I can do next?'

'Soph, I love you but shut up, you know that's not it,' Mya scoffed. 'What I will say, though, is that there is something missing. Your videos aren't the same as they used to be.'

'You don't seem as excited by it any more,' Polly said softly, before she resumed biting her lip.

'They're crap.' Sophie jumped, not realising that Paige had moved until she was sat down on the sofa behind her. 'They are and if you want to do this seriously, something has to change. There's only so many times I can watch you talk about how make-up suppliers come up with the names of the latest shade of lip gloss or whatever.'

As Paige's words sunk in, Sophie stopped to think about what her friends had said. She didn't doubt their honesty, though perhaps it would have been more welcome before she'd uploaded the wrong video. But even in her current frame of mind she knew that she could, on occasion, be a little precious about her ambition, and maybe, just maybe, wasn't the most open to criticism.

But was she becoming bored with it all? No, she knew that wasn't true. She still loved talking to people about make-up; how to put it on, how to combine it, what the latest looks were. She'd been playing with her mum's make-up and experimenting on her sisters' faces since she was little. And sharing her passion on social media always made her giddy, her heart beating that little bit faster just before she pressed the record button and again whenever her latest video was posted. The addictive thrill of seeing the likes and the comments and the stats increasing. Or she did when they were increasing in any case.

'I am serious about it. I want to continue, but the stats are pants.' Sophie took a deep breath, and rolled her shoulders. 'Oh God that's enough whining, I'm doing my own head in.

Give me suggestions on what I can do. I want this to work, I need this to work. Presuming that I haven't lost thousands of followers from my last video.'

If her friends were shocked at her request for their feedback they didn't show it, thankfully. Sophie knew that they were right and the only person who could really change anything was her, but she could ask for support and advice. After all she was not going to allow herself to fail. She had worked too hard at this to give in so quickly and her dedicated fan base wouldn't want her to give up either. If nothing else, Sophie was immensely proud of the small but mutually supportive community she had cultivated. Yes she had trolls – well, just the one – but any trolls were usually silenced by her supporters. Her videos on YouTube were watched fairly regularly by those that subscribed and by non-subscribers that stumbled across them by accident or recommendation. But there was nothing new happening. There was no way YouTube would be sending her any awards anytime soon. And the absolute last thing she wanted was to prove her mother right.

'OK,' said Polly, with the most reassuring smile she could muster. 'What about some specials? The one where you gave Mya a makeover got loads of views, so maybe you could do another one of those.'

Mya smiled and pouted, dropping her face towards her shoulder. 'I'm more than happy to have another makeover.' Mya didn't need a makeover, she was always flawlessly put together, one of those people that were effortlessly glamorous, not a glossy luxurious hair out of place, her golden brown skin always glowing. Sophie really wanted to dislike Mya sometimes.

'You're too gorgeous. You put people off. But, yes, maybe, I mean you did get the most hits, but then that could be randomers who aren't watching the videos for my make-up tips, if you know what I mean.'

Sophie raised an eyebrow and Mya grinned as she tossed her shampoo advert-ready hair over her shoulder, winking as Polly laughed at Mya's trademark move. Men and women all seemed to respond to Mya, as if she were some sort of siren. At college it had taken Sophie a few weeks before she could even say hello to Mya, she had been so in awe. When she did, she was immediately greeted with, 'Well, it took you long enough. When are we going out for a drink?' One very hilarious but completely drunkard weekend later they were best friends. Sophie had discovered that Mya's personality, and her attitude, was highly entertaining, if not sometimes troublemaking. Needless to say, while Sophie became a qualified make-up artist, Mya did not. What Mya did become was anybody's guess but she had quickly earned enough money in her mystery job to buy her own house and Sophie rented a room from her.

'What about where you do them? You've always said that the lighting wasn't that great?' Polly asked.

Before Sophie even had a chance to respond Mya cut in and announced, 'You're not remodelling my house just to get some light. I am not made of money. Besides, you're the one with the ideas, this is your baby, it really needs to come from you.'

'Well, I record them at the kitchen table, but I have to keep the curtains closed otherwise I would run the risk of having some of the garden in the background, and... well, you've seen the state of that. It's a shame because with the curtains open the kitchen gets the most natural light in the house, but unless we could afford—'

'I've told you already; I'm not made of money. Not yet, but we'll have to wait and see what happens on my next business trip. On that note, I need to get going as I have to pack before my early flight tomorrow. I assume you're staying here for a bit?' Mya asked as Sophie nodded. 'Don't worry, Sophie, you'll figure it out, if anyone can do it it's you.' Mya quickly poured and necked a shot of tequila, before grabbing her limited edition Mulberry handbag. She blew them all a kiss as she turned to leave, stopping only for a second to remove the kitten that had gotten into her bag, and handing her back to Paige.

'You have impeccable taste, but back to Mummy you go, my darling. Bye, ladies.'

The door shut and Mya's footsteps could be heard as she made her way down the metal fire escape stairs.

'I still don't understand what it is Mya does for a living. I know she said she was in finance, but what sort of finance? How can she be the richest of us, and yet we have no idea what she does? I mean she could be doing *anything*.' Polly was always asking Mya what she did for a living. It had been going on for so long now that Mya thought it was hilarious and therefore even more determined not to give anything away. There was that one time Polly put a tracker in Mya's bag, and Polly followed it straight into a strip club. They had all laughed about that for ages afterwards, but it still didn't answer the question as to whether or not Mya actually worked there. Unfortunately Polly was not the type of girl to have hung around long enough to find out.

'What are you suggesting, Pol? Do you reckon she has a secret dungeon somewhere and men pay her thousands upon thousands to be told what to do?' Paige asked.

Polly belly laughed. 'Probably not, although I'm sure I won't be able to get that image out of my head from now on. But just think if you could tie that in with your vlog – pun intended – you could have your subscriptions up in no time.'

Sophie snorted as the pair of them fell about laughing. Then Polly's phone began vibrating on the table.

'Have you been swiped right again?' Sophie asked as her nosiness got the better of her – it always got the better of her, and she was grateful for the distraction. She tried to look over Polly's shoulder to see what was on the phone.

'No, don't be daft. It's just Marcus texting me about— oh,

wait, hang on. I have *the* best idea. Marcus needs to build up his gardening business.'

'What? You think I should lease out advertising space on someone's face?'

'Er, no. I was thinking that he could do your garden and you could feature him in some of the videos. It's a win-win. I'm texting Mya now.' Polly's face disappeared as her head bent down towards her phone, her hair shielding her from view as the kitten in her lap started to stretch as it woke.

'No wait, Pol... er, I don't think that's a great idea. I mean, how do you fit a gardener into a make-up vlog? It would never work. It would be too much mess. We can think of something else. I can think of something else.' Sophie could hear the pleading tone in her voice.

Polly's phone lit up, and so did her face. 'Mya says it's a great idea, but only if it's at a reduced cost. She said she'd pay for materials. I'm going to go and call Marcus now and tell him what a clever sister he has.' Polly quickly placed the tiny kitten on the floor and ran off with her phone already clutched to her face.

Sophie's head fell back onto the sofa and she stared up at the ceiling. No, not him. This wasn't going to work. How could this possibly help?

'Here.'

Sophie straightened. Paige was stood directly in front of her and she smiled in thanks as Paige put another shot of tequila in her hand. Maybe the drink would help her come up with some new ideas. As she felt the hot burn of the tequila hit her stomach, Sophie sighed relaxing her head back on the sofa again and closing her eyes. The alcohol taking effect she felt her body start to warm up, especially her feet. No make that foot, no wait. Sophie opened her eyes, staring at the kitten that had been playing in Mya's handbag just moments earlier, now peeing on her foot.

Perfect.

11

Chapter Two

Sophie sat at her makeshift desk that just happened to double as the kitchen table, though the small galley kitchen was through an adjoining archway. Her laptop was open, displaying different graphs and figures, something about 'reach', 'activities' and 'engagement'. While the laptop was upright, Sophie was not. She had drunk a little too much at Paige's. OK way too much, and after a taxi ride home she had attempted an impromptu blog, hoping it would be light-hearted and fresh for its lack of preparation. What it was, was the ramblings of a drunken twenty-something desperately trying to get a break in a career that, if she was honest, was really only 'sort of' a career. Sophie groaned, knowing that by the end of the day her mum would have seen her video and be gearing up for another one of her *inspiring* phone calls. They were monthly and about as welcome as her period. They usually went along the lines of, 'What are you doing with your life? Playing around with make-up isn't a career. What will you do for money? How are you going to get your own house? You can't live in Mya's house forever. It's hard enough these days. Your sisters are managing, you're the only one your father and I really worry about.' And so on and so on.

'Oh God, you look like crap. Have you been up all night?'

Sophie's hands shot up and immediately clutched her head, trying to keep the loud volume of Mya's voice from splitting open her brain, while at the same time trying to stop the heavy weight of her head from slipping off her shoulders.

'Mya, shhhhh. What time is it?' Sophie slowly raised her head until she was sat up.

'Five a.m. I'm going in a few minutes, just waiting for my taxi. But seriously, have you been to bed at all?'

Mya dropped her designer handbag on top of her matching

suitcase before walking through the archway into the kitchen. From the table Sophie could see she was messing about with cups and the coffee machine, but somehow sounding more like a percussion section warming up.

'I must've slept for an hour or two at the table. I was trying something new for YouTube.'

Sophie stared at the screen, still thinking about her sisters and what they did for a living. It sucked being the youngest when everyone else had already figured their lives out. It had taken her sisters a little while to become what Mum would call successful, but there they were.

At first it gave her some breathing room, but lately there was nothing else for her family to discuss, at least until her sisters started settling down and getting married, which Mum had assured her was likely to be happening any day now, their lives being so perfectly on track.

Until then, the family WhatsApp group was full of helpful 'normal' career suggestions with a small sprinkling of, 'What are you doing with your life?' GIFs. Sophie would've rolled her eyes but despite the volume of liquid she had recently consumed, her eyeballs felt like they had holidayed in the Sahara.

Mya leaned from the counter towards the doorway so she could shout. 'So what was it? What were you trying to do?'

Sophie waited to answer until the coffee machine had finished its drum solo. 'Here come and see.' Sophie clicked a button and the screen lit up, displaying exactly what she had recorded. The mad ramblings of a drunken woman complaining about a new garden. Exactly what a social media influencer wannabe should be publishing, right?

'And so you get it, don't you? You get why the garden can't be done. I mean, it's not even about the garden, well it is about the garden, but imagine if you were me, I mean, you get it right, you see it's not about the garden, or about him, it's about the garden – no wait, I mean. Yeah. You get me.'

'It goes on like that for another fifteen minutes.' Sophie groaned again.

'Drink this, and let me press this little button here for you.'

Without any warning, Mya simultaneously handed Sophie the nectar she desperately needed and lent across to the laptop, dragging the file and dropping it into the recycle bin. 'You need some new ideas, but, just so you know, that wasn't it. What were you trying to say anyway?'

Sophie shrugged as she considered Mya's question. She had a feeling she knew what the answer was, but it wasn't something she wanted to look at too closely. Besides she had more pressing issues at the moment, firstly a literal pressing in on her head. Instead, she took a sip of her coffee and began inspecting Mya.

'Where are you flying off to today and how long are you gone for?' she asked, gently cradling the warm hug that was the coffee mug.

'Well, Mother, I'm just off to Barcelona, and I'll probably be back in a couple of days. It will depend on how business goes. You know what it's like.'

'No, I really don't. You won't tell any of us what it is that you do.'

Mya laughed. 'I know, but I love to keep you guessing.' She smiled wickedly, like the bad influence she had proven to be on more than one occasion. 'Anyway, Polly messaged and said that Marcus might be interested in the garden project. You have my emergency card details, you can use that up to the value of two thousand pounds, but listen, I don't want ponds, or fish, or any sort of calming trickling water feature. I want something modern, something simple and preferably with a fire pit.'

'Don't you think we're better putting this off until you get back, so that you can work with Marcus on your dream garden? You seem to know what you want and I don't want to get it wrong, after all I'm only your lodger.' Sophie sighed, she certainly didn't want to be working too closely with Marcus.

'If you refer to me as your landlady one more time, I'm going to kick you out. No, it's important, this could be exactly what your vlog needs. Besides, if Marcus is as good as Polly says, then we need to snap him up on this offer before he hikes his prices up, gets too busy and we no longer qualify for mates' rates.'

Sophie grimaced, she wasn't sure that they did qualify for mates' rates, not any more at least. There was a time when they may have qualified for a substantial discount but that was over before it had even begun. 'You can afford this house, you fly off all over the world. Do you even need mates' rates?'

'I'll have you know that most of my flights are paid for by my sponsors and I won't say any more about it.' Mya's phone buzzed, she looked down and said, 'Saved by the buzz. My car is here. Have a great time and don't get up to any mischief with the staff.'

Mya was laughing but Sophie had a sudden vision of exactly what that would look like and felt herself heat up. Knowing full well that her blush would give her away, Sophie tried to hide her face in the coffee mug. Mya laughed even harder, grabbed her sunglasses from the worktop, then kissed Sophie on the head and said, 'See you soon, darling.'

'Message me when you get there.'

'Of course.' With that Mya was out of the door to work, doing God knew what. Sophie looked around her, the room suddenly quiet and still. Mya was so vibrant and so full of energy that she always seemed to take it with her when she left. Sophie looked back at her notes. She had planned on doing a simple make-up tutorial for a clean, professional look. She sighed, how many more ways could she do that? Turning the camera back on, Sophie actually shuddered, and very nearly screamed when she saw herself.

'No one wants to see a make-up artist looking like this.' Sophie began putting some primer on, then she suddenly stopped.

'Wait, no, it's exactly what people need. They need to see a transformation. Let's give it to them.' She began setting everything up that she could. She threw all the lights on and the extra desk lights that she had – she didn't need to close the curtains to the garden as she hadn't opened them yet this morning. She angled the camera and positioned her mirror. She checked all the levels and balances were OK, making sure that all her equipment was in reach without impacting on sound quality. Taking a big gulp of coffee and a final check that she had all the make-up she needed, she put her mug down and gingerly ran to the kitchen for some much needed sugar. Sitting back down and getting herself settled she took a deep breath and clicked record.

'If you're having a morning like I am, whether you're hungover or overworked, underworked, or hung up on someone, you're going to thank me for this life-saving tutorial, my first tutorial that includes coffee, and chocolate Hobnobs. Cheers. Let's just hope I don't stab myself in the eye with the mascara wand again.'

Chapter Three

Marcus dragged his hand through his hair, pushing it off his head. He'd had enough. It wasn't even ten in the morning and he was already over this day.

'Listen, Pol, I'm just not sure that this is such a good idea.'

'Come on, Marcus, it's a great idea, and you know it. Since the handover from dad your business is going nowhere. This could be just the thing you need.'

'Bit harsh, Pol.'

'Your words, M.'

Marcus studied Polly as they sat at his breakfast bar, Polly drinking from her favourite mug, the one she had bought specifically to stay at his flat. The pair of them drank a ridiculous amount of tea, a trait undoubtedly gained from their parents. Thinking of his dad, he felt sure he would agree that this was a bad idea. Having said that, his dad had been so reluctant about handing over the gardening business, that he very nearly didn't, so maybe not all of his ideas were to be relied upon.

'The business needs to expand slowly, if I do this and get famous overnight, then I'm not going to be able to keep up, and Dad's regular clients would suffer. They'd tell him and then I'd suffer.'

'You should be so lucky, besides aren't Dad's old clients just after maintenance? You said yourself you wanted more, and look, I shouldn't say this but Sophie's videos aren't hitting millions of followers, not yet. So it's not like you are going to be inundated, but this will help a little, I guarantee it.' Polly looked so determined her brown eyes wide open, but Marcus couldn't help but raise an eyebrow.

'How? How exactly is this going to help if she isn't even that popular? All I know is that rather than making a profession out of gardening, all this is doing is getting me to makeover someone's garden for little, maybe even no profit.' Marcus went to stand up but Polly grabbed his hands.

'Marcus, look I don't know all the details, we can figure that out, but I do know that Sophie likes to use natural light and the garden is a state. The audience will see it improve, and then I'm sure that Sophie would do a special with you so that you can flog your wares.'

'I'm not being on camera.'

'Did I say that you needed your eyebrows plucking? No. You will be doing the garden, you won't be on camera.' Polly paused. 'Having said that, you might want her to look at your eyebrows. Now quit making excuses and just do it.'

Polly let go of his hands and just glared at him. The same way she did when they were kids, and she needed her older brother to do something for her. Usually something that would end up with both of them getting in trouble. He knew from that stare that she wasn't going to back down anytime soon, and that if past behaviour was an indicator she would just get more annoying, more petulant, until she got her own way. He could easily forgive her this habit, because more often than not, she needed something from him in order to help someone else, and perhaps this time was no exception. Yes she wanted to help her brother, but she also wanted to help her friend.

Marcus began mulling it over, scratching the scar on his eyebrow as he did so. He wasn't sure why he was so reluctant, only that it didn't seem like he would be getting much out of it. Except having to spend a lot of time in the presence of a diva. No, that's not true, Polly was right, once the plans were sorted he could just get on with it. But still, it felt like they were getting a free garden out of it, on the premise that he may or may not reach the dozen or so followers that Sophie might have. Marcus groaned. He knew that he had little to no knowledge about how Sophie's work might impact him.

He wasn't a luddite, he sort of used Facebook and Twitter for his business – occasionally – and his numbers on Instagram were pretty impressive, even if he said so himself. He was even friends with Sophie on all of them, which is why he knew that this plan wasn't going to work. Who would ever put make-up and gardening together? He looked across at Polly, who was sat calmly sipping her tea, continuing to stare him out, a smile on her lips that suggested she knew she'd almost got her wish.

'I just don't get—'

'Look, come on let's go and talk to Sophie, you can get the business workings out from her and you can have a look at the garden.' Before Marcus could say another word, Polly was walking towards the door, the keys to his van in her hand, her mug of tea in the other. 'Come on, dear brother, let's go.'

Marcus was silent as he drove, his mind working overtime trying to figure out the pros and cons without cutting his nose off to spite his face, as his Mum would say. Polly was drinking her tea and messing about with the radio as she always did, finding a song and quietly humming along, before changing her mind. She was always doing something, always flitting from one thing to the next, seemingly without a care in the world. It's when she went quiet and still you had to worry, he'd learnt that from a very young age. Quiet and still meant she was plotting. Thinking about Polly's habits didn't do anything to calm his anxiety about going to Sophie's house. He wasn't sure why he was so bothered. He was usually the laid-back to Polly's fidgety nature, but his stomach muscles were tense and he was struggling to maintain his usual calm manner. The result of which was putting him in a bad mood. A quick glance in the rear-view mirror confirmed that his face was scowling. The effect that woman had on him made his teeth clench. How could she be so infuriating and he hadn't even seen her properly in ages? Well, apart from in Paige's bar where she worked, but the only conversation they had there was him ordering a drink, but now seeing more of her would be an everyday occurrence if he took this job on. He groaned inwardly. This was going to be a bad idea. He was going to go in there and tell her that he was sorry, but that it wasn't possible. Maybe he could make something up about new clients he had managed to bag himself. Whatever, he would come up with something, or maybe he wouldn't, maybe he'd just say no, he didn't want to. Simple really. He didn't need to justify anything to her.

When they arrived ten minutes later, he couldn't help thinking that it wouldn't be that bad a commute to work. He parked up on the street and got out of the van, reminding himself that he wasn't taking on the project anyway. Polly practically skipped to the front door.

'Let me check that she is in first.' She stopped and looked at Marcus. 'Don't you need some stuff, you know to measure and draw, make plans, that kind of thing?'

'Wait, does Sophie even know we're coming over?'

'Not specifically, hang on I'll see if she's in. Go get your stuff.'

This time Marcus groaned out loud before walking back to his van and getting his folder. It was the folder he took to all new clients, it contained the usual; papers, pencils, tape measure and a small sampling of the work he had already completed. There wasn't much to go on, most of his customers just wanted the garden maintaining and so he was usually just tidying up, weeding, mowing. But his passion and training was in renovation and transformation.

'Marcus! Come on,' Polly was shouting for him.

Marcus stood up and looked over at the house. Polly was standing chatting to Sophie, he couldn't hear what they were saying, but he could see her and that was enough. As always, for a split second, Marcus found himself floored by Sophie's beauty. Not that it lasted. Instead a bitterness rose up from his stomach, and gave him a bad taste in his mouth. Yes Sophie was beautiful. Stunning, even, but high maintenance to the extreme. Who the hell needed that much make-up at ten in the morning?

His face must have shown what he was thinking because as Sophie looked over at him her face dropped. She'd gone from smiling openly at Polly, to looking at Marcus with something close to revulsion. She'd be crap at poker. He didn't care if she was unimpressed or even repulsed by him, it wasn't like he was running up towards the front door to greet her in a hug.

'Shall we get this over with then?' Marcus said as he approached the doorway.

'Good morning to you too. Is this how you treat all your clients? It's no wonder you don't have many.'

'You're not the client. Mya is the one that is paying, and as it looks like you are getting a garden for next to nothing, we both know my charm isn't necessary here.'

Sophie stepped back and let them into the house, her teeth gritted and her eyes fired up. Marcus was trying not to notice that she looked more appealing that way. The glow on her cheeks down to anger rather than blusher.

Polly stood between them. 'He's just grumpy this morning. Ignore him. He'll be happier once you and he can figure out how this will be mutually beneficial.'

Marcus and Sophie's eyes met for a brief moment, before Polly bounced into the house and went straight to the kitchen to put the kettle on. Marcus followed, wondering how this plan of theirs could be mutually beneficial. He couldn't help looking around as he did, trying to get a feel for how Sophie and Mya lived: were they messy, tidy, cluttered, hoarders, minimalist? He needed to take it all in if he was going to come up with a plan for the garden, which he reminded himself he was fairly certain he didn't want to do. Everything was tastefully decorated, a bit neutral in his opinion, but the finishing items were catalogue worthy. It was lived in, but calm. It was smart without being clinical. Except for that one wall in the lounge. He only caught a glimpse of it through the doorway but it looked to be a wall completely covered in photographs. Not the artistic kind, but of many adventures and drunken times and holidays. Apart from that, he had a feeling they would want something modern, which would suit him no end. Modern was where he was particularly enthused, it was also where his portfolio was lacking. He wondered if he would be able to talk them into a central sunken fire pit with built in seating space. What the hell was he thinking? He was going to say no, wasn't he?

As he got to the kitchen, he turned around and found Sophie was still seething. Marcus thought he must be mad but he was starting to warm up to the idea of doing the garden. The benefits of adding a contemporary garden transformation to his portfolio would be significant without the media attention from Sophie. It also helped to know that he had rattled Sophie a little, although he wasn't sure why that mattered.

'Tea?' Polly asked as she set about making herself at home. She must do that everywhere, Marcus thought.

Sophie walked over to the kitchen table that was piled high in paperwork and products. 'Let me just clear some of this stuff out of the way and then we can sit at the table.'

Polly had disappeared through the archway into the galley kitchen where he could see her pottering about. He turned back towards the table and the French doors as Sophie began putting all of the make-up into little boxes all clearly labelled and organised. She kept the brushes to one side and began moving the equipment. Taking her laptop and her lights to the end of the table, she moved her make-up boxes, all of them, through the archway onto the kitchen counter, before finally grabbing the brushes and moving them towards the sink. It was a small insight into just how much work was involved in what she did. Marcus would've been impressed, if he could figure out why. Eventually all of the products, equipment and paperwork were tidied away, the brews were made and they all sat down.

Polly looked from Sophie to Marcus and back again expecting one of them to say something. Marcus knew that he had been rude enough already and decided not to say anything, except for a mumbled, 'Thanks' when he got his brew.

'I think that before Marcus says yes to the project, he is concerned about how this will impact his business.' Polly sat between them acting as a mediator.

Marcus still didn't say anything, after all, as much fun as it was to wind Sophie up and although ideas were forming in his head, he wasn't completely sure that this was a project he wanted.

Marcus looked at Sophie as she went to get some paperwork from her mini kitchen office.

'Well, as you can see from this,' she turned around the paper and pushed it towards him, 'my business plan shows you where I would like to be in the next six months. This is where I am currently, meaning that any work you do for my vlog and other social media will be currently seen by up to fifty thousand people. I have dedicated followers in the thirty thousand range, but with shares and engagements, it usually hits nearer fifty, if not more. If we do a simple before and after then you will get exposure to those people twice. Here is a detailed account of the level of activity, the yield so far, the revenue from advertisements...'

Sophie went on, in a very professional and very astute manner. Marcus wasn't an idiot, he knew what she was saying made sense, he was just taken aback that it was her saying it. He had always had her pegged as a diva. Her make-up always over the top, her brown shoulder length hair always lightly curled to perfection, fooling no one with the 'just got out of bed look' that probably took her five hours to create. He looked again at her make-up supplies and her equipment; she was clearly taking this all very seriously. He thought about some of the stuff of hers that he had seen. She was thorough, she was very clear, at least from what he could gather having no hands on experience with make-up himself. Surely with this sort of drive, intelligence and organisation she could be some sort of high-level boss, so why was she wasting her time with make-up? He looked at her closely as she continued to talk about 'being on brand'. She was beautiful. Her eyes, currently hidden under a shit tonne of eye shadow and eyeliner and mascara – OK so he had watched maybe a couple more videos than he cared to admit – were a gorgeous chocolate-brown. Her face was perfectly designed and when she smiled, he begrudgingly acknowledged, it was impossible to look away. Well it had been for him, for longer than he cared to remember. But especially last year. He thought back to that moment, the planets must have been in some weird alignment, they had both been quite cheerful, she had seemed at ease then, more fun and carefree, she certainly had been when they were kissing.

He moved about in his seat trying to get comfortable, as he remembered the feeling of her body pressed against his, the memory far too easily recalled.

'So, as you can see my target audience can only increase and short of giving you actual advertising space on someone's face, which we've already ruled out, I think that you should be able to see some real benefit from it.' She sat back, not quite managing to hide the small look of satisfaction at having laid her cards out and believing she'd won.

He took a sip of his brew before saying, 'It could go down.'

'What do you mean?' Her eyes flashed with fury.

'Your figures could drop.' He didn't like her slightly belittling fed up tone; it was the only reason he could think of as to why he enjoyed winding her up so much. When she was angry she was far easier to talk to. 'You need me as much as I need you. Your business plan, although detailed and thought through, isn't accurately reflecting your current numbers. Like I say, you need me as much as I need you.'

Her eyes flashed again. He wasn't sure if he had hit a nerve, or if she had picked up on his actual meaning. Either way, Marcus knew from the fire in his belly and the way his body was responding that there was no way he was turning the project down. Spending the next few weeks with this diva was going to be fun.

Sophie was gritting her teeth and he had no doubt that if she could, she would be telling him to piss off. Polly coughed and looked at Marcus before kicking his leg under the table.

'What sort of garden transformation did you have in mind?' he asked almost professionally.

If she said modern, he'd do it. He would just have to talk his labourers into doing it as a favour for him, so that he could keep the cost down and get it done as quickly as possible.

She deliberately rolled her eyes before replying, 'Mya would like something modern, no water features, no pond and she said something about a fire pit.'

Marcus grinned, and stood up. 'I'll do it.'

Sophie took a deep breath looking less than thrilled with the idea of having him around, but forced a smile. 'Great.'

Marcus grinned wider.

Chapter Four

'OK so, once I have blended in the last block of eyeshadow, you can see how I have created a subtle ombré effect. I'm going to add false lashes and then fill in with this eyeliner. Then once you can see the impact, I'll do the other eye.' Sophie continued to apply her make-up, looking carefully at the screen to make sure that she didn't move too much and that she remembered to keep her breathing even. In her first few videos, she was concentrating so hard, that she was holding her breath, and made make-up application sound more like she had just finished an hour of an advanced spinning class. The same class she once did with Mya. The same class where she discovered it was impossible to die of mortification, and despite all her pleading, she was obviously not appetising enough for the ground to open up and swallow her whole. Basically, she couldn't get off the bike without the help of both Mya and the instructor, while the rest of the class looked on in horror.

Re-focusing she applied the glue to the eyelashes, and when ready, she delicately applied them. When she was finished she fluttered her eyes at the camera, loving that the gloriously sunny morning was giving her the best natural light, but grimacing at the bits of garden any eagle-eyed viewer could make out. But that was the point after all – they needed to see the garden transformation as it took place.

'See what a difference false lashes can make? I always try and experiment with the lesser-used pallet colours, if for no other reason than to try and make the most of the make-up, but sometimes it creates something new and a bit different. OK, I'll do the other eye now and you can see the complete look.'

Sophie took a deep breath and— KNOCK KNOCK. She rolled her eyes and hit pause. As she stepped away from the table she assumed it would probably be another delivery for Mya. Or maybe it would be a parcel for herself, maybe some fabulous new make-up brand wanted to send her loads of free stuff so that she could review it for them. The idea made her smile wide as she pulled the door open. Her smile ran down off her face faster than cheap mascara and wine crying as she saw Marcus standing there. He was looking over his shoulder at his van, so she took the opportunity to quickly give him the once-over. He had a cap covering his hair, a plain grey T-shirt that clung unnecessarily tightly showing his muscular arms, and was that a six-pack? He had on cargo shorts, the ones with the obscene amount of pockets – like really, if you need to carry that many things get a bag – finished off with thick socks and work boots. He was quite tanned and for a minute Sophie wondered what fake tan he was using.

'Hi, I thought I would come and take some... erm, measurements.'

Marcus was looking at Sophie with a strange look on his face. Sophie felt herself redden. Had he realised she was checking him out? Well, not checking him out, she reasoned with herself, more giving him a professional once over as was a requirement of her job. She realised she was looking at his T-shirt again, trying to see if she could make out any more muscle definition. With a cough she looked back up, telling herself to get her act together.

'I didn't know you were coming today. I'm actually working.'

'That's OK.' Marcus stepped over the threshold and around Sophie. 'I just need to take some measurements, just go ahead and carry on doing your work.'

The way he said 'work' made Sophie's lip curl. She took a breath as she remembered she had promised herself to stop letting Marcus antagonise her. Cheeky git had stopped to put the kettle on, on his way to the garden. There was a back door through the kitchen itself to a side entrance, as well as the French doors behind the table she was currently working at. Fuming, but trying to remain calm and mature, Sophie went back to the table to go over her notes regarding what she had been recording, and what products she was reviewing. Next she would need to look at how best to title and tag the videos for her social media. Well, she was trying to, but it wasn't working. With her back to the French doors, it was very unsettling knowing that Marcus was behind her. She couldn't read the notes that she had written, and she was fidgeting in her seat. Was he looking at her? Could she turn around and look at him? She should've kept the curtains closed after all. Deciding that it was her garden – well Mya's – she could look at whatever she wanted to look at, whenever she wanted to look at it. She turned around. He was at the bottom of the garden with his phone, clipboard, pencil and tape measure. He was clearly just getting on with his work, which just made Sophie mad. Why was she so affected by his presence, and on what planet did he go around being the professional one?

Clenching her teeth and sitting up straighter, Sophie went back to her notes determined to focus. She heard the side door open again and she found herself wanting to look especially productive, but from the corner of her eye she watched as Marcus made some notes and also started to make himself a brew. 'Ahhhh,' Sophie screamed in her head. Why is he so annoying? Why does he come in here like he owns the place? Why am I so bothered?

'You look like you're working really hard, so I'll keep it short OK?'

'Fine.' Sophie forced the response through her clenched jaw, knowing that if she said what she really wanted to, they'd be arguing again.

Marcus mumbled something under his breath before saying, 'I think I have all the measurements I need for now. I have done a few designs. But the first thing I am going to need to do is some excavation and clearing away. I'll email you with the plans and you can let me know what you like most. But for now I'll get the truck and the digger here as soon as possible and we can get started. Weather looks fine for the next few weeks so I'll get cracking. Is that OK with you?'

'Weeks? How long is this whole project going to take?'

'Well, it certainly isn't going to happen overnight. It will probably take a couple of weeks, but that will depend upon which plan you like.'

'Fine,' Sophie grumbled, feeling and sounding like a spoilt brat, with a limited vocabulary.

'You could say thank you, you know.' Marcus was back pottering about in the kitchen.

'Thank you so very much, I am greatly looking forward to the interruption of my work over the next few weeks.' Sophie smiled sweetly batting her eyelashes at him, or trying to, for some reason it didn't feel quite right. Marcus laughed, the sound making Sophie's sarcastic smile retreat as her eyes studied his face as he smiled. She knew it was a genuine smile because his eyes were doing that twinkling thing and she was struggling to look away from them as he started walking towards her, mug in hand. The cheek of it, she still couldn't believe that he would just swan about her kitchen as if he had every right. Why was he looking at her like that?

He bent down towards her and rather than look away, Sophie stayed focused on his eyes. They were a green-brown blend, perfect for a gardener as they reminded her of mud baths and lush lawns. Unfortunately for her when he smiled, and it was rare in her presence these days, they gleamed as if the smile started there rather than his mouth. Suddenly she was looking at his lips. He continued to slowly lean closer towards her, bending down towards her face. Her breath held, the same way it used to when putting on mascara. He placed something next to her hand.

'Flattering your eyelashes at me will probably work better when you have them both on. Enjoy your brew, see you later.' Marcus laughed as he abruptly straightened up and began walking to the door, still chuckling to himself as he left.

What the—? Sophie quickly reached for her mirror. Oh God. The video, of course. Yeah, she looked like Two-Face. It wasn't a strong look, and she felt her face redden, her embarrassment further fuelling her anger, but then again she didn't care what he thought anyway. Right?

Sophie threw herself back into her chair and away from the mirror. She took some deep breaths to try and relocate her calm. She slowly sorted out her make-up as she catalogued where she had been up to and what she would need to do next. Her eyes kept moving back to the mug. The brew had been for her. That was actually, well, it was sweet, but also presumptuous. She studied the cup wondering whether or not to drink it. To drink it would mean that it was a welcome gesture almost admitting that he was a nice person, to leave it to go cold felt like the only way she could win whatever had just happened between them. Oh God, he really was going to drive her insane. If this garden thing was going to take weeks, what sort of state would she be in by the end of it? At the very least she might be dehydrated. She needed sugar. She got up and went into the kitchen to look in the biscuit tin and miraculously found a Ginger Nut. Walking back to the table she sat down, studiously ignored the cup of tea, and turned the camera back on.

She took one last deep breath, plastered a smile on her face and pressed record.

'OK, let's carry on with the left eye.' Sophie took a quick slurp of her brew. 'OK so… dammit!' She put the mug back on the table. 'I'll definitely have to edit that bit out.' She looked back at the brew that she hadn't wanted to drink. 'Fine, Marcus you win.' She picked up the mug and biscuit, occasionally drinking it as she chatted to the camera.

Chapter Five

'Mya got back to me about the budget and final plan approval. We'll make a start today in terms of prep. I will need to start ordering the supplies and coming up with a full plan of what's happening as well as who you can expect and when. It's not something I normally go into great detail about for my clients, but I know that you will need to do your filming around it. So let me know if anything really doesn't work and I'll move around what I can, OK?'

Marcus waited, to see if this really was all right, or, as her face seemed to suggest, that this whole thing was going to be a problem.

'Yes, thank you that would be really helpful. I can talk to Paige as well about picking up shifts that will give you more time without me here.'

He could tell from her tone, and also the fact that she was being civil, that Sophie was trying to be on her best behaviour. He could see through it though, he knew she was still miffed about the whole thing. 'Who else is working on this with you? Surely you can't do it all by yourself?'

'Bailey is going to be here as often as I am, and Joseph will be helping out on the labour intense days. But, yes, that will be it, so it will take longer than if you had a full team on hand. We'll do it as quickly as we can though.'

Sophie was nodding and her face smiled slightly, only slightly mind, at the mention of his best friend Bailey's name. It suddenly occurred to Marcus that he wasn't sure of Sophie and Bailey's relationship. He knew they knew each other from the bar, and the rare occasion someone decided to be brave enough and throw a house party, but a cold shiver suddenly went through him at the thought that she might be into Bailey, or perhaps something had already happened between the two of them? Marcus rubbed at the scar on his eyebrow, trying to get his thoughts back in order.

'In fact, Bailey should be here soon. I'm going to go through the design plans with him and start roughing out a project plan.' He tried to study her face to see if there was anything to give it away. Feeling sour at himself for caring so much, the flip was switched and he was immediately in the mood to provoke. 'Assuming that's all OK with you, princess?'

'Don't call me that. Yes that's fine, the sooner you get started the sooner this will all be over.'

At that moment the door knocked and was immediately opened.

'Knock knock, it's your one o'clock here and very ready for our scheduled shag,' Bailey shouted loud enough for all the neighbours to hear before closing the door. He was laughing as he made his way into the kitchen. Sophie grinned, and Marcus's jaw had never been clenched so tight, it was making his temples beat.

'Are you going to shout that every time you walk in?' Sophie asked.

'Hmm, maybe, or maybe the neighbours are used to it, perhaps I'll make up something better next time, really get them talking.'

He winked at her and Sophie smiled, her eyes lighting up at the playful banter. Marcus looked on feeling like an outsider, and as he watched Sophie and Bailey continue to chatter back and forth he mentally kicked his own arse. He really needed to get over himself and stop sounding like a schoolboy. This was about business, *his* business.

Interrupting them he said, 'We're going to need some really good "before" pictures.' Marcus held up his phone and motioned to Bailey.

'Are you using that?' Sophie was clearly aghast at the thought.

'What else would I use?'

With a tut Sophie picked up her DSLR camera. 'Come on, you need to get really good, I mean professionally good, "before" pictures. Otherwise, what's the point?'

Marcus held open the back door as Sophie walked out with her camera and tripod. Marcus and Bailey watched as she set up her equipment in the middle of the backyard – in its current state you couldn't actually call it a garden. It was uneven, with lashings of crazy paving, some random hedge on one side, a thin rickety fence on the other and a general sense of a grey seventies palette. Despite that, looking around again gave Marcus the same thrill it had the last time. It was a generous enough space and he knew he could turn it into something wonderful, something worthy of being a backdrop, even if it was only for some diva's make-up videos. Sophie was messing about with the settings and Bailey was looking at the plans again, a look of concentration on his face as he got a feel for how it was going to look.

'You really want to do all this? Is it really going to be worth it?' Bailey asked.

'Yes,' Marcus said, watching Sophie as she bent over her camera, 'it will pay off, I'm sure.'

Bailey just laughed and continued to study the plans.

'Afternoon!' shouted Polly as she made her way into the garden and walked towards them. Standing next to Marcus, Polly stage whispered, 'What is she doing? I thought the point was that the garden needed a makeover not that it needed to be a location setting?'

Marcus smiled at his sister. 'What are you doing here, Pol? No more awful dates for you to be on?'

'Erm, no.'

Polly's hesitation was enough to get Sophie's interest and she looked up in time to see Polly blush. 'Thanks again for the rescue the other night, Bailey.' There was a definite redness making its way up Polly's throat.

'No worries.'

Sophie looked over to Bailey. She couldn't have explained why, but something about his response had her studying him. Getting nothing she cast a glance at Marcus who gently shook his head, with a definite, 'don't ask' vibe.

'I thought I'd come over and see you guys in action,' Polly said, her eyes scanning the garden, or avoiding eye contact, Sophie wasn't sure which. 'But now I'm confused. What's with the camera set-up?'

'She's taking "before" shots,' Marcus answered.

'Oh, that's a really good idea. You could do a show-reel. The sort of thing that could go on your website.' Polly nodded.

Sophie began slowly moving the camera around three hundred and sixty degrees.

'Unless you lot want to be in as "before" models I suggest you move inside!' Sophie shouted as the camera slowly approached them.

'Right, I told Sophie I would do a full project plan with timings and dates so that she can do her "work" around us and vice versa,' Marcus said as they moved away and Bailey just nodded.

'Why do you say it like that?' Polly asked.

'Like what?'

'Like her work isn't really work.'

Marcus just shrugged in response. He made it clear, from both his tone and expression, that he didn't think it was work. Not really.

'She works flat out on this non-stop. She has business plans, a brand, a five-year plan. Have you seen her website? It's one of the best. Remind me again, what's your website traffic like?'

Bailey laughed. 'She's got you there. Doesn't your mum's knitting blog get more traffic than you?'

Marcus stared at Bailey but didn't say anything as Bailey grinned.

'I'll edit this for you and pull some stills, and then you can add it to whatever you need to, websites, Facebook etc,' Sophie said as she walked back in tripod in one hand, camera in the other.

'OK, thanks,' Marcus grumbled. 'I'll go and get a scope on how long it'll take to get some of the supplies and pull together that project plan for you.'

'Thanks.' Sophie began packing away her camera.

'Wow look at that, you can be nice to each other when you really try.' Bailey was grinning as Marcus and Sophie scowled. 'Or not.'

Chapter Six

'Yo, Joe, pass me that measuring tape, please?' Bailey shouted over from the back end of the garden.

'Call me Joe one more time, boy, and I'll have you doing this work by yourself.'

'Come on now that's not very gentlemanly of you is it, Joseph?'

'What would you know about being a gentleman, hey, Bailey?' Joseph retorted.

Marcus loved working with these two. They were, for the most part, always happy to get stuck in and have a laugh. More importantly, Joseph knew when to lead by example and shut Bailey up and when to get stuck in.

Marcus looked around the garden, once again taking in all the work that would be needed, but also the monumental difference they would see in a matter of days. His portfolio would benefit, no doubt. But that wouldn't be the only thing. He'd done some research and firmly believed that they would add a significant amount of value to Mya's property too.

'So, skipper, what are we doing today?'

Joseph and Bailey looked at Marcus awaiting instructions. Marcus laid out the plans on the uneven concrete and pointed to the relevant sections. 'The general plan for the next few days is to get rid of all the top, the patchy turf, the crazy paving, in this area.' He pointed to a section just off the middle. 'That's where we are going to have the sunken fire pit and inbuilt benches. So that will need digging out significantly. Depending on what we have underneath that, I suspect we may need to look at reinforcing. With regards to the outer edges, I want all that digging up as well. We are going to add some fencing to create more privacy, but in getting rid of the hedges that should help to open up the garden some more. From there we can start creating a solid, and, more importantly, straight foundation to landscape the rest of the garden. Once we have done that we can then add on the decking over there at the back, which is a suntrap, and also look at planting some trees and other accessories so that it looks modern but not barren.' When he had finished talking he looked up and saw that both Bailey and Joseph were busy studying the plans and the garden.

After a while, they both looked at him and Bailey whistled. 'It's no small job, is it?'

Joseph looked closely at Marcus. 'And you're doing all of this so that you can get more publicity, and therefore more business?'

At that point, the back door opened and Sophie stuck her head out. She was wearing her usual jeans and T-shirt, meaning that she was probably going to work at the bar. As she stepped out, Marcus very quickly looked at her from her shoes to her hair and was immediately affected – as he always was – but how he wished he wasn't. Whenever he saw her the weight shifted onto the balls of his feet as if he was about to run toward her, his heart picked up pace and his body instinctively wanted to get closer, and each time he had to fight his response. She fascinated him, it was that simple. Added to that, he enjoyed winding her up to see what her quick mind would come up with next, and yes, she was gorgeous with and without make-up. But the woman giving him a strange look right now, this was the Sophie that he had kissed all those months ago. Not the diva with all the make-up and the big hair, making strange faces at the end of her make-up tutorials.

'Is this a good time? I don't want to interrupt, but I just wanted to give you this. I didn't realise that you would be having post delivered here. Is this whole thing a scam just so that you can move in?'

Sophie was waving some sort of magazine around. As

he slowly made his way towards her, Marcus couldn't stop himself thinking about what it would be like to live with Sophie. She'd be a daily pain in the ass, he had no doubt, but it made him grin. It would be fun. Going to sleep and waking up next to her, their constant back and forth, the shared work escapades – thoughts about how his life could be left him feeling a bit empty. Uncomfortable with his train of thought, he looked around to get his bearings and realised that Sophie hadn't been formally introduced to everyone yet. She was still scowling at him, stood at the back door, and didn't exactly look friendly, but now was as good a time as any. Marcus leaned forward and took the sample catalogue he had had delivered here, simply to annoy her, and it had worked. He'd do it again.

'Believe me, princess, I wouldn't want to live here if you paid me.' Before Sophie could come back with anything he continued, 'Let me introduce you to the people that will be in your garden for the next few weeks. You know Bailey, of course.'

Bailey smiled and bowed low. Marcus rolled his eyes shaking his head at his best friend's usual behaviour.

'And this is Joseph.'

Joseph laid down the shovel he was holding and immediately walked over to Sophie holding his hand out.

'It's such a pleasure to meet you, Sophie. I promise that we will be as quiet as we can and disturb you as little as possible. But should you need anything at all, at any time, just ask.'

Marcus watched as they shook hands, Sophie's face immediately softening and warming under Joseph's gentle nature, giving him a full smile that he himself hardly ever managed to provoke. He'd seen Joseph pull that charm over many an anxious customer, it must be something about his warm gaze and his silver hair, he should have realised that it would work on Sophie as well.

'Thank you, Joseph, that's really lovely of you. I'm a bit

worried about the noise and the interruptions, but I'm sure it will all be fine.'

'It will. I guarantee it. I'll make sure these boys stay in line.' Joseph winked as Sophie laughed.

'But let's not forget I'm the boss around here,' Marcus cut in.

He immediately regretted saying anything at all. Turning back round he ripped the cellophane off the catalogue, with slightly more power than was necessary. It wasn't like him to pull rank. Joseph had worked for him for years despite being a decade or two older. Once again being around Sophie had got to him and he had lashed out unnecessarily. Why did she always manage to make him feel like an inadequate twelve-year-old, like he had to prove something to her? He certainly hadn't felt that way towards her when he was twelve. Back then she barely even registered on his radar, she was just his younger sister's friend, although he could admit to himself that she was fun to wind up even back then. No, this was all no doubt linked to their near hook-up last year. The kiss they had shared that was over before it started, but that for him at least, he couldn't seem to forget.

'He is you know, and he's always been a great boss so you don't need to have any worries at all. He's brilliant and your garden is going to look amazing. Now, do you need to get going, we don't want to keep you.'

'Thanks, Joseph. Do you need anything before you begin?'

'Well, we would always say yes to a cup of tea, if you have time?'

Sophie smiled at Joseph and Bailey but when her glance got back to Marcus it turned hard again.

'OK. How do you take it? Actually it's OK, I'll make a pot and you can all help yourself.'

Sophie turned and walked back into the kitchen. Marcus was amazed at Sophie's transformation. She was never that quiet and, well, nice when he was talking to her. When

Marcus suggested anything she usually rolled her eyes and came back with a cutting remark. Mulling it over, he realised he'd rather that she was antagonistic to him. It meant that he was getting to her.

However, he had to admit he was embarrassed at how he had reacted, pulling rank like that. He didn't want to get into it with Bailey and Joseph so he just looked down at the catalogue making a big deal of studying it in great detail.

Joseph walked over to Bailey and whispered, 'I wasn't sure about doing all of this work on the off chance of some publicity, but doing it for love, now that I *can* do.'

'Don't hold your breath, Joe, they've been fighting like cats and dogs for ages now.' Bailey grunted as Joseph elbowed his stomach.

'Well, this will be fun then, and I told you don't call me Joe. Besides me and Harriet started like that and we've been blissfully married for thirty years now.'

Sophie walked out with a tray holding the teapot, three mugs, a small milk jug and separate sugar bowl. Marcus leapt up and grabbed the tray from her, their fingers brushing, not completely accidentally on his part. He waited until she was looking at him, then smiled and in his best manner and voice said, 'Thanks, Sophie.'

Sophie looked puzzled for a moment, before slightly shaking her head. Waving at Joseph and Bailey she turned around shouting, 'Bye,' as she shut the door.

Chapter Seven

Sophie was glad it was Thursday as it meant that the bar was steady enough to keep her occupied but not that busy that she would need to wash spilt beer out of her hair later. Giving a customer their change, Sophie decided to nip out to the other side of the bar to collect empties, partly because it was her job, and partly because Mya and Paige were chatting at the quiet end of the bar, Polly was due any minute, and Sophie really needed to be further away.

She didn't want to join in their conversation because she knew they would want an update on her videos and the garden. Two days in, and it had already proven to be more distracting than lipstick on teeth, but maybe perhaps not in the way she had imagined. Accidentally recording Marcus taking his shirt off had been distracting. As had accidentally capturing him in shot as the sun caught his ridiculously toned body as he dug up the hedges near to the French doors. For some reason these images of Marcus were somehow burnt into her retinas, probably nothing at all to do with the number of times she had needed to re-watch the same clip. For editing purposes. Obviously.

Sophie was suddenly fizzing with energy as she moved quickly towards the next table, and the next, until her arms were full of dirty glasses, and she made her way back to the dishwasher behind the bar, her entire concentration on ensuring the glasses didn't crash to the floor. Managing to get the glasses to the dishwasher without having to pay for breakages, Sophie began wiping the bar top, her eyes scanning around as she did so. The bar was a decent size. Paige had really done well with it. It was on the outskirts of Manchester city centre itself but the area had its own indie scene. It was decorated in dark colours, but Paige had used different light fittings and light shades to almost completely cover the ceiling and walls. It had the twinkly effect of the light section in B&Q, mixed with the darkness and grunginess a decent bar was supposed to have. It wasn't a posh cocktail bar, so didn't need to have sharp lines and glass everywhere. There were no cliques either; sometimes there were loads of students in, sometimes hen and stag parties warming up. Sometimes Paige put live bands on the tiny stage at the back. On Saturdays one of the many food trucks would be parked out front.

'What do you want me to do, boss?' Sophie asked, trying to wipe beer residue off her T-shirt with little success as Paige approached. In comparison Paige looked gorgeously dishevelled, in another of her hoodies, and skinny jeans. She was rocking the side undercut hair, had jewellery on nearly every finger, earrings going up her earlobe, and dark eyeshadow that showed off that shrewd look of hers, but, more than anything else, she carried herself like she simply didn't care what anyone else thought about it. Paige was the perfect bar owner, and with her height and confidence, she was more than capable of throwing out anyone that got out of hand. More often than not, too often in fact, it had been her own friends. Sophie included on more than one occasion.

'You know, you really should let me do your make-up for my videos one day.'

'You keep asking me and I've already told you I will, but at the moment it's tricky, now that I am a temporary kitten momma, not to mention the bar. People insist on coming here and drinking, I mean, what's that all about? You may have noticed them on occasion?' Paige looked Sophie up and down.

'We could always do it here?' Sophie chose to deliberately ignore the jibe about her bartending abilities, instead thinking about how a kitten video would pull in a different audience.

Paige's eyes moved across Sophie's face. 'What's the matter with you?'

'What do you mean? How are my gorgeous nieces and nephews? Can I come up and see them and take some more pics, maybe a couple of videos?'

'Sure, just not while you're on shift. I'm still trying to run a business here,' Paige said sternly.

'Paige, that would sound a lot more convincing if you weren't making that sound. Are you purring?'

Paige surreptitiously glanced down at the mega pocket at the front of her hoody.

'This one is struggling to settle without me.'

'Sure he is.' Sophie reached forward and stroked the little black kitten face that was sticking out of the pocket. 'And what are you going to do when they get adopted?'

'I'll probably cry for a little bit, but then I'll remember that they're in their forever homes, and I'll finally remember what a full night's sleep is. And I know you're trying to change the subject. What is wrong with you?' Paige asked again, trying to look stern, the tiny kitten purr somewhat diluting the effect.

'Nothing, honestly. Why don't I check the liquors and restock?'

With that Sophie immediately took off. While it was a good idea to avoid Paige's insightful glare, the spur of the moment task actually took her nearer to Mya, shit.

'Here she is!' shouted Mya as she approached their end of the bar. She lunged over the bar and grabbed Sophie's face and planted a huge kiss on her lips.

'What are you doing?' Not completely unusual for Mya who was always one shot away from outrageous behaviour.

'The plans for the garden. I can't believe it. I saw them on the table when I got home. They are incredible. It's going to look awesome. I wish that we had done this sooner.'

Sophie shrugged. 'Well, in that case, kiss Polly as it was her idea.'

'Oh yeah, it was, well I will when I see her. So how has it been?'

Sophie tried not to groan, this was exactly why she didn't want to be around her friends today. She wasn't sure how to act. She didn't want to be petulant, and she knew that she needed to be grateful, but Marcus was annoying the hell out of her. He was either suddenly looking away from her, or else he was looking far too good as he worked and she found that she was looking at him. Was she blushing? Sophie quickly turned away and grabbed her paper and pen so that she could make a list of all the bottles that were needed.

'Oh, it's all good, a bit disruptive but should be worth it in the end.' Phew, that felt like a neutral response. Why was this such hard work? Sophie blamed Marcus for disrupting her ability to function naturally.

Paige walked over and stood on the customer side of the bar next to Mya. 'Is it affecting your videos?' she asked as both she and the kitten studied Sophie.

Sophie felt herself try not to shrink under Paige's probing stare. Sophie blamed Paige's height, she had an unfair elevation, her field of vision always clear and vast.

'No, there's been a slight increase in views but that could be down to anything, it's certainly not indicative of any major changes. They are just as likely to drop down next week.'

'Oh I loved the last one you put out, the "What to do about your Hangover Face" one. You looked so rough, I was showing all my colleagues in Barcelona.' Mya laughed so hard she nearly threw herself off her bar stool. 'But then again the transformation was stunning.'

Well if Mya had been showing her friends that would probably account for the small increase in views that she had seen. Sophie frowned, she had been secretly hoping that it was the start of an upward curve but probably not in that case.

'Mya tell us about work. How was Barcelona? Did you make lots of sales?' Sophie asked, desperate to move the subject on.

'I'm sure one of these days you're going to guess right, and who knows, when you do I might finally tell you my job title. But for now, Barcelona was the usual, lots of fun, but look here comes Polly. Has she got another date tonight?'

Nicely diverted Mya, thought Sophie, having aimed to do precisely that herself.

Before Polly could say anything Mya grabbed her and gave her a huge kiss on the lips. Polly just smiled as if this was a perfectly normal welcome.

'Hi, gang. How are we all?' Polly pulled out the next bar stool and sat down.

'What are you drinking, Pol and do you have a date again tonight?' Sophie asked.

'Don't say it like that, and no, I am having a small break. Don't ask me why as I don't want to talk about it, and I'll have a Corona, please, Sophie. Paige when can I see your kittens again?'

Polly squeaked as she realised there was a kitten ready to be petted. She plucked the kitten out of Paige's top, unaware of the effect her words had had.

News that Polly was taking a break from dating was like announcing that the internet was just going to switch off for a day or two. The rest of the group were stood stock still as they processed what they had just heard. Gently placing Polly's Corona on the bar, Sophie waited, wide-eyed with everyone else. Polly looked up at the lull in conversation and took in their expressions.

'Please, it's not that big a deal. I just haven't been able to think straight lately and so it wasn't fair on my dates.' When still nobody said anything, Polly continued. 'Well, gee, thanks for your support everyone.'

'What happened?' Mya asked, putting an arm around Polly's shoulders.

'Nothing, well, nothing I want to talk about anyway.' Polly continued to pet and stroke the black kitten, looking as though they were both calming down as a result.

Sophie sympathised, she had plenty she didn't want to discuss or think about too closely as well.

'Does it have something to do with Bailey?' Paige asked quietly.

Mya squealed. 'Ohhh, what have I missed?'

Sophie was startled to discover that her inkling about Polly and Bailey had been noticed by someone else.

Polly looked shocked, not shocked like what an outrageous thing to say, more shocked that someone had uncovered a secret, but she still played it cautiously though. 'No, of course not, why would it have anything to do with him?'

'I kind of thought that perhaps the lip-locking that took place here the other night might have sent you a little off course?' Paige was smirking.

Mya grinned salaciously. 'Have you been sneaking around with Bailey?'

Sophie stayed quiet as she watched Polly's face. Her red hair and fair complexion giving her no barrier against the blush that had started on her neck and worked its way up her face. Polly tried for indignant and spluttered on her drink.

'What kiss? What are you talking about?'

'Am I the only one who saw it?' Paige asked, looking at Sophie.

'I have no idea what you are talking about,' Sophie said, finding it unusual that instead of goading Polly for more information like she would've done normally, she was instead trying to help Polly protect her privacy. Who'd have guessed that this thing with Marcus would make her a better person?

'So you didn't see Polly in the corner having the most boring date ever, while her brother and his best friend were getting more and more drunk over here? That Polly needed saving from the date but she couldn't get Marcus's attention and so Bailey stepped in, and gave her what looked like the most spectacular kiss ever?'

Sophie shook her head and nobody said a word, but they were all staring wide-eyed at Polly patiently waiting for more.

'Firstly,' Polly started, 'if you could see I was having a bad date, why didn't you come and rescue me? Isn't that part of the code, that's why I meet people here so that my friends can help me when I need them to?'

She looked accusingly at Paige, who simply shrugged and said, 'It was boring not dangerous. There was no rush.'

Sophie looked at Paige and, not for the first time, felt like Paige was let in on some cosmic knowledge because she always looked like she knew what was happening next, or what should happen next at any rate.

'Secondly, shouldn't you have been working rather than paying attention to what was happening with me and Bailey?'

'Ha! So something did happen with you and Bailey!' Mya screamed.

'God, shhhh will you. No, nothing happened. Like Paige said, I was having a bad date.' Polly stopped to look at Paige accusingly, but Paige just smiled slightly and shrugged. 'And even though I was signalling to Marcus for his help, he was too far gone to notice but Bailey did, and he came over and helped extricate me from the date.'

'Helped you how? Did he help you all the way back home? Did he help you out of your clothes too?' Mya wolf whistled.

'No, he, er…' Polly cleared her throat, her eyes focusing on the kitten in her lap, as her neck became redder by the second. 'He kissed me and pleaded for me to take him back. That made the guy I was with leave rather quickly. It really was the perfect get out.'

'You like him,' Mya accused.

'No I don't, he was just being gentlemanly, helping out his best mate's sister, that's all.'

'It looked like one hell of a kiss from where I was standing. I don't think it would've stopped if Marcus hadn't interrupted it.'

'What did Marcus do?' Sophie asked a little too sharply.

'I just think he was shocked to see his best mate kissing his sister and asked us to stop. We did, and, if memory serves, Bailey then went on to take some random customer home with him, so clearly not a big deal for either of us, OK? Paige, when can I see the rest of your kittens again?'

'Yeah, it'd be just like Marcus to stick his nose in other people's business and interfere in their lives.' Everyone looked at Sophie, who immediately turned back around to face the liquor once again, pretending to look busy.

'So why the no dating then?' Mya asked Polly.

'I just… I can't.' Polly took a deep breath. 'Fine, yes, the kiss was out of this world and I haven't been able to stop thinking about it. It wouldn't be fair on the people I might meet, I can't… I mean, I couldn't get Bailey out of my head. But like I said, he went off with someone else, so it really doesn't matter, does it?'

'Of course it matters. I can't believe Bailey would treat you like that!' Mya was clearly outraged.

Polly sighed. 'Like what? It's not as if that isn't his usual behaviour, is it?'

'He didn't go with her,' Paige interjected quietly.

'What?' Polly turned to stare at Paige.

'He didn't leave with her. In the end he got her an Uber, and went home alone.'

'You have got to be kidding me? Why the sudden change?' Polly asked.

Mya raised an eyebrow, looking like she had a rough idea, Paige stayed silent and Sophie half turned to observe her friends.

'What because of the kiss?' Polly said. 'I don't think so. I don't think one kiss, one meaningless kiss on his part, will suddenly make a leopard change his spots. Besides it's no big deal to me either, I just need a couple of days to get my head back on straight and all of this will be forgotten about. Look, please, just forget I said anything, OK?' Polly finished the rest of her drink in one go, and passed the kitten back to Paige. 'I've got to go, I'll text you later.' She jumped off the bar stool and walked very quickly to the door.

Mya necked the rest of her Martini. 'I'll go and make sure she's OK. See you later.' She blew kisses at Paige and Sophie and ran after Polly.

'Tell her she can come hang out with my babies tomorrow. They'll help cheer her up!' Paige shouted after Mya.

Sophie cleared away their glasses, cleaned up their mess and wiped down the bar top, all the while aware that Paige was still stood next to her.

'Hers isn't the only kiss I've seen, that no one else has.'

Sophie stilled. 'I don't know what you are talking about.'

'Oh, I think you do. House-warming party last year, you and Marcus. He's still in your head too, right?'

'As I said, I don't know what you're talking about, and I need to work.' Sophie turned away and walked into the back room where the bottles were kept, having absolutely no idea what liquor was needed, the list nothing but doodles. She randomly picked up some bottles and in no way did she allow her thoughts to remember her own version of an amazing kiss. The kiss that had nearly carried her away, nearly made her change her dreams. The kiss that was over before it truly began, and would absolutely remain that way.

Chapter Eight

Sophie gently chewed her thumb, as she wondered about this 'brilliant' idea of hers. She was seconds away from pressing the button, enabling her to do her first ever 'live' social media event. Usually she recorded herself, which would take an hour or two depending on the topic, or how much make-up was being applied, but then it would be at least a day spent editing. Editing to make sure that all of the formats and filters that may be needed were put on, not to mention the hours it took for her to cut out every 'ummm', 'ahhh', 'shit' and 'bollocks'. If a mistake was made, like the time she almost took her eye out with the mascara wand, they could be edited away on screen, wiped away on her face too and she could start again with no one the wiser – as long as she remembered to upload the right version, of course. These are the sorts of things, in her opinion, the public didn't need to see or know about. They wanted flawless make-up demonstrations and conversations about when to use specific colours for different skin tones, different occasions, etc. They didn't want to know that she cried like a baby when the mascara wand threatened to perforate her retina, or that she couldn't put a contact lens in on camera because watching it back and seeing herself touch her eyeball on screen made her want to vomit.

Sophie's hand shook over the pad she would be pressing and reminded herself of why she was about to do this. Going 'live' would mean that she would be visible to a whole new audience, it would increase her online presence and, more importantly, it was relatively different. Not a lot of make-up artists had done what she was about to do, because of all the reasons she'd listed over and over. But if it did work, then the potential impact on her market positioning could be substantial.

Sophie had a quick look behind her. Through the French doors she could see Marcus working away in the garden. As it was a Saturday Joseph and Bailey weren't around. She would rather do this without Marcus or anyone working in the garden, but the gorgeous summer light was bright and perfect, cleverly bouncing off the mirror in front of her without any glare, and she needed to do this video now or else it might not work to its full potential. It really was now or never. A final look at the kitchen door, it was definitely shut. Right, deep breath, let's do this.

Click... 1... 2... 3... LIVE.

Sophie coughed and smiled as she internally scolded herself, great start Sophie really professional. Taking a second to smile she mentally reiterated the importance that she take her work seriously. It was the only way she was going to become something, the only way she was going to succeed.

'Hi, it's me, Sophie. I know it's unusual for me to do a live video, but why not? Oh, I can see some of you have joined me already. So hi, Trina, hi, Leah, hi, Ashley.

'OK, so let me explain what I am hoping to achieve today. Instead of my usual tutorials, I wanted to do a live video of one of my "quick" everyday make-up routines. I thought that some of you might wonder what kind of "magic" happens behind the scenes to make it look so flawless. Even though I don't change anything on my vlog, I do edit bits out, usually where I am stammering or saying something I shouldn't, also I do have a tendency to swear. Anyway, I thought if we do a live one you can see how I do it in real life, so to speak. That way you can watch it back at a later date and follow along, and you'll also see what is possible in a short time. Oh wow, lots more of you are joining us now. Hi, everyone. OK so I have already cleansed and moisturised, and next, I will add a primer. I am not going to do the full contour, but I will do a little bit, because like I have said already, the idea here is that this is my "quick" everyday make-up. Oh gosh, my hands are shaking, I am not used to doing this live it's a little nerve-wracking.'

Sophie stopped to pick up her primer. Looking back up at the screen she could see herself and the numbers of her followers as well as the comments and 'likes' they were sending her way. The numbers were comfortably in the hundreds. This was why she chose to do this type of thing on a Saturday morning. Her demographic, mostly women in their twenties, would be able to watch it, and practice it before going out that night. Sophie looked back at the comments again.

'Oh, you're all being so sweet, thank you. That makes me feel loads better. Yes, Tracey, in answer to your question, this is genuinely the make-up routine that I do more often than any other. I also work at a bar, so I am tired and running out of the house with little time to spare. So what I am about to do is my "go to" if you like.'

Sophie spent a minute or two applying the primer, trying to disguise the fact that her hands were shaking. 'This is one of my favourite primers as it dries really fast and my make-up tends to stay on longer. OK, there you go. Right, next is my Flawless twenty-five hours foundation.' Sophie held it up to the camera her hand more steady now that she was getting into the flow of it. A quick look at her numbers indicated that they were heading towards five hundred people watching live, and lots of people were tagging their friends in. As part of her business plan, Sophie was hoping to get maybe two thousand live viewers and then an increase in the number of views as people who missed it live could watch it back afterwards. Applying the foundation Sophie was explaining why it was her favourite and why she used the particular sponge she used.

'Like I said already, we're not doing the full contour today, this is a quickie.' Sophie smiled and then laughed at the comments. 'Yes, it's quick enough to put on after a quickie!'

Grabbing her contouring kit and the next brush, Sophie got in the flow and was applying her usual make-up effortlessly. So far so good, no major cock-ups. The views had crept up to the thousand mark and were remaining relatively steady, with some dropping and some adding, which she had anticipated.

'OK, so next I am going to add some powder – oh bollocks, I mean crap, oh sorry.' The powder had gone everywhere, she quickly scooped up and recovered what she could. 'Ah can't believe I swore. I'm so sorry and this is exactly why most make-up artists wouldn't want to do this type of thing live. Anyway, I am a swearer so there's your warning, I am likely to swear again so sorry in advance!' Sophie was laughing as she was applying the powder to her face. Next, she picked up her blusher.

'I am going to open this very carefully. Phew, there we go. I love this one and I have done a tutorial all about blushers recently, so make sure to have a look on my YouTube channel for that. I will try and answer any questions you may have after this, but as always you can message me or leave comments in the usual places. So, let's put a little blush on, not clown blusher but a healthy glow is what we're aiming for. Right just need to do the eyes and then the lips and then we're good to go. As you can see this has only taken maybe five minutes, eight including the moisturising I did beforehand. Another five minutes to do the eyes I reckon, two for the lips so twenty minutes max. OK on to the eyes.'

Sophie held up more products and brushes to the camera and had another quick look at the numbers. They were still the same and the comments mostly encouraging, she'd have to break down the stats after and maybe experiment with doing one on a Sunday evening, that seemed to be another time for peak social media traffic. There seemed to be one person that was giving her a bit of agro but she didn't have time to pick up on that right now.

Sophie picked up the palette that she had been using

recently and grabbed for the next brush, all the while talking to the viewers and seamlessly applying her make-up, but also wondering what she could do to enhance her viewing figures and engagement.

'Once I've finished the video I will put a link to all the products in the comments, and then if you want to, like I've said already, you can copy me exactly.' A quick glance at the comments, to make sure everything was OK. 'Oh that's a brilliant idea, Xan. Maybe next time I can tell you the sort of products to prepare and we can do our make-up together.' That really is a great idea and it seemed to get a lot of likes. Thanks, Xan, whoever you are, thought Sophie.

'OK, here is the mascara that I am using at the moment. In fact, there's not a lot left. That's embarrassing, I probably should've checked that first. Anyway, we will do what we can.' Sophie kept her hand still and prayed to the Maybelline gods that she didn't blind herself, although that would probably get more views in the long run. 'Ha! I am sorry but I have to hold my breath when I am doing mascara and eyeliner. Is that just me? Not to mention the face that I have to pull with my mouth!'

Sophie spent a minute or two pulling faces at the camera before remembering what she was supposed to be doing. Laughing it off, she finished her eye make-up before she picked up her lip liner.

'OK, it's really coming together now in no time at all. Just going to put on some lip liner. I am using this one today because I want to enhance my natural lip colour.' Sophie took a deep breath and applied the lip liner thinking that she had nearly done it. She had nearly completed her first ever live video without too much of a problem. She was excited to break down the viewing figures and painstakingly traipse through the comments. Picking up her liquid lipstick she explained why it was good and when she used that over other similar products, before applying it.

'I love the colour of this one. Again this is one that I am running out of.' What with concentrating on the make-up, the video, the figures, not swearing etc. she didn't hear the back door open before suddenly, Marcus burst through the archway.

'Hey, Sophie, sorry to interrupt you but I need to make a brew and wondered if... oh shit, sorry, am I interrupting something?' Marcus smiled slightly his eyes shining as he waved at the camera. 'Erm, hi.'

Sophie rolled her eyes at her viewers. 'Sorry, guys, we're nearly done anyway and Marcus was just leaving.'

Sophie looked over at Marcus who was now stood beside her. He was smiling fully, causing his cheek to dimple, his eyes taking a mischievous look as he read the comments on the screen. Oh God, thought Sophie, what the hell? She couldn't tell him to get lost that would be rude and she couldn't explain that he was the gardener as it might look like she had 'staff'. Closing her eyes and just praying that he would leave didn't seem to be working either.

'Why hello there, Claudia, Ava and Henry.' Marcus gave a little wave. 'OK, what does that say? These comments are moving too quickly for me. Hang on. Ha ha no, I am not her boyfriend. I am her mate working on the garden in the background.'

Oh great, he's going to use this time to promote his garden. Why not, it's not like it could get any worse, thought Sophie. Plus it was why he was doing the garden work, after all. Taking a deep breath she knew she needed to try and get some control over the situation.

'Sophie, look at this. Everyone's putting their drink orders in. I don't think that we have a kettle big enough, but I'll read them out and you can make a note.' Marcus winked at her, clearly having the time of his life.

'Marcus,' she said, patting his arm to get his attention, momentarily distracted by the hard muscle underneath her palm, 'if you're making a brew for all these people then you're going to need to go and get a *lot* of milk.'

'Hmmmm, OK, guys we don't have the milk for all the brews. Sorry, maybe next time. Ha ha, Shauna you cheeky minx, I wasn't expecting that sort of a request.' Marcus grinned but carried on, 'It's certainly not that sort of show.' He looked at Sophie. 'Is it?'

Sophie read the comment and her jaw dropped, Marcus was certainly appealing to the viewers and a quick look at the numbers stunned Sophie into silence.

'But I must say, doesn't Sophie look beautiful? She's not going to in a minute when she's kicking my arse for interrupting!'

Marcus laughed again, and Sophie shook her head in disbelief. Did he just compliment her? Why was he being so nice all of a sudden? She knew why she was being nice. She didn't want to appear rude, but Marcus could be his usual antagonistic self, why was he instead choosing to be playful and apologetic, and why wasn't he plugging his gardening business?

'Anyway, ladies, oh and gents, I should probably leave you to it. What was that comment? Oh hi, Steve, well yes I am single at the moment, but I'm probably not what you're after.'

Marcus laughed before looking back to Sophie.

Time to regain control, thought Sophie, try and salvage as much of this as possible. 'Right OK, let's wrap this up. So this is the liquid lipstick and you can see how it's dried.'

'Face me, let me see.'

Sophie turned to Marcus tilting her face up so that he could see. He gently held her jaw and bent to look more closely. Sophie's eyes widened as she felt his rough fingertips gently holding her face.

'Wow, it really does dry well, you wouldn't know that was a liquid. Amazing.' He let go of her jaw and leant back again.

Sophie quickly took a breath unaware that she had been holding it, her heart beating erratically, she was still looking at Marcus's eyes, or at least she was until he turned away to face the camera.

'Shows what I know, right?'

Sophie coughed to clear her suddenly dry throat. 'So there you have it, my first ever live make-up tutorial. Joined by Marcus. Please like the video if you have enjoyed it, leave any feedback or questions in the comments and I will do my best to go through them. I'll have my usual video up on Tuesday night so why not subscribe to my YouTube channel, or you can like my page and get the links on here. OK thanks, guys, see you soon, bye.'

Sophie blew a kiss like she always did at the end of the video and clicked to finish it, catching Marcus waving as she did so.

The screen display changed indicating that it was uploading the video and that it would take a minute. She slowly turned towards Marcus who was looking incredibly sheepish.

'Shit, Sophie, I really am sorry, I had no idea what you were doing. I promise I won't make that mistake again. I'm just always going to assume you're working from now on.'

Sophie looked at Marcus, he was genuinely upset that he might have ruined her video. She shook her head and decided to let him off. 'I probably should've told you what I was doing. Don't worry about it. But listen, I have to ask, why didn't you mention your gardening business?'

'I didn't really think it was the right time. But, yeah, I probably missed a trick there, huh? Never mind. I'll go make that brew now and get out of your way. Sorry again.'

Marcus was looking right at her, making her body malfunction again, her breathing had stopped so that something warm and exciting could start low in her belly. Marcus's glance changed and he suddenly looked confused, but before she could do or say anything else he got up and went through the archway into the kitchen, enabling Sophie to breathe comfortably again. Taking a deep breath she looked at her screen. 'Shit,' she muttered, 'I can't believe it.' The view counter was increasing in front of her eyes, already at the four thousand mark, and the comments just kept coming and coming. Her heart began beating wildly, she was so giddy that it had worked even better than she thought. She had been nervous about using 'an everyday' make-up tutorial, avoiding a more dramatic makeover but they must have really liked it. She decided to go and check the comments.

Oh my God he is hot!

They must be together, right?

Did he say he was doing the garden? He can come and do my garden anytime.

Oh shit, Sophie thought. It wasn't the make-up. It was Marcus. Sophie was furious, yes she wanted the numbers, the engagement, but she wanted it for her make-up, not for the gardener.

Shit, shit, shit.

Chapter Nine

'Why are we here? Why must we always come here? There are other drinking venues, you know,' Marcus said with a groan, dropping his head into his hands as he reached the bar. Bailey was spinning his head around like he was trying to make it pop off, whatever he was looking for he didn't find.

Bailey slapped his hand on Marcus's back. 'You know full well why we keep coming back here, why we always come back here. It's the same reason you have all of us doing a garden for free.'

'I don't know what you're talking about,' muttered Marcus as he looked around trying to spot Sophie without looking obvious. Who was he kidding? He was obvious, and a glutton for punishment. The second he spotted her round by the back of the bar, collecting drinks and chatting with the locals, he sat up taller and checked to make sure that he wasn't having any wardrobe malfunctions. Knowing that he looked OK, he steered his glance back towards Sophie, unable to look away for long. Her brunette hair was tied back out of her face, the loose curls bouncing from the top of her head, her eyes seemed even brighter than usual, probably a new mascara or something. He really had to stop watching her videos. It also meant that when she smiled it went right up to her eyes and he could tell when she was being genuine and when she was being polite. Unfortunately for him, apart from at the house party, the only smiles he got these days were the polite ones, if any. It didn't matter too much, because when she got irritated her eyes lit up and her cheeks flushed and she really looked at him, and that was better because that was real.

Trying to look away from her, if just for a minute, he noticed that he couldn't keep his hands still, he was fidgety and restless. She would have to say hello at least, and even if he only got a polite smile it would be better than nothing.

Bailey nudged his ribs. 'What are you drinking?' he asked with a huge grin on his face.

Marcus spun around, his attention back to Bailey. 'Sorry, what?'

'Drink at the bar, what are you having? Man, she really gets to you, doesn't she?'

'I'll have a Beck's with a side of "mind your own damn business". Besides, where were you today? I know it's Sunday and all but I thought you were helping me out at their garden?'

Bailey turned around. 'Well, yeah, but I— Hi, Paige, how are you doing? Can we have two Beck's, please?'

'Hi. You both OK? I'll get those drinks for you. But, word to the wise, Marcus I would stay sat at this end of the bar tonight unless you want my number one bartender to kick your ass.' With that Paige wandered off to get the drinks.

Marcus rolled his eyes and groaned. 'What is it with Sophie? Why is she always pissy at me?' he asked.

'I have a few ideas,' mumbled Bailey.

'Me too,' winked Paige conspiratorially as she sat the bottles on the bar.

'Marcus, what did you do?' Bailey handed the money over to Paige.

'It was nothing really, just a mistake. I walked in on her when I shouldn't have.'

Marcus was feeling very uncomfortable with all the attention on him. It was making him squirm. Truthfully he had felt bad walking in on Sophie's live video, it had been a genuine error, but they had had a bit of a laugh about it, or so he thought at the time.

'What do you mean walked in on her…? Did you see—'

'No, you idiot, she was doing a live make-up video and I walked in on it. It was pretty funny actually, all these people were commenting and... Why are you looking at me like that? I didn't do it on purpose.'

'Yep, sure.' Paige handed the change over to Bailey and walked away to serve another customer. It was early evening on a Sunday night and there was a steady stream of customers, but it was unlikely to get too busy.

'So, did she give you an earful?'

'No, actually she was very nice about it at the time. But now she's mad? That would be just like her. She can never just tell you the truth.' Marcus made a noise of exasperation as Bailey tried to not snort his drink everywhere.

'If she was doing a live broadcast she couldn't exactly kick your ass in front of her viewers, now could she?' Bailey took a long swig of his drink as Paige returned and got her phone out to show Bailey the video.

Marcus tried to process what was going on with Sophie. So she had been mad, but hadn't acted mad and now she was likely to kick off with him when it was a genuine error. Why did he have to have a thing for the most complicated person in the world? At that moment Marcus decided to look around for her, and as he did, Sophie looked up at the same time and her expression immediately changed from one of concentration as she cleared away a table, to a look of rage. Oh, she was pissed all right. Well, bring it on, thought Marcus.

Sophie cleared away the glasses putting them on the end of the bar as she made her way towards them. Marcus slowly stood up, watching her every move, deciding to appreciate her body before she kicked off at him.

'What? So as well as seeing you all the time at home, you have to come to this bar as well?'

'Yes. We are supporting our friend's bar. Paige wouldn't like it if we spent our money somewhere else, would she?' Marcus retorted, casting a quick glance to Bailey who was casually sitting on the bar stool taking it in turns to watch the act in front of him unfold, but also watching the video on Paige's phone. Paige was stood across the bar from Bailey, watching Marcus like all she needed was a big bag of popcorn.

'I have seen far too much of you recently,' Sophie goaded.

Deliberately misunderstanding, Marcus smiled. 'You really haven't seen *that* much of me at all.' As he glanced down at himself and back up, his eyes returned to her face to judge her response. If he wasn't mistaken her eyes did linger over his chest and maybe her cheeks had gone a little red. That bolstered Marcus's confidence no end. 'But of course I can arrange that if you'd like?' Just as quickly the heat in her eyes was replaced with cold steel.

'Oh, please, as if I want to see that. I've seen enough of it already and calendar material you are not. Besides, you know what I mean. It's like I can't get a minute away from you. We need to talk about that little cameo stunt you pulled. You can't just barge in like that when I'm working.'

Marcus had been apologetic at the time, but it was clear she was spoiling for a fight, and he was frustrated enough to want to fight her back.

'No, actually, I was the one working, you were the one doing your make-up.' Oh yeah, that did it. As if a match had been struck Sophie ignited, her eyes blazing with fury, her arms shaking in anger.

'Oh, I get it, being a gardener is such a noble profession, so much more sophisticated than a make-up artist, and tell me how many years at university did it take for you to become a professional? Or better still you can tell me just how you're managing to meet the needs of *all* your customers? How's that business plan working out for you?'

Marcus turned to look at Bailey, who along with Paige had suddenly decided that the other end of the bar desperately needed their attention.

Marcus didn't want to admit how his veins were buzzing,

the adrenalin coursing through his body. He knew he had been deliberately mean about her work, but in that instance he couldn't resist and now that she was glowering up at him he couldn't help but smile. She was powerful, confident, and hot as hell and he liked all of it... a lot. More than he was comfortable with.

'Well, like I said at the time, I won't be interrupting your work again. So you don't need to worry about it. But if you really are "working" then maybe you should remember to look at what you're doing rather than watching me in your garden.'

It was a complete shot in the dark, nothing more than a volley in the conversation, but Sophie was suddenly blushing, her cheeks were definitely redder, and she dropped her eyes just for a second but he caught it. Oh my God, she had been checking him out when he was working. Ha! He found himself praying for warm weather tomorrow, either way he was certainly going without his T-shirt from now on, even if he had to freeze.

Sophie's eyes narrowed. 'Maybe if you were actually working on the garden and not sticking your nose into other people's business you would have finished by now.'

With that Sophie turned on her heel and walked away. Oh no, she's not getting the last word. Marcus ran after her, touching her arm, prompting her to turn around.

'What?!' As he looked at her, he could tell that her breathing was fast, the skin on her arm, hot under his hand. She was staring at him refusing to break the eye contact. Marcus had every intention of getting the last word in but suddenly found himself speechless. He was looking at her flushed face, watching as she tried to breathe normally and failed. She really was as affected by him as he was by her. He looked at her mouth as she bit her bottom lip. Was he leaning forward? Oh shit, he was leaning forward to kiss her. Suddenly remembering what happened last time and how quickly she had cast him aside, he dropped his hand from her arm. If she wanted him she would have to make the first move, there was no way in hell he was up for being rejected a second time, he was already pathetic enough pining after her now.

He lowered his eyes. 'I'll stay out of your way,' Marcus said softly, before turning around and walking back to the bar.

As he sat down on his bar stool, he turned to face Bailey, putting his back towards whatever Sophie might be doing, and took a long drink. Before Bailey could say anything at all Marcus said, 'So Monday, you coming to work on their garden then? The sooner we get that finished the better.'

'Actually no, I have some other appointments on Monday, but Joseph will be there.'

'What other appointments... oh, never mind. Will you be there Tuesday?'

'Yes, of course. Tuesday is fine.'

Bailey got Paige's attention to get another round, leaving Marcus to wonder exactly what appointments Bailey had that were so important. It was better to think of that, rather than what Sophie was or wasn't doing at that moment in time.

'Is Polly coming in tonight?' Bailey asked.

Marcus shrugged. 'I've no idea, but probably.' Marcus was so focused on his drink and not looking at Sophie that he missed the look on Bailey's face, but Paige didn't.

Chapter Ten

Sophie pushed the breath out of her mouth simultaneously rolling her eyes as an image appeared unprompted on her laptop screen, accompanied by a toe curling alarm and the announcement that she knew had been coming but had wanted to avoid regardless.

'Shit.'

The ringing kept going, and for a second Sophie's eyes shot around the kitchen desperate for some place to hide. Seriously contemplating jumping under the table – real mature – Sophie knew if she didn't answer it now, it would be ten times worse if she called back again later.

Clicking 'Accept', FaceTime connected and Sophie had a few seconds to throw on a smile before her mother appeared on screen.

'Hi, Mum.'

'Darling, there you are. I haven't seen you in ages. What have you been up to?'

Sophie very quickly went through the options available to her. Her instinct was to go sarcastic, but knew that that would bring the conversation back round to her failures all too quickly. The best thing would be to keep the topic on her mum.

'Oh, you know, the usual. What about you? It's nice to see you.'

'You know this doesn't count. When am I going to see you in real life?' Her mum made it sound like she lived on the other side of the world. They were only forty minutes away, just over the hills, in fact. Sophie's parents had a fabulous house with magnificent views that they bought a few years ago now. It was really very lovely, but it came at a cost. The cost being that Sophie would be accosted for every minute she was there about why she wasn't doing more with her intelligence, more in the way of a career, and if that didn't work, why she wasn't settled down with someone, etc. etc.

'Soon, Mum. It's just so busy now.' Sophie smiled brighter, but inwardly she groaned having realised she had set her mother up with the perfect way in to talk about work.

'You're busy with what, darling? With your make-up?' Here we go. Sophie zoned out, but kept a smile on her face as her mother went on about how she needed to take life more seriously. Sophie studied her mum and saw some of their shared features staring back at her. Her brown eyes, with naturally curly lashes, the same loose curls that fell onto her shoulders, albeit in different shades. Sophie wondered if she would be as lucky as her mum to have youthful looks in her fifth decade. She also wondered just what her mum would have done if she'd hadn't had kids. Her mum had mentioned once that she had been offered the chance to head up a recruitment business overseas. Apparently, the offer had come at the same time as Sophie's dad's proposal. Her mum hadn't mentioned anything further but given that they were north-west England based, and her mum and dad had been married for thirty-three years, the same age as Sophie's eldest sister, Sophie could make an educated guess as to what had happened. Still nobody could say her mum hadn't been successful. Early retirement isn't a gift for everybody, hence the gorgeous house in the hills, but Sophie couldn't shift the 'what ifs' when she looked at her mum.

'We just worry about you, don't we, Nick?' Sophie watched the screen as her mum took the phone over to her dad.

'Hi, Dad, you OK? How's your back? Did you try that cream I sent you?'

'Hi, love, I did and it worked wonders, thank you. Where did you find it?'

'I didn't. Mya found it on one of her travels.'

'She's a smart cookie that one, just like you.'

Sophie beamed at him. While her dad confessed that he had little to no knowledge of what Sophie was trying to do online, his faith in her never wavered despite Mum's insistence otherwise. Then again he was the blusher to her highlighter and always had been. Complete opposites that somehow made it work. Her dad was laid-back and as steady as a rock, her mother always moving from one thing to another, always busy. Always having a go.

'Anyway, so how is it going? Are you achieving your goals on your business plan?' and there it was. As much as her mum might disapprove, she was a shrewd one, but then she had been Chief Executive of her own recruitment company for a number of years before she sold the company and ran for the hills.

'Mum, you know if it wasn't for your critical eye my business plan wouldn't be as good as it is.'

'No, love, you did all the hard work, you're a natural, like me. That's why I don't get it. Why don't you apply yourself in another area? Any other area. You could make a fortune and have a real career. I still have some contacts in recruitment, you know, just say the word.'

'Mum, please. I've got this. It's all on track and everything is going to work. You'll see.'

'Hmmmm. Well, when are we seeing you next? Your sisters are coming over next Sunday. I'm doing a roast. Are you coming?'

Sophie looked at her calendar praying that she was working at the bar.

'Sorry, Mum, I can't. Paige has me down for a shift on Sunday.'

'Likely story. Let me see.'

Sophie held up her calendar on screen. 'See.'

'OK, well you need to come and see us at some point, you can't avoid your family forever.'

'I can't avoid you full stop,' Sophie said, with a smile.

'Watch your cheek, lady. We miss you, that's all. It's not the same watching your YouTube videos.'

'I didn't know you still watch them?'

Her mum's mouth opened wide in shock. 'Of course we watch them, don't we, Nick? Well, your dad doesn't watch them that often, but me and Debbie watch them all the time. She's shown them to her daughter too. You went to school with her, Clara. Do you remember her?'

Sophie did remember, but wouldn't have put the girl from school as the same person who would watch her make-up videos. As she seemed to recall there was no love lost between them.

'Thanks, Mum. I love that you watch them.'

'So when are we meeting Marcus?'

Sophie was stunned silent for a moment. 'What?'

'When are we meeting Marcus? Why didn't you tell us you were seeing somebody? Debbie and I agree he is absolutely gorgeous. Isn't he Polly's brother?'

'Erm, yes.'

'I thought so, I said to you, didn't I, Nick? I've told your sisters to watch it too.'

'What?'

'Your sisters, I mean as much as I don't like only seeing you on YouTube it's very helpful to be able to share parts of your life with other people. But really when are we meeting him in the flesh? I bet he's very muscular, isn't he?'

'What are you talking about? Marcus is doing the garden over. There's no more to it than that.'

'Hmm, that's a shame. Anyway, we'll see. Speaking of your sisters, it's Jenny and Olive's third anniversary next month. We're hoping that they are going to get engaged, although I was talking to Debbie about it, and she said which one of them proposes? I told her I have no idea. As long as one of them does and the other says yes, what does it matter? I'm so excited. I'm so happy that Jenny is finally settling down. Did you know that Hollie and Thomas are going on a mini-break in October? Who knows we could have another engagement on our hands.'

Sophie just watched in shock as her mother bounced up and down on her chair barely able to keep the phone still.

'How's Mya? How's Polly, Paige?'

'Yes, they're all fine, Mum.'

'I do love those girls. You might not have your head screwed on when it comes to business and love, but one thing I never have to worry about with you is friends. They're as solid as they come.'

Sophie was nearly lost for words as she finally managed to agree with her mum about something.

'They are the best. Have you been drinking, Mum?'

'Me? Well, I might have had a daiquiri or two with the girls at lunch. Why?'

That explains it, thought Sophie. Her mum was never usually this complimentary. 'So what's new, Mum?'

'Nothing much, love, I've just started archery. I have the time so I thought, why not. Your father is talking about going away again.'

'Haven't you only just come back from the last holiday?'

'Yes,' said Sophie's mum smugly. 'But you see you can have lots of holidays when you work hard in a profitable career, and retire to enjoy the spoils. Hint hint.'

'Right, got it, Mum. I need to go. I have to get ready for work.'

'I thought getting ready was your work.' Sophie's mum chuckled away to herself.

'OK, Mum, see you soon, love you, love you Dad.' She could just about make out a grunt in the background that suggested her dad was saying bye.

'Love you, darling, come and see us soon, and bring that delicious gardener with you.'

'Bye.' Sophie quickly pressed 'End' and watched as her mother disappeared from the screen. She took a deep breath as she rolled her head round her shoulders. Well, it hadn't been as brutal as she thought it would be. It wasn't pleasant but not as bad as some of the other conversations they had had previously. Obviously she just needed to time the conversations around her mother's cocktail consumption.

Sophie knew that her mother loved her, and wanted the best for her, but it was hard. She didn't fit in the mould her mother had created for her, and she didn't want the relationship goals her sisters had. She just wanted to work hard and succeed at bringing her passion to life. Why was that so hard for them to get? Still, Sophie couldn't help but smile at the thought that her mum was still showing her YouTube clips to her friends. She might not be able to come out and say that she was proud of her, but her actions maybe hinted otherwise.

Chapter Eleven

'Marcus! Greg's here with your digger,' Joseph called over his shoulder.

'About sodding time.' Marcus made his way over and shook hands with Greg.

'I know, I know. We got held up at another drop off. They had no space for the equipment... anyway I won't bore you with it. Here sign this. So what you doing then, some sort of water feature?'

They both laughed, Greg heartily, Marcus sarcastically as they remembered the first time Marcus had borrowed a digger for a complex water feature and managed to nick the water mains instead.

'No, it's a sunken area for seating and a fire pit. Besides, you know I can handle these things now.'

'So you say. See you in a couple of days. Give me a bell if it needs picking up before Friday.'

'Cheers, Greg. Will do.'

Marcus waved Greg off and neatly folded the paperwork up before putting it in his back pocket. He had a quick glance at the French doors and could see that Sophie was working again. It was the light he could see more than anything else, she looked more like a shadow, but he couldn't stop himself from staring every couple of minutes or so. He simply couldn't tear himself away for too long. She was absolutely right, if he could focus more on the garden they could be done quicker, but then what? Granted they weren't exactly on the best of speaking terms but at least this way he got to see her every day, but it was costing the business and more than anything else he hated how pathetic he sounded. His eyes picked up a change and he realised that her make-up spotlights had been switched off and she was up and moving about. Would she come outside now? Did she have reason to? Realising that the digger was an eyesore and it was going to be incredibly loud, it suddenly occurred to him that he had a legitimate reason to talk to her. If she was doing a live video again, well that would be fine because then she would have to be nice to him, wouldn't she?

Striding over to the back door, he stomped his feet to clear the mud away before walking through the kitchen. Marcus slowly peeked through the archway.

'Pssst.'

Without looking up from her screen Sophie said, 'You can come in. I'm editing.'

'OK great, I didn't want to steal your limelight.' He saw the corners of her mouth turn up, she was clearly trying not to smile. 'Anyway I won't keep you, I just wanted to let you know that the digger has arrived, it's going to be noisy and a bit of an eyesore but we need it. We'll make sure it's done as quickly as possible.'

Sophie finally looked up at him. 'OK not to worry, you put it in the project plan so I've done most of my recording for the next few days. I just need to upload and schedule them. Thanks for letting me know.'

'OK, no worries.'

Marcus wanted to wait around and say more but knew that he had been dismissed, she was clearly not in the mood, and for once he didn't feel like provoking her. She was quieter than usual and he worried that something might be bothering her. His mind wandered back to the comments on their live video. Most of them had been encouraging, some flirty, but there were one or two that were outright hateful. She had never mentioned having any issues with online abuse, but maybe that's what was bothering her. Or actually, it might be him and his constant mithering. He really wasn't sure. He was still perturbed by the realisation that he would miss seeing her every day. It was a worry that he felt so strongly about her, when she was clearly not as bothered or at least trying to not be bothered about him. Walking back through the kitchen and outside he grabbed Bailey.

'Can you use the plans to mark out the area that we are digging? I'll get started in the middle.' Reaching for the supplies he grabbed a can of spray paint and chucked it at Bailey.

'Yes, boss.' Bailey saluted, grabbed the plans and began measuring out the area under construction.

'Joseph!' Marcus shouted over to him, he was pulling out the last of the hedges and beginning the prep for the fence posts. Joseph stood up and turned to face Marcus with a nod.

'I'm gonna start with the digger in the middle while Bailey marks out the edges.'

'You want me to do it?' Joseph asked, nodding at the digger.

'No, it's OK, thanks though.'

With that, Joseph nodded and returned back to digging out the last of the hedge roots and Marcus jumped into the digger. He turned the ignition and moved towards the middle of the garden. It was starting to look like a much bigger space now that they had pretty much pulled everything out of it. It was brown mud and clay as far as the eye could see, but Marcus could visualise the end result and it was going to be magnificent.

This stage of the transformation was always the most exciting for Marcus, the canvas was blank and he was about to make his first mark. Well, it should've been exciting but in the same way, it felt like the beginning of the end. It wouldn't take long, the hardest part is almost always the prep. His mind started to wander, once again, with the idea of what would happen next. Would his business grow? How often would he see Sophie after this, and not just at the bar?

Marcus was pulling the lever and moving the excavated ground to one side where it would be put into a skip. Ideally, they would have a skip ready but the last one had been filled and needed to be taken away, another one was due to take its place at some point later today.

Suddenly there was a strange pullback on the mouth of the digger, a tension before there was a snap. Marcus stopped the digger and jumped out to investigate. At first, he couldn't see anything, and was about to jump back in thinking it was a sinewy twig when a small bit of black plastic caught his eye. He'd gone through a wire. His heart started galloping... not again. Please don't let this be an important wire, already knowing with a sense of dread that it was definitely going to be the—

'Have you guys hit any wires or anything? My broadband has just gone right in the middle of my video uploads.' Sophie was walking towards Marcus, the look on his face obviously giving him away. The frayed wire in his hands not helping the situation.

'What's that?' Sophie asked, clearly hoping that the Cable Gods had just had a blip and that the now in half cable that Marcus was holding was something else and not internet related.

'I'm going to guess it's your broadband cable.'

Bailey and Joseph ran over to see what the commotion was. Bailey's eyes were peeled wide in shock. He, like Marcus, knew that Sophie was about to explode.

'Are you kidding me!?' Sophie screamed. 'I know that you don't think much of my work but really, Marcus? Do you have any idea what you have done? This could set me back weeks, months if my subscriptions drop because my videos aren't there as promised.'

Marcus just looked at her. He felt awful. It had been an accident, but there was no way she was going to believe that, he could feel himself becoming defensive.

'Look I didn't do it on purpose, OK. It can't have been buried in the right place, besides can't you just use the Wi-Fi at the bar?' Marcus suggested, as Bailey groaned and Joseph quietly chuckled.

'You don't care about my work at all, do you? You've now gone out of your way to sabotage it. Twice. Well, thank you, thank you so much!' Sophie had tears in her eyes and Marcus didn't think he could feel any worse than he did right then.

'Come on, Sophie.' Joseph gently held Sophie's elbow, escorting her away from the scene of the crime. 'Let's go and get you a cup of tea and we will call the broadband company and see how quickly we can get this patched up, OK?'

Sophie followed Joseph back towards the house. Marcus looked at Bailey who just shrugged. Standing in the middle of the dug up area Marcus wished it would open a little more and swallow him whole. He was really going to have to make this up to her. He'd just need to figure out how and hope that she'd let him.

Taking a deep breath, he realised that the damage was done so he might as well carry on digging now.

Sophie was beyond fuming, her body shaking, her chest tight. She stood against the kitchen counter trying to get her breathing under control, desperately holding back hot angry tears, while Joseph filled the kettle.

'He just has no idea what he's done. And no, I can't use the sodding Wi-Fi at work, the speed is shocking and it's going to take forever to upload my videos. I'm going to have to though, because what's the alternative? Use a library? That would take even longer and I have a video due tonight!'

Joseph carried on making a brew, occasionally nodding sympathetically but mostly letting her blow off steam.

It was taking Sophie a little while to cool down to a rage level rather than a killing level. How could Marcus be so inconsiderate? She thought he was supposed to be a professional, but cutting through a broadband cable had to be a rookie error, surely? She was absolutely sick of it; of him.

She hated the noise, the disruption. How she always sat up straighter when he was outside, how she couldn't concentrate because she kept looking behind her. Or better yet constantly looking at her make-up mirror, using the reflection to try and see what he was doing, what part of the garden he was working on and worse, to see if he was looking at her.

She hated that in truth, she didn't need to work on the kitchen table as much as she did, but that every time she thought about working from her bedroom, her body just didn't move. She really disliked how she felt like a schoolgirl, all giddy at the start of the day and at the end of the day when he would have to come in and talk to her, and then wind her up to such an extent that she got angry again. He was doing her head in and now this. Well, it was the blast of cold water she so desperately needed, and a firm reminder of why she was right to stop their one and only kiss. She'd stopped it then because she knew he was trouble and her social media career was just about to take off. She had been absolutely right and yet look where it had left her. He had still managed to ruin her career without them even having had a relationship. Sophie looked down at the cup she was unaware of holding.

'That might help a little,' Joseph said quietly, nodding towards the cup.

Sophie looked down again and took a sip. Apart from being a little sweet, she guessed for the shock, it was nearly perfect, and very nearly calmed her down an inch or two. At least to the point where she could see again rather than the black rage that had been affecting her vision.

'You know, when I first starting working as a labourer, I blew up this girl's kitchen.' Sophie looked up at Joseph, it took a minute or two for what he was saying to sink in. 'No one was hurt, and the kitchen was mostly a shell as we were in the middle of doing it up, it had the essentials like an oven and what have you, or it did have before there was a definite explosion, albeit a small one. I remember how mad she was. When she came home and discovered what had happened, I watched her colour change in front of my eyes. She had seemed so carefree before that point. She then went on to tell me that she was a caterer, and she accused me of ruining her career. I felt awful, I could see she was really upset, and I knew that my incompetence had cost her work. Being a labourer, I knew what it was like to wait for the next job to come in. I went away that day and kept walking and walking trying to come up with a solution – until I found myself outside the village hall. I happened to know one of the keyholders, and when I explained the situation they allowed me the key for the next two days. They explained that the main hall was being used for piano grading and that people would be in and out to take piano exams, but that the kitchen was completely free for use.

'I went back to the house I had partially blown up, and held out the key. She looked at me and smiled and said she was sorry. I asked her why she was sorry, she wasn't the one who had destroyed part of her house. She said that she had overreacted and had already figured out where she was going to do her cooking from for the next few days as a backup, in case she wouldn't be able to use her kitchen. She explained that she was going to use her mum's kitchen, but that it would be rather cramped. I asked if she would come with me, and she did.

'We walked around the corner, me with my head still hung low because I was so ashamed, and I opened up the village hall and showed her the spacious kitchen in the back. She was delighted and I spent the next two days, either refitting her kitchen or helping her in the village hall. When she was finished, I managed to convince her to dance with me while one of the grade eight students was taking their piano exam. So you see it all works out in the end, it really does.'

Joseph patted Sophie's arm and started walking away,

before stopping and turning around again. 'It really was a great village hall, and it was the perfect reception venue for our wedding a year later. In a few months we're celebrating our thirty year wedding anniversary.' Joseph chuckled as he walked away.

Sophie's eyes opened wide at his casual remark that he had married the woman whose kitchen he had once blown up. Well, she certainly wouldn't be marrying Marcus, she didn't even want to be in the same room as him, but, she thought, it could be worse. He could've blown up my laptop. At least this way, she could keep working, even if it did mean waiting ages for uploads. As she got to the end of her brew, her breathing had returned to normal, and Sophie could grudgingly admit, albeit only to herself, that perhaps she had overreacted a little. Maybe.

Chapter Twelve

It was possible that she wouldn't even open the door. She had been steaming mad, beyond mad, and if she had had anything nearby or in her hand, she would've tried to kill him with it. Marcus sighed as he approached Sophie's front door. He had gotten himself into a routine of letting himself in but figured that would be a really bad idea right now. So instead he knocked and waited, shifting the heavy Japanese Red Acer plant over onto his other hip. He'd picked it up last night at the garden centre, it was going to be perfect in their garden, it produced the most stunning red colours that would work so well against the green lawn and the charcoal grey they were using in the sunken seated area.

Marcus took a deep breath. He hadn't known what to do with himself after Sophie left the house yesterday. He knew he needed to make it right, he just didn't think that she would let him. He might be an idiot but he wasn't a coward, and after a night of shuffling around his bed, he thought he had an idea that could make it a little bit better. After making some early morning calls, and calling in a favour, it would all be for nothing if she didn't open the door.

The door did finally open, but it was Mya who smiled at Marcus.

'Hi, if you're looking for "pissed and angry" she's still upstairs.' Mya opened the door fully and motioned to let Marcus in.

'She's still really upset then?'

'Yes, and so am I. But lucky for you I have the option of working away again for a few days, so a few days using hotel Wi-Fi, when I am not in the spa, is going to work out in my favour. Is that for her? It's lovely.' Mya pointed down at the Acer.

Marcus coughed, still feeling embarrassed, but not as upset as yesterday, at least now he had a plan. He always felt better with a plan. He would win her round, he needed to, and once he had he could text Bailey and Joseph and tell them that the coast was clear. 'Yes, it's my start of an apology.'

'Start? In that case, SOPHIE!' screamed Mya as she leaned towards the stairs.

The sound of a door opening and feet appearing at the top of the staircase made Marcus hold his breath. She was revealed to him step by step, her toenails painted red, moving up her long legs towards her washed and worn denim shorts that stopped mid-thigh, her grey sweatshirt hanging off one shoulder revealing her honey coloured skin and the delicious curve of her neck. He had seen so much of her neck lately, that and her hair, it was the only part of her he could see while they had both been working. However, just as her face was revealed, his primitive instinct meant that he looked straight into her eyes as he sensed that's where the danger would be. Yep, she was still furious. Understandably.

Marcus coughed to try and get some air to his throat. Mya was still stood holding the door open, she obviously wanted to bear witness to his pathetic attempts at grovelling. He would've preferred to do this without an audience but what the hell. Straightening his shoulders and making sure that he looked as non-threatening as possible he held out his hopefully peace-making red Acer tree towards Sophie.

'Here, I know it's not the broadband that you need, but it's a peace offering. Well, the start of one. It's going to look great in your garden.'

Sophie took the plant and mumbled a quiet 'thanks', before moving the mini-tree into the lounge, immediately returning to her spot in front of the stairs, facing him as he remained on the threshold of the front door.

'I know that you're not working at the bar today, because I messaged Paige, and because of my cock-up yesterday there's not much more we can do until the cable has been fixed, but I think I've thought of a way that we can both work today and I can hopefully make it so that you hate me a little less. What do you think?' Marcus watched as Sophie looked away and then looked pleadingly at Mya.

Mya's eyes opened up wide and she laughed as she shrugged her shoulders and feigned ignorance. 'I don't know why you are looking at me. I'm not the one being invited, but that's OK as I need to pack again anyway.'

Marcus watched as Sophie all but shouted at Mya, albeit with no sound whatsoever.

'But isn't there that thing we need to do?' Sophie asked, her eyes practically falling out of her head.

Wow, thought Marcus, this was going to be harder than he thought. If she really didn't want to go with him, there would be absolutely nothing he could do about it, and she would have what she'd consider a very legitimate excuse for keeping him at arm's length.

Mya was still laughing only now she was clutching her stomach, 'No, my darling Sophie, we have absolutely nothing to do today, and I absolutely insist that you do whatever Marcus has in store.' With that, she winked at Marcus and turned away to go up the stairs.

'Come on, grab your shoes and your laptop and whatever else is it you might need to do your other work.'

Sophie's eyebrows rose in shock, before bending down to put her flip-flops on. Well, he guessed it was the first time he had actually referred to her vlogging as work, without sounding sarcastic. It was true though, it most definitely was work. Marcus had been going through some of it last night and also thinking about her business plan and how hard she was working, he knew he had potentially messed her up completely.

Sophie disappeared to get her stuff, and while she did, Marcus sent a text to Bailey and Joseph telling them that the plan was going ahead. It was a shame on a beautiful day like today that he couldn't be doing the garden work himself but he knew it was going to be worth it. Suddenly Sophie reappeared with her stuff.

'So where are we going?'

Marcus nearly laughed at Sophie's attempt at surly, but held it back, just.

'You'll see.' Looking over at her he felt his heart, and other places jump with excitement that after all this, they were going to get to spend the day together, just the two of them. As she turned and closed the door behind them, Marcus had to try and remember that he was apologetic and therefore should lose the huge grin spreading across his face.

'Why are we at a garden centre?' Sophie asked as they pulled into the car park. 'Isn't this for old people, and people like you?' she continued, giving him the side eye. Marcus hadn't said much as they were driving here, he was probably trying to keep himself out of trouble thought Sophie. Too late for that. Sure, she'd managed to get the most important video uploaded at the bar last night, but it had taken ages. She had loads of videos and social media bits to schedule as well, but that would take a long time, and not to mention decent Wi-Fi to sort it all out. Instead, she had decided to take it one day at a time. The company fixing the broadband couldn't come out for another couple of days, and she just needed to remember that it was an innocent mistake.

'You OK?' Marcus asked as Sophie covered up her snort with a cough.

'Yes, fine. So why are we here?'

Marcus parked up his small van not much bigger than a car and opened his door.

'Don't forget your bag and follow me.' Marcus led the way as they walked towards an open plan, slightly roofed area that had beautiful flowers everywhere. The sound of dripping water made her look around for the source and realised the hosepipes now hung up on the walls must have recently supplied the plants with water. The colours were grouped together forcing her to look from one lot of flowers to another, from the reds to the purples and so on. As she was looking around she saw Marcus was about to turn the corner and head towards the built-up area of the garden centre.

She wasn't sure what was in the main entrance as her attention had been caught by something else entirely. Something that she really shouldn't be looking at. While the beautiful flowers, and the display of colours had momentarily calmed her mood, checking out Marcus's bum in his trousers was only making her angry again. Angry because although she would've liked to, she was finding it very difficult to look away. His jeans were a faded blue – there was nothing special about them at all – but they were working magic. She could just about admit to herself that as a gardener he was bound to have a lean body, what with all the heavy lifting and so on. But that was about all she was ready to admit to herself. Certainly not that she found his green eyes captivating, and that when he smiled he tended to smile with one side first before the other cheek joined in, and that when she was looking into his eyes, she could forget everything that was going on. Nor would she admit, that during the one kiss they had shared, that she had stroked her way up his thick muscular biceps feeling them tense underneath her palm, before her hands pulled the hair at the back of his head, moving his body closer to hers.

Marcus suddenly turned around. Crap, she was fairly sure she had just been caught checking out his bum. That would be bad on a normal day, but on a day when she was supposed to be supremely mad at him was much worse. Still the reminder that she was mad, and the fact that she had been caught was just what she needed to make her stomach tighten and her scowl deepen as she recalled why they were here in the first place. She was now angrier than ever, and it was in no way defensive because she got caught checking him out. No way.

Marcus had turned back around straight away, presumably checking that she was following and was now walking towards the garden furniture. He stopped next to a gorgeous slate coloured outdoor sofa and sat down. He patted the space next to him. For good measure Sophie sat down, but as far away as was possible.

'OK, I've brought you here because as you can see on a day like today it's incredibly quiet. There are no weekenders killing time, it's mostly trade people and pensioners. Anyway, the point is that their WiFi is fantastic. I happen to know the manager and he said you can use the staff Wi-Fi, and that you're welcome to work here for as long as you need to, whenever you need to. I thought that you could either work here on one of the sofas or through here.'

With that Marcus jumped up and grabbed Sophie's hand, pulling her up and off the sofa. She went to pull it away but stopped when they rounded the corner. The restaurant or cafe area should've been nothing to write home about, just your standard garden centre eatery, but it wasn't. There were glass windows everywhere on nearly all sides. On one side it backed onto the flowers. So many flowers. So if you wanted, you could sit next to a kaleidoscope of colour. Or on the back wall there was a slightly darker area as part of the seats were arranged beside the fish ponds, each had their own tranquil water feature. Not her cup of tea, but the sound was none the less soothing. Finally, the other corner was showcasing some stained glass windows alongside the outdoor lighting range. All together the space should've been chaotic, but it was resplendent, calming and beautiful, and Sophie was at a loss but to look around at everything and try and take it all in.

Her attention was suddenly diverted from her surroundings as there was a gentle pull on her hand.

'I'm going to go and get us some drinks while you figure out where you'd like to sit.' Marcus looked at Sophie and pulled his hand again. 'You need to let go.'

Sophie threw his hand away, and Marcus laughed, the dimple on his cheek making a rare appearance. Sophie quickly looked around happy to have a task to cover up the embarrassment she felt at not actually letting go of his hand when she could have. It made her realise that actually, she liked holding hands. It had been ages since she had had a boyfriend, and the kiss she had shared with Marcus had been the last physical contact she'd taken part in in a long time. Not through lack of invites, but because of her dedication to try and make her work a success. Every spare minute was put into her videos and her social media, she didn't want a single 'what if' when it came to her career. It was exactly why she had shut Marcus down last time.

As Sophie walked towards the chosen table, she looked at her hand. It still tingled from Marcus's touch, but she thought, that could be loneliness, rather than an attraction to Marcus – Marcus the man who annoyed her daily and then sabotaged her career by cutting through the broadband. Try as she might to regroup and get back some of that angry fire that had spurred her earlier; the bright colours, the calming water and the gorgeous scents made it impossible to stay mad. She had chosen a table with her back to the stained glass, but with a view of the flowers and the sounds of the water just close enough to hear, without her feeling like she needed to pee the whole time. She was playing her hand through the colours and shapes on the table cast by the stained glass when Marcus came back holding a tray with two mugs and a pot of tea.

'Oh, this is the table I normally pick too. I love how the stained glass reflects on the table.' Marcus smiled gently at her, his eyes showing her how cautiously he was playing it.

Sophie took a deep breath suddenly feeling a bit mean

about making him feel so bad. Accidents could happen. They happened all the time. Like her checking out his bum, that had been an accident. She went to open her mouth to apologise when Marcus beat her to it.

'Look. I really am sorry about the broadband. I know that it is really important to your work. I would never have cut the line intentionally. I mean, why would I?' He was scratching the scar on his eyebrow. She knew that he did that when he felt uncomfortable or stressed. 'Yes I've taken the piss a little bit about your work, and I'm sorry for that too because I know it's important and the amount of time and energy you put into it really shows.' Marcus took hold of Sophie's hand. The tingle was there again and this time it shot straight up her arm. She knew he didn't do it on purpose, but she still wasn't sure if she was buying into the whole 'I believe your work is important' line. He'd made it clear far too often that he thought it was some sort of elaborate hobby. Either way, she knew she had to put him out of his misery.

'I'm sorry too. I overreacted. I was able to get yesterday's video online using the bar's Wi-Fi. I'm sure that the broadband will be fixed soon, and if not then I'll just have to keep manually uploading each video as and when I need to. Maybe I can do it from here. It would make a nice change from sitting at the kitchen table.'

It would be a nice change certainly, but as lovely as the current scenery was, it wasn't anything compared to watching Marcus work in the garden. She felt her face flush and looked down at their hands.

Marcus coughed and let go of her hand to pour the tea. 'So the bar Wi-Fi worked enough to upload your Tuesday video, but what are you going to do about your Throwback Thursday video? Can you use a link to one that you've done before?'

'Yes I can, but I usually do an intro and explain why I've picked it. I mean, that's fine I've already done it, but I will need to edit the two pieces together and upload it from the bar,' Sophie looked around her again, 'or here.'

'What topic have you picked for Saturday? Are you going to be doing another one of your ready for town makeovers?'

Sophie's eyes shot up and she really looked at Marcus. She'd thought he was going to take the piss, or that he didn't really know what she did, but he obviously meant what he said. He was taking her work seriously.

'You watch my videos?'

'No, well some, I mean not all of them.' Marcus coughed and looked down, a definite blush appearing over his cheekbones. He looked up at her through his obscenely long eyelashes and grinned. 'Bailey made me watch the Mya makeover one.'

'Ha. Yes, that's not surprising it happens to be my most popular video of all time.' Sophie rolled her eyes as she smiled.

'Polly's watched them at mine from time to time, so I've seen a few of them.'

'You know I can have a look and it would take me all of one minute to find out if you are a subscriber.' She was winding him up on purpose, wondering how he would respond.

'Well, obviously I am a subscriber, I mean what are friends for?'

'So you're watching online videos about make-up and lifestyle because you are a friend?'

'Of course, it has absolutely nothing to do with the stunning creator running the show.' Marcus smiled wickedly and Sophie had to busy herself with her drink to pull herself away from his eyes.

'Right, I have some work to do in here myself so I'm going to head over to the trade bit. Once I've finished I'll come sit with you and then when you're done we'll go and get some food.'

Before she could say no, he'd already stood up and tucked his chair in and walked away. He'd only walked a few feet when he turned around and caught her checking his bum out again. He laughed as he turned around and carried on walking. Figuring she had already been caught she brazenly studied all of him as he made his way out of the cafe. He had been long gone before she managed to pull herself out of a dream world, where she was holding onto his thick muscular arms, as he held her close enough that she could feel all of his equipment. Flushed she drank her tea before reaching into her bag to get her laptop out and begin her work.

Chapter Thirteen

Marcus merged into heavy traffic. 'We just need to do a quick drop off at your house before we go out to get food. Are you working at the bar tonight, Paige mentioned she might need you later? I can drop you off after if you like?' Marcus looked at Sophie, trying to stifle the grin on his face. After the last few hours, and the promise of more time together, Marcus wasn't sure that he would stop smiling for quite a while.

'Yeah, she's asked me to go in but why don't we just eat there? Saves time and it means I won't be late for work.'

'Sure.' Marcus decided to believe that it was so that they could spend more time together rather than just being efficient, but knowing Sophie as well as he did, he couldn't help but think it was probably more the latter.

'So did you get what you needed from the garden centre?' Sophie asked.

'Yes, I was just pricing up some options. I need to get some bark and other big items. I'll either need my van for that or get them to deliver. I can look into all of that later though.'

'So how is the business going? I know that you need a little help promoting, hence the garden, but generally is it OK?'

Marcus cast a quick glance in Sophie's direction as they stopped at the lights. She was looking at him, her face more open than usual. He nearly laughed out loud as he realised it wasn't that it was more open, it was because she wasn't scowling or giving him the stink eye. He took a moment to appreciate how different she was when she wasn't mad at him. Her gorgeous dark eyes were lit up and her skin glowed and tempting him to get closer, to touch, to taste. He just wasn't sure if or how he could make that happen. Just as quickly, he reminded himself of how it felt being shut down last time. He took a deep breath and changed his focus towards answering her question.

'Yes, I have a lot of steady regular customers. They came to me once my dad retired. I need to think of a more realistic schedule actually, so that while I am doing your garden I can still make sure that they are being seen.' Marcus looked thoughtful for a moment. 'But that's not what I want to focus on.'

'It's not? What then?' Sophie asked, sounding genuinely interested.

'Transformations.' Sophie looked puzzled. 'Like what we're doing with your garden, for example. Bringing it back to nothing and creating something spectacular. Your garden is going to look amazing. I want to do that, the landscaping, the planning the engineering. It's what I've trained for. All of it, not just cutting lawns and digging out. But, you know, I can't let my dad's customers down. I'd never hear the end of it.'

It wasn't that he begrudged it, it was just that once he had told his dad he wanted to garden like him, his dad had gotten the wrong end of the stick and so thought he was helping Marcus out when he asked his customers to use him instead. He just hadn't been able to have that conversation with his dad yet, and after his small heart attack scare a couple of years ago, the right time just seemed to move further away.

'Does your dad know that's what you want to do?'

Marcus shook his head and half smiled. 'No, but it doesn't matter. He's retired now and most of his customers aren't too much trouble.'

'No probably not, but they are taking up your time. Time when you could be planning and organising more transformations.'

Marcus indicated before parking up on the street outside Sophie's house. He turned to look at her.

'It really hasn't been a problem until now. I think that it's only recently that I have become more focused. Then again I think it's only recently I've realised what it is that I want.' The double meaning wasn't lost on him. The only difference being he'd known he wanted Sophie for a long time.

'Maybe it's my influence.' Sophie laughed. 'After all we both know how focused I've been. Perhaps too much at times.' Sophie pulled her eyes away and looked down.

As he looked at her face he suddenly realised that she was talking about them. That they were both talking about 'them'. Did that mean she regretted shutting him down? Had she changed her mind? Sensing there was a potential shift in their relationship he watched closely as her face changed. Putting the polite smile back on her face, she looked at him in what he could only describe as a professional way. Just like that, she'd made the same decision again. She was going to put her work first.

'I'm sure that you're going to do great. The plans for the garden sound amazing, even if I have been struggling to visualise the end result.'

Marcus opened the door and motioned for Sophie to do the same. As he got to her side he took her hand again. The first time he had done so was an accident, a spur of the moment thing, then when he did it again he genuinely thought that she would push him away. But having got away with it twice there was no harm trying a third time. Besides, it felt wonderful holding her hand in his, and it felt natural to try and hold it whenever he could, it also surprised her so much that each time her professional mask would fall away.

'Funny you should mention that. I have another surprise for you. Follow me.' He began walking to the front door, letting himself in, but not letting go of her hand, as he led them through the hallway to the kitchen and out the back door. 'As you know with work sort of suspended until your broadband can get fixed, sorry again about that.' Sophie pulled on his hand, the unexpected pressure making him move his weight to his back leg, she reached for his shoulder, gently pushing so that he could bend slightly and then kissed his cheek.

'It was an accident so you can stop apologising. It's OK.'

Marcus was stunned.

Sophie coughed and pulled at his hand, 'You had something to show me?'

At that point, Marcus had a few different things he wanted to show her.

'There you are! Come on we've done it!' Polly shouted from the other side of the garden. Sending a silent thanks to Polly for interrupting them before he did something stupid, Marcus looked over at his hand holding Sophie's.

'Why is Polly here? Wait, what are Bailey and Joseph doing?'

'Just before we get properly outside, I want to say that I felt bad about disturbing your work, albeit temporarily, and wanted to try and show you that it was going to be worth it, what your garden is going to look like. As my team had some unexpected downtime they wanted to help out too.' Marcus stepped forward bringing Sophie with him. 'Ta-dah.'

'What am I looking at?' Sophie stepped forward and Polly took over.

'Well you know how much I hate my job right, but one of the few perks is that I get to use the printer.' Everyone knew how much Polly hated her HR job, but no one could figure out why she stayed.

Polly continued to explain. 'So Marcus sent me over the plans. Basically what I've done is print them almost to scale so that you can get a feel for how it's going to be.'

Marcus looked at the garden and felt his heart speed up, and not for the first time today. It was as close a visual as they were going to get before the work was finished. It really was going to be amazing and he gave himself a little cheer for having had this in his mind's eye.

Polly dragged Sophie around, showing her where and what flowers would be planted in the pots. How big the sunken fire pit would be, where the outdoor furniture would go, the colour schemes. The decking details at the back where the suntrap would be and so on. Marcus watched Sophie closely to make sure that she liked it. Her face was beaming with each new feature uncovered. Interrupting only to ask relevant questions with Joseph or Bailey answering. As they started to go back towards the house she looked up at her usual spot through the French doors, where she usually sat at the kitchen table.

'So there's going to be a small decking area behind the doors?'

'Yes, it was Marcus's idea. He said that it would... what did you say Marcus, about symmetry?' Polly asked.

'It will match the one at the end adding a pattern and symmetry to the garden. It will also allow you a flat surface so that you can work outside or so that you can put your light reflector on there to get even more natural light for when you're doing your filming.'

Sophie grinned, spinning around on the spot, pure delight shining out of her face. 'I can't believe it. It really will be amazing. When will you have it done by?'

Marcus laughed and took a moment to try and capture Sophie at her most beautiful, so he could remember it the next time he undoubtedly pissed her off.

Chapter Fourteen

The knock on the door made Sophie jump, she hadn't realised how much she had been concentrating on her six-month plan. Looking up she heard Marcus shout a hello.

'In here,' Sophie shouted back, residing in her usual spot at the kitchen table.

'So has the engineer called? Any idea when the broadband is going to be up and running?' Marcus asked as he walked past her into the kitchen, getting two mugs down making himself at home as usual. 'Oh and you got some post too.' Marcus dropped an envelope on the table and went back to the kitchen.

Sophie figured he was making them both a brew. He was a serious tea drinker. She had never seen anyone drink as much tea as he did – it almost matched her addiction to biscuits. It made her chuckle, thinking how domesticated they appeared. It was nice, although living with him would cost a fortune in Yorkshire Tea. Sophie's smile slipped from her face as she remembered that it was temporary. When the garden was finished they'd both be back where they were before. Her stomach dropped and she recognised the feeling for precisely what it was, remorse. It wasn't that she regretted what happened to their relationship, well she did, but it wasn't that straightforward. She had needed to focus on her work, she still did and it was so close to paying off. But she could admit that it had come at a price. A price that had become all too obvious of late. As much as she could get used to his company, and having him around, the occasional hand-holding had become a bit of an addiction, and the pressure of forcibly restraining herself from kissing him was getting harder, but she knew the damage she had caused when she turned him down last time. She certainly knew that she couldn't hurt him like that again, and ultimately she hadn't 'made it' yet, so she needed to try and continue with a single-minded focus on her career. Not wanting to wonder what might have happened with her career if she gave in to his pull – then or now. It was just getting more difficult, but she assured herself that it would be worth it in the end.

Her concentration was broken when a mug was put in front of her. Marcus put his hand on her shoulder and the butterflies that flew around her body were yet another indication of the mistakes that she had made, and how her once ironclad resolve was crumbling under pressure.

'You OK?' Marcus asked, concern unhidden on his face.

'Yes, sorry, just concentrating on work. How come you're here? The engineer can't come out until tomorrow.'

'Oh, that's what I just asked. So one more day, huh? How behind are you?' Marcus pulled out the seat next to her and sat down blowing on his tea.

'I'm not really, well, not that my subscribers would notice I don't think. Besides I made up some time after I mistakenly uploaded the wrong video. Surprisingly, it grabbed me some more subscribers. Whether they stay or not when they realise I'm not always such an idiot, remains to be seen. I've lost a little bit of time in my six-month plan, but that's what I was working on now. I think it's nearly done, I just need to think of some more pieces that are a bit different but still within my brand, you know? Anyway, I think I've covered my plan with as much as I can do. I need to do a couple more recordings, then it's going to be a busy few days editing and uploading, then I should be back on track.'

'So what are you doing today then?'

'Look, Marcus, you don't need to do any more gestures or any more apologising. It's OK.'

'Ha, actually I was going to ask if you wanted to help me in the garden? Joseph can't work today, and what with the broadband still down there's not a lot I can do, but there are some bits and pieces I thought you could help me with?'

Sophie's eyes opened wide in shock. 'You want me to help you in the garden?'

'Yes, your garden, you're going to need to know how to look after it when I'm gone.'

She could have sworn she saw a brief look pass across his face, and she wondered if he was worried about this finishing too, maybe he would miss it as well.

'Or are you one of those girls that's too afraid of a little mess?'

Oh man, that was like a red rag to a bull. She wouldn't be able to say no now, it wasn't in her nature to back down from a direct challenge and she suspected he knew that and had used it to his advantage. Well, thought Sophie, not about to be bested, game on.

'Fine, give me ten minutes to type this up and straighten my stuff away and then I'm all yours.'

Marcus grinned and winked. 'Can't wait, that sounds fantastic.'

Sophie laughed, and then took a sip of her tea. Her mouth parched thanks to the images that flashed through her mind at the thought of being all his.

'OK, it's really simple. All we're going to do is measure and dig the holes for the fence posts. If we have time we might try and get the posts at least part way in. It means less work for Joseph and Bailey tomorrow, or the day after if the engineer is here.' Marcus, ever the optimist grabbed Sophie's hand and began pulling her towards the edge of the garden where the hedge used to be.

As soon as she could, she removed her hand from his. She was really struggling to keep the distance that she had put in place after *that* kiss, and he wasn't helping matters. She saw a look of confusion on his face, but frankly, that was easier to deal with than accidentally leading him on. She was making herself dizzy. She could admit that he was having quite the effect on her. It was really cheesy, if she was honest with herself, it reminded her of a schoolgirl crush. She couldn't wait to see him; she was now exclusively working from either the garden centre or the kitchen table – both places where she could either see or think of him. The effortless way he just made himself at home and always made her a brew before he went to work. The hand-holding and the breath-stealing looks and glances that heated her up from the inside out. More than anything, and the main reason she found herself pulling away wasn't just work, it was the fact that she couldn't bear to think about what it would be like when he was finished and was gone. Although looking around at all the dirt and dug out holes, it would seem that was a way off yet.

Marcus had handed her a small shovel and pointed to the area she was going to dig up. She did as he asked for two minutes before her knees were killing her and she began sweating. It was too hot a day for gardening, but she wasn't going to let him think that she couldn't keep up. She jumped up.

'You had enough already, princess?' Marcus laughed.

'Nope, I just need to go and get changed, it's hot out here.' Sophie ran upstairs into her bedroom and tried to find something to wear that was cooler. If it also had the benefit of winding him up, well then that was just perfect. She pulled open her drawer and looked at what was in front of her. A bikini was pushing it without a doubt. Also not practical, as even though she might want to push his buttons she certainly didn't need her boobs falling out every two minutes. She grabbed a blue sports bra from her gym pile, and grabbed a pair of what could only be called short shorts. They weren't obscene but they were probably more suitable for holidaying than gardening. Throwing them on, she stood in front of the mirror grabbing her hair up into a messy bun. Yup, perfect. She would show him. She'd be able to work no problem, she was fit and didn't doubt that she could keep up with the physical demands, she was a regular gym-goer, so long as it wasn't spin class. She felt she had to be for her work, and, as for getting dirty, she had absolutely no problem with that. Marcus, however, might have a slight problem trying to keep his attention on the job at hand. Running downstairs and out into the garden she desperately tried to keep a straight face but almost fell over her own feet when she saw Marcus had taken his T-shirt off and was working in just his light brown work shorts. Work shorts that hung dangerously low on his hips showing off a delectable V shape underneath the most perfect six-pack she had ever seen, not to mention his delectable happy trail. Trying to get her head back into the game, she straightened and pulled her shoulders back, dragging her eyes up his body ready to see what Marcus was going to make of her outfit.

'OK, then, princess, you ready to keep going?'

What the hell, how was he completely unaffected? She almost growled before reason kicked in and she remembered that she actually didn't want to provoke him, especially not with her body. Sinking back to the floor, she began to dig in earnest, this time not to make a point, but more to keep herself busy and out of trouble.

Marcus had measured the same area at least five times. Luckily he didn't think Sophie had noticed but figured he should look over at her again to make sure. Oh shit. His tongue was glued to the roof of his mouth, which was fortunate really because otherwise he was likely to drool or say something he might later regret. But she looked absolutely incredible. Her legs folded underneath her as she worked, making him want to unfold and stretch out those legs preferably on either side of his own body. He enjoyed nothing more than staring at her ankles and casting his eyes up over every exposed inch of her legs. Her shorts, if you could call them that, were the main problem. They weren't tight, but they were short, obviously, but they kept threatening to show him a glimpse of her perfect bum. Her sports bra, though, was behaving admirably and with a thoroughness he could not applaud. Then again if it wasn't working as efficiently as it was, he would probably fall down in a heap on the floor.

He tried to laugh at the situation. He'd known the second she had declared she needed to change that she would do something like this. He enjoyed winding her up and calling her princess. He knew that if he indicated in any way that she couldn't keep up with a task it immediately got her back up. But knowing that she might wear something provocative and looking right at it, were two very different things. He would never ever get the image out of his head of her stood there in front of him, the sun shining over her skin, her eyes blazing before they dulled. He would do anything to stop them from dulling, it was worse than the professional mask he saw her put on. When she was just 'her' she was everything, and anytime she pared it down, he felt robbed. Her eyes didn't shine as bright, her smile was forced and practised. Instead, he wanted to see her brown eyes turn almost golden, her face when she properly laughed and how it made her nose slightly scrunch up.

He grinned to himself when he thought of the look on her face when she saw him. He'd taken his T-shirt off as a pre-emptive strike. It had worked. He was very proud of his six-pack and was just incredibly lucky that gardening allowed him to stay on top of it, that and the weights he had at home. OK so, if he was honest, he had spent a lot of time sculpting his abs, and he knew that at times he could be quite vain about it. But it had definitely been worth it when he saw how she struggled to drag her eyes up to his face. The only disappointment was the look in her eyes. The fiery look of challenge was quickly doused by what he thought looked like disappointment. The Sophie he knew wouldn't do that, but he was at a loss to figure out why. Momentarily puzzled but not giving up he continued to measure out the areas they needed to dig up, this time successfully. Once he had done that he went back over to where Sophie was. She was focused as she worked hard digging out the mud and clay. Of course, she would be, she worked hard at whatever she was doing.

She looked up and smiled one of her non-smiles. 'Is this OK?'

'Yeah that's great, we just need to keep going and go a bit deeper.' Marcus waited for a moment, gathering his nerve. 'So listen, I have another favour I wanted to ask you?'

Sophie looked at him suspiciously. 'You want a makeover?'

'No, I think I have my skin tone matched perfectly, but thank you.' He watched as she smiled, realising that once again he had let slip just how many of her videos he had been watching lately.

'No, I wondered if you would help me with my business plan.' He carried on digging even though Sophie had stopped. He had hoped she would agree to it. Her business acumen, he had learnt recently, was second to none.

'You want me to help you with your business plan?'

'Yes, look I know that I was a bit of a dick about your work at first, but I have seen just how seriously you are taking it and how much you put into it. If anyone can make what you do a success, well it would be you. I need some of that to rub off on my work, now that I have this new found focus.'

'Marcus, look at me.' Marcus looked up, feeling embarrassed although he wasn't sure why. 'I'd be more than happy to help. I think that you are going to have an amazing garden transformation business and I'll help any way I can. Although I think you should probably make sure you use your labourers for this bit.' Sophie grinned. 'So generally speaking what is your plan? Where do you see your business in five years?'

'Well, as you know I want to do transformations. I'd like to build up my portfolio and eventually do large-scale transformations.'

'Yeah, but that's more medium term. In five years to the day, what would you be doing?'

For a brief minute, he saw himself here, working side by side with Sophie as they each managed their successful businesses. Shaking his head, he said instead, 'Planning a huge transformation.'

'OK. Residential or corporate?'

Marcus hadn't considered corporate transformations. He stopped digging for a second as he gave it some thought.

'Honestly… erm, I think residential.'

'OK and presumably you would like to have a steady stream of them. So, quick short-term question, what are you going to do about your current customers?'

'I'm not sure. I can't give them up yet as they are my main source of income, but I know what you mean when you said the other day that they are taking up my time. I could see what Bailey wants to do, but you know him, he's not one for taking anything seriously.'

'Hmmm. It sounds to me like you have a few areas you need to think about. But I can help. You may want to think about Bailey though, if he is serious he could be a major asset.'

'I'm not the one that has the problem with thinking seriously about Bailey. Bailey is the one that has problems thinking seriously.'

'Where is he today?'

'I don't know, and doesn't that just tell you everything. He told me that he was busy and that he was working on something. But I could've sworn I saw his car parked outside Mrs Rollinson's house as I drove over here. What on earth could he be working on? It's not the first time recently that he's been unaccounted for. Mrs Rollinson certainly took a shine to Bailey, and he was happily flirting along.'

'Are you trying to suggest that Bailey is sleeping with your customers?' Sophie was shaking with laughter until she saw his face. 'No way, come on. You don't seriously think he's sleeping with your customers, do you?'

'No, but she was trying to set him up with her granddaughter. I know that he isn't seeing anyone at the moment. Why else is he at her house? It's not the first time either.'

'Look, I really don't think that he is, but if you're worried about it, just ask him.'

'I've tried that but he is always so vague. You know what he's like.' Marcus shrugged.

'Maybe one day you could follow him. I mean, I don't think that's the way to go, I think you should try and speak to him, but if it's going to put your mind at ease then…'

'Yeah, only I'm not sure I want to see that in action, you know.'

'I think with Bailey he's going to be either an asset or a liability, there will be no middle ground.'

Marcus groaned. He loved his best friend dearly and they had been through so much together but Sophie was right, she had him nailed. Unfortunately, the way Bailey had been behaving lately he just really hoped that he wouldn't have to fire his best mate. Sophie had started digging again leaving him to his thoughts. Not coming up with anything he wanted to act upon, he carried on digging too.

'Oh, I need to say thank you,' Sophie said as she sat up, Marcus turned towards her.

'You do? Why?' He used the back of his hand to brush his hair out of his eyes.

'The live video we did. It's gotten a huge response.'

'I'm sure that was just because you—'

Sophie actually blushed as she interrupted, 'Er, no, you want to read some of the comments. You definitely played a part in it. Maybe you could come in on another live video, you could talk about your business. It's about time you got some promo out of the nearly free garden you're doing for us.'

Marcus grinned. 'OK, sure. Just let me know when. Will I need to have a makeover?' He chuckled feeling relaxed and happy in Sophie's company.

'Hmm, well you do owe me. You could help out at my work; after all, I am currently helping out at yours. We'd need to clean your face up though, it's filthy.'

Taking off her gloves Sophie reached forward and held his jaw in her left hand as she tried to wipe away some of the dirt with her right. Marcus felt his eyes widen in surprise. He nearly jumped when her soft fingers gently held his face. He was gone, immediately captivated and completely enslaved. Whatever she wanted to do next he was game. He tried to focus on her eyes as they got closer but he was drawn to her lips. Were they getting closer? Did her grip on his jaw tighten slightly? Was she gently pulling him towards her? Then just as quickly Sophie blinked and brought her hand up to rub the dirt off his face.

'Right let's get this finished and we can talk more about your business plan as we go.' Sophie moved with speed back to her previous position, deliberately not looking at him.

Marcus knew that she was as smitten as he was. Yes, he realised, he should feel bad about being pushed away again, but he felt relieved that he wasn't going crazy. That the attraction was definitely mutual. He had seen her heart beating faster as her pulse raced in her neck, saw her pupils dilate as she leaned in towards the kiss, her tongue briefly licking her lips. While it would've been much better to be actually kissing at this point, simply knowing that she was hot and bothered for him, like he was for her, gave him a huge confidence boost, as well as a future game plan.

Chapter Fifteen

Having spent most of the day at the garden centre, Sophie took her laptop to the bar to get the last few videos uploaded before her shift started. She'd gotten quite a lot done at the garden centre but then she'd started to feel uncomfortable. She obviously wasn't used to being out in the wild on her own as she kept getting the feeling that someone was watching her. It was particularly unsettling when she had her laptop and other expensive gear out on display. So she'd decided to head to the bar instead.

She knew that the boys were working in the garden today and after the near kiss with Marcus the day before, Sophie was ashamed to admit that she needed to spend some time away – OK she was avoiding him. There, she'd admitted it to herself. How could she be so stupid? She'd nearly kissed him, even now she wasn't sure what had happened that made her stop. It wasn't thinking about the business, or about what had happened before at the house party. Her mind had gone completely calm, as her body took control. Her pulse was going nuts now just at the thought of it. Butterflies chasing around her stomach. The effect was too strong, and that was without actual physical contact. She couldn't be trusted to keep her hands to herself. That's why she was at the bar, muttering 'come on' in an attempt to encourage the broadband to be just a little bit faster.

The bar was quiet and Paige had just come downstairs after making sure the kittens were fed and was currently chatting to India, one of the bar staff. Sophie had lined India up to be one of her makeovers in the next month or so. Looking at India's face she wondered about what colour palette to use. Her skin was a gorgeous brown and her features soft and pretty. India's personality was a little bit wilder then her facial symmetry would suggest and Sophie wanted to try and incorporate that into it somehow. She jumped when her laptop chimed and her mum's face suddenly appeared on screen.

'Now's not a good time, Mum,' Sophie whispered to herself, hesitating over the 'Decline' button. Figuring that she could tell her she had to start her shift might make it a mercifully short conversation, Sophie clicked 'Accept'. It took a second or two to connect and the picture was a little fuzzy but viewable, damned stupid Wi-Fi.

'Hi, Mum. You OK?'

'Hi, my darling. Where are you?'

'I'm at the bar. I can't chat long as I'm about to start my shift.'

'Oh, where's my gorgeous Paige?'

'Hi, Mrs T.' Sophie jumped as Paige appeared beside her.

'How are you? It's so lovely to see you. You are just as stunning as always. I'm going to come to the bar soon. It looks so cool and trendy. I hear that you're a fur mama now too.'

'You're welcome anytime Mrs T, you know that. And yes, my darling kittens, they're so cute with their little bellies, and their tiny purrs. But I only have them for a few more weeks. Their adoptions are going to start soon. Anyway come see us anytime and I'll make you a Pornstar Martini. You'll love it.'

Sophie watched as her mum threw her head back and laughed. 'Oh, Paige, you do make me chuckle. You'll have to come for dinner one night, you can even bring my daughter with you if you like, but you don't have to.'

Deciding to interrupt Sophie said, 'Mum, what can I do for you?'

'I just wanted to check in and see how you are and see if there was any gossip?' The gleam in her mum's eye and the small smile on her face suggested that there was and she already knew it, but wanted to hear it again. Sophie was at a loss.

'No, same old, same old.'

'Oh, it's just that Debbie had mentioned that her daughter Clara had mentioned a romance?'

'Mum, what are you talking about?'

'You and Marcus, of course. Why did you deny that he was your boyfriend? I told you he was gorgeous. He looks athletic, is he?'

'Mum, I—' Sophie looked around and realised that more than one of the patrons were listening in on the conversation and India was grinning. Sophie felt her cheeks heat up.

'You're blushing, how sweet.'

Sophie took a deep breath, her jaw clenched. 'I'm blushing because we're having a private conversation on FaceTime in the middle of a bar and people are listening in. There is nothing going on with Marcus.'

'You don't need to shout. You don't want everyone knowing your business.'

Sophie shook her head bewildered.

'It's a bit late for that,' Paige muttered.

'Paige is there really nothing happening between Sophie and Marcus?'

Sophie looked up at her friend.

'They're not sleeping together no,' Paige said sincerely.

Sophie wasn't impressed with the answer, as it sounded to her like there was a 'yet' missing. Another glance around and the few patrons who hadn't been listening in certainly were now.

'Sophie, look at me.'

'Yes, Mum.'

'What's wrong? You've not mentioned a boy in ages, must be well over a year. Are you a lesbian now like your sister, or no wait, are you asexual?'

Wondering why the broadband seemed to be working so perfectly for this conversation to be shared with the entire bar, Sophie considered whether she could just close the lid of her laptop and walk away. No, she'd never hear the end of it.

'Well?'

Sophie didn't know what to say but as she looked around everyone in the bar were still obviously pretending to not listen but listening intently, everybody it seemed, waiting for an answer.

'No, Mum, I've told you, I'm just trying to focus on work.'

'Well, it's a waste. A gorgeous boy like that. If I didn't have your father...'

OK, thought Sophie, that's enough. 'Sorry, Mum you're cutting out. The broadband here it's really—' and with that Sophie hit the 'End Call' button and closed the lid, before glaring at all of the people in the bar, daring them to say anything else. Paige just smiled serenely.

'You weren't exactly helpful.' Sophie scowled.

'I couldn't lie to her. You're not sleeping together and that's a fact. I don't think that you will ever sleep together and I don't think that you should. I love you, Sophie, but I'm not sure you're right for him.'

'What. Why?'

'You don't want him. You've made that very clear. He's free to play with whomever he wants to play with and you are free to focus on your work. Right?'

'Right,' Sophie mumbled, her head a mess. What did she mean? Why shouldn't they sleep together? No, wait. Hang on.

'Can I have his number then?' India shouted with a grin.

'No!' Sophie shouted her reply, a little forcefully even to her own ear.

Unseen by Sophie, Paige smirked as she walked away and winked at India.

Sophie was completely lost in her own head, but she did notice that the bar suddenly got louder as people stopped listening now that the show was over. What did Paige mean that she wasn't good enough for Marcus? She wasn't a bad person. Her mind was racing with a million and one reasons why she would be good for Marcus, why they would be good together when she suddenly realised what she was doing. Her head shot up, her shoulders squared.

'For the last time,' Sophie muttered, 'it's not about me and Marcus, it's about me and my work. That's why we're not sleeping together.'

'Shame,' said a random customer as they walked passed.

Chapter Sixteen

Sophie looked up from unwrapping her parcels as once again Marcus walked straight into her house saying 'knock knock' as he came down the hall. She wished they didn't, but the bubbles and butterflies filled her stomach, and she had to give herself a cursory glance in the mirror to make sure she looked good. Trying to be nonchalant, reining in her smile, but she was too giddy with Marcus turning up as well as the new development with her work. She wasn't sure if that was in the right order or not.

'Hi, so what's the plan today? Is the engineer coming?' Marcus asked.

'Morning, yes, the engineer is due in a couple of hours. But I'm not sure how long it will take.'

'Hmmm. OK, so are you working this morning? I can't decide what to do. I need to work on your garden and if the engineer is going to be done soon then I may as well wait around here, if not then I need to go do something more productive. I'll text Bailey and Joseph and see what they have on today. Brew?'

'Please.' Sophie smiled, getting used to the way Marcus thought out loud. She watched as he walked into the kitchen, his tall body filling the space, taking all of the air with it. Just wishing and trying to be unaffected by him didn't seem to be working. She needed something to cool him off, something that might make him unattractive to her in some way. Looking down at her exciting parcels she was suddenly struck with an idea.

'I am working this morning but do you think that you could give me a hand?'

Marcus popped his head up from brew making. 'Oh, man, you've got a wicked look about you. Is this going to be a good thing or a bad thing?'

'Make the brew and then I'll tell you.' Sophie carried on opening the packages making a note of everything from the packaging to the labelling to the colour range and name. It was her first official 'freebie'. It was exciting because Sophie's numbers had finally started rising again, and were continuing to rise steadily, and at least one make-up brand had noticed and, as a result, she was now looking at a contouring range that she was tasked with reviewing on her vlog. It had come with instructions about how to properly reference the company and particular guidelines that she needed to follow regarding the clarity of affiliated gifts and advertising. A lot of it was legal speak, but she was too delighted to care, this was a game changer.

Sophie knew that she would review the product fairly, whether it was free or not. It just wasn't her style to do otherwise. She wasn't selling out, neither was she going to risk letting her audience down if she wasn't fair. She knew as well that her audience had developed a soft spot for Marcus with more than a few comments asking if there was more to the relationship, and if not, could they see more of Marcus either way. She hadn't broken down the figures yet but she suspected that the increase in subscribers might have something to do with him. Finally, she figured that she had had a torturous time with Marcus in the garden the other day and he owed her. It would be the perfect way to review a product, but for it to be a little different, with the added effect of dampening down her attraction to Marcus. Sophie was beaming at her genius idea, as a cup of tea was put down in front of her.

'Right I've texted Bailey and Joseph. What's got you so happy?' Marcus asked as he sat down next to her.

'I've had a really good idea for my vlog, but I need your help to do it. But you can say no, it's OK. But it's all really exciting.' Sophie was practically bouncing up and down on her seat. Her eyes shining as she grinned.

'OK.'

'What do you mean, OK, you don't know what it is yet?'

'Whatever you want from me is OK.' Marcus cleared his throat in an attempt to wipe away his outburst. 'What I mean is, you're a make-up artist, you probably want to give me some sort of makeover. It doesn't take a genius. So, sure.'

She studied Marcus, his answer unexpected. She looked closer trying to figure out what the catch was, but all she saw was his gorgeous green-brown eyes, slightly raised eyebrows, the scar on the left one subtle yet roguish, small smile on his full lips. Basically she saw that he was game, and happy to help. She realised that he would always be like that; with the right person he would give them the world if they asked.

Once again the tightness in her stomach reminded her that he wasn't hers, that she had already caught and released him. But then she remembered that this was for work, his as well as hers. She'd make sure that they talked about the garden so that he could get his exposure, so it would benefit them both.

Marcus's phone vibrated. 'That's Joseph. He says he's got to watch the grandkids today so he can't work anyway. So it's all good. I've not heard from Bailey though so…' Marcus's voice trailed off as a look of concern crept onto his face. Without conscious thought, she held his arm.

'I'm sure he's fine.'

'Yeah, I know you're right. It's just that there is definitely something going on and I just don't know what it is.' She wondered whether or not to tell Marcus about Polly and Bailey. Then again what was there to say? For all she knew there had been a kiss, that was all. The same could be said for them, she tried in vain not to remind herself of that kiss. Kiss seemed too bland a word for the experience they shared last year. She swallowed, her face flushing slightly at the affect Marcus and the memory of their kiss had on her.

She cleared her throat and got back to the make-up in an attempt to steady herself. 'OK, if you're sure. It's a good job you shaved this morning. So all I want to do is a simple contouring video. Look, I got all this cool stuff today. I don't know if it's any good or not, but we can try it on you and then I can review it.'

'Oh wow, companies are starting to send you free gear now huh?'

'Yeah, my numbers are really on the increase lately. This video should really help. It's so exciting. It's a major breakthrough. Hopefully, they'll like my review and then send me more stuff and other companies will follow. If they share it on their social media I could see some huge numbers in a really short timescale.'

Sophie nearly squealed she was so excited. Marcus was just looking at her with a little smile, occasionally sipping his brew.

'OK, so talk me through it, or at least tell me the do's and don'ts so that I don't ruin your video.'

'Well, it's not a live one, so we can pretty much just see how we go. I'll just record the whole thing and then edit out any mistakes or anything. I'll obviously ask you about your gardening work so that you can get some exposure too.'

Marcus raised an eyebrow looking concerned. 'Hmmm, surely in this video you want to focus on the brand that has sent you the stuff? If I start going on about my gardening business, isn't that going to look a bit weird? They're less likely to share it on their social media pages, aren't they?'

'Oh shit, yes, I hadn't really thought of it like that. I haven't exactly planned it all out. OK well, we'll maybe do another live one then soon so that you can start getting some airtime. Are you still OK being my model?'

'Of course.'

Sophie actually did jump up and down in her chair and gave a little squeal. 'Fantastic. Thank you so much. Just sit there and enjoy your brew while I get everything ready.'

She started to get all of her equipment together, placing

the seats just right – she was using the same set-up for her most recent makeover with Mya so she knew roughly where everything needed to be.

'Would you mind grabbing the biscuits while I set this up?'

'Of course, boss.'

Marcus headed to the kitchen as Sophie started checking her white balance and noise levels, thinking about how the video was going to look. She was also refreshing her memory as to how to contour a male face. It had been a while since college but she was confident she could do it. If not, then they would keep going until she could. Hopefully.

Marcus came back in with the supplies.

'OK, just sit here while I check all the settings.'

Marcus sat down as directed and amused himself watching Sophie running around sorting out all the equipment, making sure the lights were good, asking him to say random words so that she could get the sound levels right. In the meantime, he just took a moment to enjoy not only the view but also to revel in her excitement. There was no dull smile, no professional smile, this was Sophie in earnest. She was spectacular and it was all too easy to be swept up in it. It also didn't hurt that she kept having to bend over the table in front of him to get the lights just right, meaning that her perfect bum in her tight jeans was practically presented to him. Deciding to refocus on what was about to happen, Marcus admitted to himself that while he was OK for her to do pretty much whatever she wanted with him, he was a little worried. He hoped it wasn't full-on drag. He didn't think he could cope with false lashes but he was game up to a point. Besides Bailey would only take the piss for a little while. Presuming that he would see him again soon.

'Right, OK. I think that's everything set up. You ready?'

'Yep.'

'I'm going to just get the make-up prepared and I might

ask you to hold it for me so that it stays in shot, things like that. We're already recording. So I'm just going to play that back and make sure that's all OK.'

Sophie did what she needed to do, and he watched it back. She was so animated. She looked completely different than she did on any of her other videos but he couldn't be sure if that was the difference between watching it back or being part of it. As he watched the video, he knew this vlog was going to be huge so long as he didn't mess it up for her. He took a deep breath. Given how he had viewed her work at first, how he had knackered her broadband, and not to mention how much he quite frankly adored her, he had a lot resting on this and he didn't want to break this fragile relationship they had started to build. Sure they still bickered, but it was fun rather than snide, and he suspected it would always be like that with them, and he had no problems with that at all, except for the duration. The garden would only take another week, maybe two at a stretch, if he really dragged it out. Then what?

'OK, that's fine we're recording again. We'll start by waving to the camera and then I'll do some filler chat while we finish our brew and eat our biscuits.'

'Is the brew and biscuit a crucial part of the video?' Marcus raised an eyebrow sipping his tea.

'It has become something I am known for, yes.' Sophie grinned.

'You never know you might have McVitie's sending you free stuff soon.'

'Ah, that would be the dream.' Sophie laughed and Marcus grinned. 'Anyway back to matters at hand. I'm just going to start by cleansing and toning your skin. I probably won't include this in the final video, bear in mind that most of my videos are about fifteen minutes long when edited but this will actually take about an hour. Longer if I have to do it again.' She grinned reaching over to get the cotton wool and a large headband.

'Here put this on.'

'Huh?'

'It's a headband. I need your hair out of my way.'

Marcus looked at it like he had never seen a headband before. He put it on like it was a sweatband, pulling his brown hair further into his face. Sophie was creased over laughing as Marcus blew a kiss at the camera.

'That's not quite what it's for.' Suddenly Sophie was right next to him, he could feel her warm breath on his cheek as she reached over and straightened the hairband out, brushing her hands through his hair, her nails gently grazing his scalp, as she made sure his hair was held back. His breath held as the feel of Sophie's nails travelled all the way down his spine.

He was in trouble.

He hadn't thought it through. Not at all.

He just hoped that the camera would be on their faces because he strongly suspected that there would be parts of him that would be affected by this close contact that he would rather weren't filmed.

'Close your eyes. I need to cleanse and tone your skin. I'll tell you when you can open them again.'

Marcus closed his eyes and prayed to all of the gods that he didn't make a fool out of himself. His body began to harden as he felt Sophie's fingertips press lightly on one side of his face as a cotton ball was wiped on the other side. With his eyes closed, everything became so much more focused. He could feel every soft touch and the feeling radiated throughout his entire body. Her breath hitting his face. He could feel the warmth of her body. He curled his fingers as he held his hands back from reaching out to hold her that little bit closer until they weren't apart at all. He wanted nothing more than to run his hands around her waist and pull her a couple of inches closer. As well as clawing at his own hands, his breathing was going to give him away. He was having to breathe through his mouth, the oxygen in the room somehow depleted. His body was responding to her and he just hoped that Sophie was concentrating too much to look down at his crotch. All of this, and he reminded himself that it was being recorded too. Suddenly she stopped.

'I'm sorry is the lotion too cold? Oh God, is my breath bad?'

Marcus opened his eyes. 'No, it's fine. Why?'

'You got all tense. I was worried I was hurting you in some way.'

Marcus coughed. 'No, not at all, the lotion was cold, that's all. Sorry.' Marcus smiled as he closed his eyes again and forced his body to calm the fuck down. Sophie carried on where she had finished but this time on the other side.

Sophie let out a little sigh. 'Look I know you think he's sleeping with your customers, but I can't see it.'

'What made you suddenly say that, and oh God would you even want to see that?'

Sophie laughed. 'What do you mean? Aren't all of your customers twenty-something make-up vloggers?'

'Are you asking me if they are all hot like you? No, they're not. Most of them are in their sixties and while Mr Hillborne was undoubtedly a fitty in his day, he doesn't do it for me.' Marcus smiled when he heard Sophie chuckle.

'It's just that I can tell you're bothered about something. I was guessing that it was to do with Bailey but we don't have to talk about it if you don't want to.'

She moved away momentarily, from the sounds of it to get some other product. Marcus considered Sophie's question. It certainly wasn't in his head before this point, but she was right it had been playing on the back of his mind. Bailey was hiding something and it made him uncomfortable. Usually, Bailey lived his life out loud. There were never any secrets or whispers, everything was full volume.

'Yeah, you're right. I need to get him to tell me what's going on. I'll try and track him down later.'

'Sounds like a plan. OK, hold still again.'

The faint smell of cucumbers wafted towards him before the scent of Sophie took over. She always smelt divine. She gently wiped his face a little more.

'OK, you can open your eyes again for a bit now.'

As he slowly did so, he saw Sophie sat back in her seat looking directly at the camera and explaining that she had received the goods free, that she was opening them there and then, that she would give her honest opinion, no matter what.

'Oh and this is Marcus, you might have seen him in some of my videos and from the "live" post I did, and for all of his background shots. Marcus say hi.'

'Hi, everyone.'

'Marcus is my willing volunteer. I'm going to be doing the contouring on him.'

'I don't even know what contouring is, but here I am. I think we can all agree that she owes me after this, right?' Marcus enjoyed playing up to the camera. He could be more cheeky, more playful and definitely more flirty.

'Don't make me tell everyone what you did to my broadband. We're even now, right?'

'We'll see what I look like at the end before we decide who owes who.' Taking a gamble, utilising Sophie's exposure as she was recording, he added, 'You might owe me dinner after this.'

'Hmmm, I think you're pushing your luck. But let's see. Close your eyes as I need to apply a primer.'

For the next ten minutes, Marcus sat there his eyes closed listening as Sophie held on to his face as she dabbed, sponged and wiped, simultaneously talking to the camera. When she stopped to open the packaging for the next product, he opened his eyes. He didn't want to look in the mirror so instead looked directly at the camera, pouted and winked.

'Do I look beautiful yet?'

Sophie had a stern look on her face as she looked at the

camera. 'Guys, don't leave too many comments. His ego is big enough as it is.' Turning back around to face him, she said, 'Don't get cocky. We've only just begun, so no you don't look beautiful yet. OK, I'm going to apply this loose powder and then we will have a completely even base to start contouring on top of. Close your eyes, beautiful, and stop grinning.'

Marcus dutifully did as he was told, although having her hands and her body so close to his had meant that the grin was hard to bite down, it wasn't the only hard thing he was trying to hold down as he felt a brush pass over his now sensitive skin. He still hadn't acclimatised to Sophie's touch and had to wonder if he ever would. Suddenly she was gently blowing into his face. He could almost feel her lips she was so close. He opened his eyes in shock. Sophie was an inch away and her lips were pursed as she stopped blowing into his face. She quickly let her hands fall as she sat back.

'Anyway, now we can start adding some depth and some shape onto this mug.'

Chapter Seventeen

She didn't remember it being this difficult when she made over Mya. Oh God, it would be all over the recording, showing the world that her hand was shaking every time she went to touch his face. That she couldn't help but take her time looking at him over and over, enjoying the opportunity every second his eyes were closed. His eyelashes were long enough to be gorgeous and totally unfair. His strong nose was perfect – he'd clearly never been in a fight, or if he had the other person had had the good sense not to break it. He was freshly shaven, which worked for today's purpose but was a shame because with his stubble he had that roguish bad boy look about him. As it was now his jaw was just perfectly proportioned, his lips inviting and constantly drawing her eyes. The only downside with his eyes closed was that she was robbed of his gaze. She couldn't help but feel that when he looked at her, she was his sole focus and nothing else mattered. It was utterly addictive. Her mind was completely scrambled. She was conscious of every little thing, wishing she had brushed her teeth before she started, worried that her breath was all chocolate digestives, trying to keep her breathing regular and unaffected, apply make-up and talk to the camera, it was a nightmare. It had seemed like such a good idea. The fact that she was about to change the shape of his face with the contouring, would, she hoped, have the effect of dampening down on his attraction. He smelt amazing. It kept putting her off as she tried to figure out what he was wearing. It wasn't heavy but it was enough to make her want to sink into his neck and breathe it in for a long time.

He seemed tense, and yet he was playing up to the camera perfectly, but every now and then his jaw would tighten and his shoulders would rise, probably just having second thoughts about volunteering, she reasoned.

'So I'm going to add this colour here, in a straight line down his nose, contrast it with the light colour that is going to go here and here.' He opened his eyes and Sophie forgot what she was saying for a moment. Getting back with the programme she continued, 'That will have the effect of slimming his nose, obviously the bits we want to help emphasise are his eyes and cheekbones.'

Sophie took a deep breath as she approached Marcus again. He closed his eyes and Sophie willed her hands to shake a little less. Either that or he was going to look like he'd been in a fight after all.

Trying to remain professional reminded her that she hadn't done much in the review part of the video.

'The colours in the palette seem to be quite varied and the fact that there are different pallets available means that you can match the contouring to your skin type. They've kept it really simple. By matching your base skin tone to the first colour on the palette you know that the rest should work for you. This is genius as it means you don't have to have several different make-up products. You can have just this one, and according to my research the company has worked hard to accurately represent many different skin colours, but please let me know if this is true to your experience. The packaging is a little difficult to open, but again in the grand scheme of things that's a relatively small issue. It's going on well so far, but we've only just started, so let's see if it's as good as it suggests. OK, I need to put a bit of the darker colour here, and here.'

The reminder that she needed to be professional was working and for another ten minutes she was able to at least sound unaffected and Marcus's face was looking less like his own, which was also helping. If she saw a man out and about looking like this, he probably wouldn't be someone she would approach in the bar, unless to ask for make-up tips or brand recommendations.

'So, Marcus, while I finish adding the final touches why don't you tell my lovely viewers a bit more about yourself.'

'Oh, OK... erm, I am a gardener, but I think you knew that already. I've never had a makeover before. I haven't seen myself yet to know whether or not I would do it again. Oh no wait, I think my sister did this to me once when I was three using some of Mum's make-up. I seem to recall Polly got told off for using something really expensive after she had covered me in it.' Marcus laughed, and Sophie smiled, thinking that his laugh made her want to be funnier so that she might get him to make that sound more often.

Sophie continued to put make-up on Marcus, intermittently concentrating and talking to the camera. With every stroke on his skin her body responded, but fortunately his face was looking more and more contoured, until they were done and Marcus no longer looked quite as handsome as he did before.

'OK, I think we're finished. Look into the camera so that everyone can see what we've done.'

'Do I have to do the poses that people do at the end of these videos?'

'Yes, it's essential.' Sophie smirked, before belly laughing as Marcus pouted and moved his arms around his face in a dramatic flourish posing here and there looking up longingly at the camera.

'How many make-up videos have you watched? That was perfect!'

'I don't know what you mean?' he said, fluttering his eyelashes at her. Marcus turned and looked in the mirror and shuddered, making Sophie laugh again.

'I know it's not your usual look.'

'Erm, no... I look, well, definitely contoured.'

'You sure do. You did perfectly. But here you go let's get that make-up off you.'

He was still gorgeous but Sophie had to admit, covering him in make-up had worked a little. Unfortunately, her body was on fire thanks to all of the intimacy, the touches, the shared breath. She responded to the smallest touch, as if he awoke every single nerve ending in her body and she had to shift slightly in her seat. Trying desperately hard to ignore the impact he was having on her she began wiping away the make-up on his face.

'Give me a wipe, I need to get my face back.'

Handing him a make-up removing wipe, she could start to make out the usual gorgeous Marcus emerging. All too quickly the effect of the make-up had worn off and now she realised that she was facing the most handsome gardener in the world. His eyes were shining as he smiled, so yes, usual gorgeous Marcus. Her breathing was faster than it should've been. She was lost for words and totally turned on.

'So was that OK? Did I do all right?' Marcus was grinning as he continued to battle with the make-up remover wipes.

'You were perfect. I think it's going to be a great video. Thank you.'

'My God, how many wipes is it going to take to get this stuff off?'

She laughed as she watched him drag wipes across his face, racing to get back to normality. 'We're getting there. I can see you again now. Close your eyes again let me just get the last of it.'

Pulling his face towards hers so that she could see what she was doing she wiped gently at his face, holding his chin in her other hand. Marcus placed his hands on her thighs to balance himself as he leaned closer. Her body tightened as she felt the heat of his heavy hands through the denim of her jeans. Her heart was beating wildly now, and her body felt too hot and too tight as she relished in this last moment of physical contact.

'OK, open your eyes...' She was hit with the full impact

of Marcus's stare, mirroring the same desire she felt. She pulled off the headband with one hand and moved his chin to make sure that she could see all the make-up had come off, allowing herself an extra moment or two simply to look at his face, his lips in particular.

'I think that's all of it.' Was that her voice, why did it sound so breathless? Why was she practically panting? Her lips suddenly dry she had to lick them, her breath caught in her throat and she was sure she could hear her racing heartbeat in her ears.

She couldn't be sure which one of them had moved the last inch but suddenly their lips had met and were pushing gently. Opening her mouth she thrust her tongue into him and they exploded as if a starting pistol had gone off. Racing to get at each other, to explore, feel, touch and taste. She opened her mouth as the kiss deepened her hands alternating between pulling at his hair and feeling the taut muscles in his arms, his hands holding on tightly to her waist as the kiss sped up.

Without realising it Sophie had moved onto his lap to get a better position, all she could hear were the moans from both of them, as well as their heavy breathing, as their tongues fought for control. His lips demanding but decadent, with little kisses interspersed with hungrier ones, in a way that was completely addictive. He tasted like Marcus would: tea, mint and something that was just Marcus. She could feel his rough hands travelling up her waist and tensed as she waited for him to go higher still. When he got to the underside of her breasts, hot palpitating electricity was flying through her body in delicious waves, leaving her breathless in their wake. She knew that if she was subject to more of his touch, she would be overwhelmed in no time at all. Feeling the hard edge of his erection pressing into her, made her wetter and she wondered if he was as turned on as she was. She was holding his neck making sure that he didn't leave her mouth for a second as she ground into him, her body completely flush on his. She pushed her feet into the bars under the chair so that she could rock against him and feel his hard length rub against her, making them both moan. She was all primitive instinct, selfish in her greed and desire.

He broke away from her mouth and began kissing her neck, the break giving Sophie a second or two of clarity. What was she doing? What were they doing? She looked down at his head before he found a sensitive spot nearer the back of her neck that made her back arch, her eyes closed and clarity was gone again.

'Please don't stop me, Sophie.' He was panting in-between his kisses covering her neck. His rough hands had gotten to the bottom of her T-shirt and were now pressing the skin at her back and waist. Pinning her impossibly closer as he pushed into her. She heard the vulnerability in his voice and realised that in his mind she held all the power. She would have laughed if she could, because frankly at this moment she felt completely powerless. There was no way in hell she was going to stop them. Moving her hands she created a fraction of space between them so that she could get the bottom of her T-shirt, removing it in one quick flourish.

'I don't want to stop this.' Grabbing his hair and returning his lips to her mouth, she pulled herself back firmly into his lap. Marcus was returning the kiss stroke for stroke, their breathing loud as they gasped for breath when they could, his hands reaching up her back to unclasp her bra. As her bra loosened his hands cautiously reached under to feel her breasts, and Sophie's head fell back as his fingers played with her nipples. Restricted by the bra, and needing so much more, Sophie reluctantly removed her hands from Marcus's hair and pulled the bra straps down her arms before dropping it on the floor beside them.

His hands reached around and grabbed her bum, standing up and pulling her up and onto the table. He moved her video equipment just a little bit further back, so there was enough space for her to perch on the edge.

As Sophie looked up, Marcus was grinning at her, holding her eye before he lowered his mouth to one nipple, as his fingers played with the other. Just before Sophie's eyes closed she saw the back garden and the outside world and realised that it was the middle of the day, on the middle of the kitchen table, and she grinned realising that that only added to her excitement, making her even wetter.

Her breasts were getting heavy and her eyes were squeezed shut as she was forced to admit she might climax from this alone, but she didn't want to. She grabbed the top button of his shorts, before hastily undoing the zip and pushing them down his legs using her feet, noticing that his tight black boxers were struggling to hold him in. She needed to feel more and with one hand she moved the boxers down and with the other moved lower to take hold of his hot and hard erection. Marcus, now unable to get to her breasts, was staggering slightly as her touch turned into strokes. He grabbed his lowered boxers and dragged them down until he could step out of them. Sophie got a few more strokes, until through gritted teeth and deep breaths Marcus laid Sophie back and began unsnapping the buttons on her jeans.

Letting go of Marcus, Sophie put all of her weight onto her arms as she lifted up off the table so that Marcus could slide her jeans off, except he had taken her knickers too, the cold of the kitchen table on her bum as she sat back down making her squeal.

Marcus laughed before sitting back down on the chair. His eyes shining as he looked at her spread out on the table in front of him. Sophie had a moment of shyness. Seeing herself spread so wantonly before him her legs started to close together. Marcus gently took hold of her ankles and began kissing his way up her leg tasting and biting, while stroking behind her knee on the other, demonstrating exactly what he was going to do once he got between her thighs. Sophie's momentary apprehension disappeared as her legs fell further apart. With every inch that he got higher and higher, Sophie was sure that she wasn't going to make it. Her body was lit up, she was on fire inside and out. She wanted to be embarrassed or at least a little more reserved but instead she closely watched him make his ascent, he was studying her body and occasionally looking up at her and grinning wickedly. She had never been more on show, but then she had never felt more turned on or so responsive. Ultimately she felt worshipped, as she was fine-tuned to his every touch and every glance. The low hum of satisfaction he was making was almost undetectable underneath her moans. She looked up for a second as the sunshine from outside cast his already gorgeous body in a glow, reminding her again that they could all too easily be seen by someone.

Reaching the end of her patience she instinctively tried to force her legs together to try and contain her pleasure but she was already too far gone. As he made her way up her thighs she was captivated by the sight of him. His rough hands holding her legs where he needed them to be, her legs placed over his wide shoulders, she moaned as he kissed the very top of her thigh anticipating where he was going to kiss next. Sophie screamed as his tongue licked her from her core to her clit. Marcus groaned before her hands instinctively grabbed his hair, pulling him closer until his mouth covered her. Her knees rising up so that she could get him at the angle she wanted. She quickly came apart with a full body shudder. Her legs clenching his head, her nails scraping his scalp as her own head flew backwards, her entire body releasing with steady pulls.

'OK, next time, I'm going to do that for as long as I like. But right now I need you.' Marcus was frowning in concentration as he lent down to his shorts, coming back up with a condom. He was about to say something else when

Sophie began stroking his erection once again. Marcus took over, putting the condom on before leaning over Sophie and bringing her right to the end of the table. Her legs spread wide, her body ready, he pressed against her core slowly, pushing himself into her, inch by inch. He was tense and his body was straining. Sophie leant forward so that her hands could grab his bum as she spread her legs further until she took him in completely.

'Shit.' Marcus breathed into her hair. 'Are you OK?'

Panting at the way she felt so sensationally stretched. Sophie was just about able to nod. Marcus pulled back slowly before thrusting again harder this time.

Happy that Marcus was now doing what she needed him to, her hands moved all over his body, her heels holding the backs of his legs. The friction building in her once again. She buried her face in his neck, licking and biting.

'Oh God, Sophie. I can't wait.'

'Don't.'

Her hands made their way to his face and she pulled him down so that they were hungrily kissing each other. The taste of her on his lips, the feel of her muscles tightening around his cock and she was ready to come again. He began to move even faster and deeper, his hands firmly grasping her hips to ensure that he could power into her again and again. His cock reaching places that took her breath away opening her legs wider, holding him closer. She looked at Marcus. He was flushed, his body glistening. She licked his neck and moaned. This was it, the climax building, her muscles tightening.

With a shout her head fell onto Marcus's shoulder as he pushed into her again before he groaned, his erection getting tighter around her muscles before he let his breath go and his body shuddered.

Shaking they tried to regulate their breathing. Marcus's hands loosening their grip but not letting go. Sophie gently moving her fingers over his back.

'Holy crap,' Marcus panted. 'I can't feel my legs. You are incredible.' He pulled back and his hands gently held her face. He kissed her softly before letting go to grip her thighs. Lifting her up he sat back down on the chair taking Sophie with him as he remained buried inside.

She smiled hiding her face into his neck, suddenly shy.

She couldn't believe that they had just done that. She wasn't ashamed, not really, it was just not her usual style. She was a three-date rule kind of person, with ample warning and preparation time, usually in a bed under the covers type of girl. Although she may have changed her mind about that now.

Marcus grinned before leaning down and moving her head so that he could kiss her. 'Wow,' Marcus said as Sophie smiled. 'Are you blushing? Surely you're not feeling shy now? Come on, that was amazing. You have nothing to be shy or embarrassed about. You are hot as hell, and we are fantastic together. I think we should do it again.' Marcus leant down and began nibbling her neck.

'You don't mean right now?'

'Maybe in a minute or two.'

Sophie pulled back in shock as she felt his cock begin to harden inside her.

Marcus just grinned. 'I've been waiting ages for this. I could probably keep going for a while yet.' He started caressing her back in long strokes. Sophie shivered, the usual gleam back in her eye as the shyness disappeared.

The sound of the doorbell and the knock that followed made her jump out of her skin.

'Oh my God,' cried Sophie. 'The engineer. Quick, get up. Find your clothes.' Sophie pushed off him and began running around trying to gather her clothes. Why wasn't Marcus moving, why was he just sat there smiling?

'Stop grinning at me and help.' She couldn't find her knickers so threw her jeans on. 'I'll be there in a minute!' she called out. Her T-shirt on sans bra, her jeans halfway up her legs.

'Get dressed, come on!'

Marcus grinned as he reached forward and smacked her bum. 'Whatever you say, princess.' Bending down to pick up his boxers and shorts he strutted off, presumably towards the bathroom, despite what they had done and the rush she was in, she still had to take a second to admire his body as he walked away. She was right; his shorts had been hiding a spectacularly sculptured bum. Fastening her jeans, she dashed to the door, making sure that Marcus was out of view, before tripping on something. Finding her foot tangled in her knickers she quickly picked them up and shoved them into her back pocket, before opening the front door.

'Hi. I've come to get you back online.'

Chapter Eighteen

'Looking gorgeous, Pol, who are you meeting today?'

Polly looked striking, with her deep brown eyes similar to Marcus, but instead of Marcus's rich brown hair, she had long red hair flowing down her back. Remembering what she had done with Polly's brother yesterday, Sophie wiped down the bar as she tried not to blush, or look guilty, or feel in any way awkward. It wasn't going well.

'He's called Ryan, and we've been chatting for a little while. He seems a little too good to be true, but today's the big face-to-face. Do you like?' Polly straightened her black dress. It was perfect, not too much for a first date meet in a bar, but it made her red hair stand out, and her red ankle boots were to die for.

'You look beautiful, Pol,' Paige said as Polly grinned.

'He must be good, you've not bought a new dress for any of your dates in a while,' Sophie mused.

Polly looked embarrassed. 'Well, he seems nice anyway, but it's not a big deal.'

'As long as you're having fun that's the main thing. The dress *is* for Ryan, right?' Sophie raised an eyebrow.

'I don't know what you're talking about,' Polly said, her face tightening.

'She's wondering if the dress is really for Bailey,' Paige said in her usual cut-through-the-bull way. Sophie slapped her arm.

'Shut up, you. So what does this Ryan look like? What do you know about him so far?'

Deciding to ignore Paige, Polly shook her head. 'He's about six foot, he works in the computer tech industry but I don't know what specifically, but I know that he does well because he's just bought a flat, and on his profile picture he looks nice, a little bit like a less defined Hemsworth, you know?'

'Wow, he sounds fantastic.' And nothing at all like Bailey, Sophie thought.

'So what time is he due?' Paige had moved round to the back of the bar, messing around on her iPad as she spoke.

'He's due any minute... oh, there he is.' With that Polly jumped off the bar stool and went over to the other side of the room to meet him.

'Bang on eight o'clock. Do you think he waited outside to be that perfectly on time?' Paige enquired.

Sophie studied Paige. 'You don't like him, do you?'

'I'm sure he's nice enough, but he's not for Polly. She'd get bored with someone that straight-laced, that together. She'd run rings around him in no time. He's no animal lover, Polly needs a cat person in her life.'

Sophie looked at Paige, puzzled, but then they both turned to watch as Ryan held out the chair for her and tucked it in as Polly sat down. It was a bit formal and old school, but some people went for that, Sophie supposed. Now that Paige had said her piece though, she was inclined to think that maybe this was another boring one. In fact, since Polly had reopened her dating apps they had all been boring, steady, serious types. Paige was right in her assessment, and the more Sophie thought about it they were all incredibly un-Bailey.

Ryan ducked down to Polly, presumably to get Polly's drink order, before making his way over to the bar. This was part of the deal. If any of them wanted to go on a tinder date, or any blind date at all, they met at the bar. They could sit far enough away and no one would eavesdrop, but they had to make the date come to the bar and order the first round. If they didn't, then as a precaution Sophie or Paige, or one of the other staff, would go and make sure everything was OK, under the guise of good customer service. More and more people were adopting this technique and the bar was becoming *the* place for a first date. It was a brilliant way for women to look out for one another and it didn't hurt the business either.

'What can I get you?' Sophie asked, giving Ryan the once over. Up close he was looking less like a Chris Hemsworth and more of a Christopher Walken.

'I'll have a glass of dry white wine.' Polly's usual date order. 'And a sparkling water, please.'

'Sure.' Sophie smiled and turned around to get the drinks but not without first catching Paige's eye and raising her eyebrow. Sparkling water? Not your usual order but OK. She felt her phone buzz in her pocket as she was getting the drinks together.

'Here you are.' He passed over his card and she took the payment, and then with the drinks in hand, he walked back to Polly. Paige came back to stand next to Sophie.

'Well, he gets points for not hitting on either of us,' Paige said as they both nodded, it had happened several times before. When that happened they usually put a small cocktail umbrella in the wine as a signal.

'But sparkling water?' Sophie asked.

'I think I would've preferred an order for tap water,' Paige said, looking down at her iPad.

'What you doing?' Sophie nodded at the tech in Paige's hands.

'Nothing.'

'Is that a nanny cam? Are you watching the kittens?'

'Maybe,' Paige replied, not looking up.

'Aww.' They both watched the screen as the kittens played together, running in and out of shot.

'You should live stream this, you'd be a huge hit,' Sophie suggested.

'I'm not profiteering off my kittens.'

Sophie got her phone out of her pocket and looked at the screen.

Marcus.

I want you again ;)

'So what does Marcus want you for, I wonder?' Paige

laughed as Sophie immediately threw her phone back into her pocket, having not realised that Paige was close enough to read her text, the nosy cow.

'I don't know what you—'

Paige stopped laughing. 'Save it. I know. So what's going to happen next?'

'You know what?' Sophie was not able to get away with nonchalant, so just avoided eye contact altogether.

'That you two got it on.'

Sophie gasped and looked up. 'How do you know? No one knows?'

Paige folded over in hysterics. 'I cannot believe you fell for that, that's the oldest trick in the book.' Sophie groaned. 'Besides it's about freaking time. So what *does* happen next? Was it good? Worth the wait?'

'I'm not answering. Besides, I thought you said I wasn't good enough for him?' Paige just smiled mysteriously, so she added, 'And besides I really need to focus on my work.'

'You're not seriously bringing that excuse back out again?' Paige rolled her eyes.

'It's not an excuse, it's the truth.'

'Yeah, and it's also a pretty good shield too. Look, don't overthink it. He knows how important your work is. Why not try and see if you can fit them both in?' Paige stood tall with her arms folded, she wasn't going to take no for an answer.

'What do I tell Polly?' Sophie asked, chewing her lip.

'I don't think that she would have a problem with it, but why don't you make arrangements with Marcus first, and see what he says. He might want to tell her himself.'

Sophie felt her phone buzz again.

Marcus

I want you… to get me a beer, please. Be there in two x

Sophie groaned before showing Paige the message. 'Looks like I'm going to have that conversation sooner rather than later.'

'Yup. Just don't forget that for now, at least, you still work here. Cover for me a minute, I need to go and check on the kids.'

With that Paige went upstairs and Sophie cleaned up. It kept her busy while her mind went through all the different possibilities. She could a) not see him again, like that anyway; b) they could keep it casual, friends with benefits type situation; c) super-secret relationship. Her stomach was a mess. The first one felt too harsh, on both of them. The second was OK, as long as the boundaries were clear. The third freaked her out again. It had been a while since she had been in a relationship and the last one finished leaving her drained. It had taken time to build herself back up after that. She almost laughed, it was no good having this conversation in her head, for all she knew Marcus was coming to tell her that it wasn't a good idea to do it again. Although, she really hoped they did because it had been exceptional sex, even if the engineer had maybe ruined it a little.

If she was really honest, she felt awkward. She would have preferred more of a post-sex debrief, make sure that they were both on the same page. She was still a little embarrassed about how brazen they had been. She might have been shy about it, but she was also turned on just thinking about it. They had been hot together. At least she had thought so. Hence why she felt awkward and wished they'd had a chance to talk. Even so, she was really animated with the idea that he would walk into the bar any second. Everything she did had a little bit more attitude, a little more swagger, a bit more sway. She was practically strutting. As well as emptying the dishwasher with style, she also couldn't help but keep looking at the door every five seconds.

Then at the doorway, he appeared, leading the way with Bailey following. He slowly smiled when he saw her and came straight up to the bar. She panicked, her throat suddenly dry, her face, and other parts, heating up. Was he going to kiss her, in front of everyone? Or was he not going to kiss her? She really wasn't quite sure what she wanted him to do. Instead, he just said, 'Hi.'

'Hi,' Sophie said back.

'Erm, hi,' Bailey said, looking at them both.

Sophie wondered if he knew and quickly glanced back to Marcus who shook his head minutely as if he had read her mind and responded.

'So what can I get you both? Usual?'

'Yes, please,' Marcus replied, his eyes sparkling brightly. She could tell he was remembering the last time they were together. Which wasn't a real problem because so was she, and it did not help to calm her down. She made short work of getting their beers and moving back to where they stood at the bar. Bailey sat himself down on the bar stool and was looking around to see who was in. At the same moment, Paige reappeared and went around the bar to join them and winked at Sophie.

'Hi, Marcus, Bailey. What have you been up to lately?'

Sophie grimaced, the small smile on Paige's face totally giving the game away. Luckily Bailey was distracted, his attention taken by something in the corner, or someone more likely.

'Oh, you know this and that.' Marcus actually could keep things nonchalant, good to know. He was giving nothing away, she just couldn't say the same for herself.

'Sure. Hey, Bailey, you need to see how big the kittens are getting, come on.' Without missing a beat Paige led Bailey further down the bar and through the private door to her apartment.

'We need to talk,' Marcus said quietly, leaning towards her.

'OK.' That didn't sound good, were they done already? Had all the build-up just been so that he could get his end away? The idea made her heart sink and she suddenly felt a bit sick.

'I'm going to lay my cards on the table, as it were.' He grinned. 'You can decide what to do with them. I don't want there to be any confusion. Yesterday was incredible. I can't see why you wouldn't want to do that again. I also know how important your work is. Well, so is mine, and I have no problem being flexible so that we can both get everything we want.'

'OK.'

'Is that all you're going to say?'

Sophie bit her lip, there was more she wanted to say but the words were stuck in her throat. Marcus looked at her closely, his eyes squinting. 'You do believe me, right? I think you are fantastic and however busy you are, any time I get to spend with you, I am going to make sure that we both enjoy it.'

'OK, look. It was great, I agree. I want to do it again too.' She stopped as Marcus grinned. 'But we both have work so let's keep it casual. I'm not going to mess around with anyone else or anything, but I can't do a full-on relationship right now. I just can't.' Sophie had spoken looking down and cautiously looked up to see how he had taken it. He was still grinning.

'OK, but I think you might change your mind. You might want a relationship with me. But I understand what you're saying and I am with you.'

'With you on what?' Bailey asked as he rejoined them.

'Helping me with some of my vlog stuff,' Sophie jumped in quickly.

'Your sister's in.' Bailey nodded towards the corner, his voice giving him away, but apparently not to Marcus.

'Yeah, she said she'd be in tonight. What's wrong with you?' Marcus was looking at Bailey who had a face like thunder. Now maybe Marcus had noticed.

He coughed and took a long drink. 'Nothing, I'm fine.'

'Where were you yesterday, by the way?'

'I was busy… sorry, I have to get this, hang on.'

Bailey got out his phone, his phone that hadn't made a sound or a buzz and walked to the other side of the bar to take a 'call'. Marcus looked at Sophie. All she could do was shrug. There was certainly something going on, but Sophie had a feeling it had more to do with Polly than it did anything else.

'So,' Marcus said. 'Now that we have the rules laid out, when can I see you again? In fact, what time are you finishing? Is Mya back yet?'

'So many questions. I'm finishing at close, and no Mya isn't back yet. She comes back later tomorrow.'

'OK. See you later.' With that Marcus downed most of his drink, winked at her and then went over to Bailey. He said something in Bailey's ear and left.

OK, well, that was weird, Sophie thought. Would he be round later? Would he be calling? In a daze and not really knowing what to do with herself, she watched as Bailey came and sat back at the bar, sipping his drink as he tried to not watch Polly. He was failing.

Sophie watched him and wondered whether or not to say anything. Bailey being this quiet was unnerving.

'Bailey, are you OK?'

'Who's he then?' Bailey asked, nodding towards Polly's date.

'Apparently he's called Ryan.'

Bailey just huffed, before finishing his drink. He leant forward and kissed Sophie on the cheek. 'See you later, Soph.'

Paige strolled back over. 'Was it something you said? You really are the world's worst bartender.'

Chapter Nineteen

Trying to look casual as he draped himself over the sofa that wasn't his, Marcus looked at his phone again to check the time. He presumed that 'close' meant half eleven. It would take thirty minutes to an hour to clean up, so she could be here any minute. He had his T-shirt and his favourite jeans on but kept toying with the idea of being naked when she arrived. The sound of the front door unlocking removed the decision for him. He had been thinking of their session on the kitchen table non-stop, she was a million times hotter than he had imagined, and he had imagined a *lot*. His only concern was with her idea that their relationship stays casual. He didn't want to be disposable, he wanted it all, but that was OK, he was going to work on that. He tried to remind himself that he had been shut down by her before and hoped that this time would be different.

'What the— What are you doing here?'

Marcus slowly got up off the sofa. She looked stunning. Her gorgeously rich dark hair piled up in a messy ponytail at the top of her head. Her face glowed, even if her eyes were slightly tired from a busy shift.

'How was your day, dear?' He smiled as he slowly walked towards her, their eye contact never wavering. 'After a long shift, do you need a back rub?' He was enjoying himself, laughing as Sophie stood stock-still in shock at the sight of him, all of him, including the hard part of himself that was pointing right at her. He reached forward to take her handbag off her arm and then taking the denim jacket down off her shoulders, turning her around in the process so that she was stood in front of him. Leaning down to whisper in her ear, he gently stroked the side of her neck with his fingers.

'I look at this neck all the time, but it really is beautiful and I have wanted to kiss it for weeks now.' He bent down putting his lips to her skin. 'Every time you're sat there working it's the only bit of you I get to see from the garden.'

He watched as she sighed and her pulse beat even faster under his lips. He took a deep breath drawing the scent of her deep into his lungs. His addiction to her building at an alarming rate. He moved his other arm around her waist holding her closer to him so that she could feel every stiff inch of him. She slowly smiled before her lips parted and her breathing got heavy and she pressed herself back into him, rubbing him. Suddenly she broke free and turned around. She leaned up putting her hands around his neck and into his hair. She pulled a little, but he preferred it when she pulled a lot.

'I need a shower, I must smell like beer and sweat.'

'You most definitely do need a shower. I insist.'

Sophie grinned, and his heart hammered in his chest. Letting go of him she turned around and set off towards the stairs.

'Come on then,' Sophie said leading the way.

He caught up with her at the bottom of the stairs, deciding to let her go up a few steps before following. He grinned as it was the perfect position to watch the most spectacular view. Unable to take his eyes off her tight bottom as she climbed the stairs he almost tripped over the last step.

Sophie reached over and turned the light for the bathroom on and then walked through the door. Marcus followed. It wasn't a huge bathroom, but it had the necessities. With them both stood in front of the bath they were nearly touching. Sophie reached behind the shower curtain to get the shower started, while at the same time kicking off her shoes and socks. She turned back around so that she was facing him, looking into his eyes as she slowly began to pull up her T-shirt, exposing her gorgeously tanned skin and toned stomach. She pulled further and her black bra was revealed. Taking her T-shirt off over her head he could tell that she was breathing heavily, her breasts pushing at the bra, her tight nipples just visible through the black design. He was having a hard time maintaining eye contact. He wanted to look at every inch of her and take it all in, but he could tell she was daring him to look away and he would not give her that satisfaction, she was playing with him but she had met her match.

He watched as Sophie licked her lips and moved her hands to the front of her jeans where she undid the top button and with deliberate slowness undid the zip and began siding the jeans down her long legs. She stood up straight, making sure that his eyes were on hers, as she stepped out of the denim.

Oh God. It was killing him. His peripheral vision not up to the job, but he was just as stubborn as she was and two could play at this game, only he was sure he was going to win. Reaching for the bottom of his T-shirt he pulled the soft cotton up and over his head, making sure to stretch and tighten to show off every inch of muscle. At that particular moment, he was so tense and pent up that he was sure his abs had never been tighter. It was his next move that meant he knew he was going to win this round. Undoing the button on his jeans, he kept his eyes on hers, as he carefully undid the rest of the buttons, his hard-on making it difficult to work around. He moved his jeans down only until they had passed his erection, before letting them fall to the floor.

Sophie smiled, her eyes blinking in an effort to not look down. He grinned, going commando had definitely paid off, and whether or not she had good peripheral vision made no difference, there was no avoiding what he had just whipped out.

Sophie just smiled, a wicked look in her eyes, as she reached behind her back and unhooked her bra. Letting go, he tried to watch-not-watch as she brought one hand to the front to hold the bra in place as she slowly slipped the straps down each arm. She was breathing heavily, but that was OK because he was all but panting too, and when she let go of her bra, it landed on the floor with a dull thud, and she nearly won.

His eyes almost dropped, almost. He was sweating now, a combination of the steam from the shower and the energy it was taking to not look down, and more importantly to not back down. Sophie lifted an eyebrow, taunting him. He could just make out her pert breasts her nipples hard. He nearly looked down again.

It was killing him, but the agony of waiting was having an effect all of its own. He just hoped that he didn't immediately peak too soon and make a fool of himself when he was finally given the chance to worship her. He could feel himself tensing up already and they hadn't touched, they hadn't even properly looked.

Sophie was biting her lip, a job that Marcus couldn't wait to undertake. Sophie's hands fell to her hips, as she took the sides of her knickers and pushed down. She had to bend slightly but still looked up at him, standing up straight again as her legs worked her knickers the rest of the way down.

He was panting now, properly, he could see Sophie's eyes were twinkling as she realised that she had met her match. She threw him a huge grin before she turned and climbed into the bath.

Giving her no time at all, he jumped in too and he was next to her, pulling her towards him at the same time she leapt into his arms, the warm, steamy water covering them both.

The feel of her wet body against his was pushing at his last bit of resolve, tightly holding onto her hips he kissed her with everything he had, unleashing his pent-up desire to see, touch and taste her. Her hands were up at his face, moving his mouth to exactly where she wanted him so that he could be devoured. That was fine for him because at this moment in time he had her wet body pressed up against his and it was taking conscious effort not to come. His hand moved lower, she couldn't miss the feel of his rock hard erection pressed up against her, but he had to know how ready she was for him. His hand moved down from her hip, until his fingers slid over her sensitive spot and moved into her. He groaned into her mouth as his fingers felt her and he couldn't wait until he could go down and devour her again. He moved his hand back up towards her clit, making her break off the kiss as she groaned and her head fell back. He took a moment to enjoy the expression on her face as she succumbed until his eyes travelled down mesmerised by the water that gathered and dripped off her breasts. He lent down to lick the water off her nipple before taking it in his mouth to lick and bite. His arm on her back got heavy as he realised that she was relaxing into him and relying on his strength as she gave in. He loved the feel of her hands as one scratched down his back and the other dug into his head making sure that he didn't move. She was crying out already and going by how wet his hand was, she was ready to come for him. He decided to press a little harder on her clit, as she began working herself on his hand. At the same time, he bit a little harder on her nipple and felt her legs begin to shake. She was moving against him faster and faster. He needed her to come he couldn't wait any longer, he slipped two fingers inside her and moved his thumb so that it was carefully in position, moving his fingers quickly until he felt her muscles tighten on him and she screamed out, his arm at her back supporting her and taking her weight when her legs wanted to give up entirely.

Once the weight was back in her legs, he removed his hands and put them back on her hips before reaching up, kissing her again.

Sophie broke off the kiss. 'I need more.'

Oh God, he wanted to give her everything. Dipping down as Sophie remained clung to him, he moved the shower curtain out of the way as felt around the side of the bath trying to find his jeans. Sophie let out a little squeal as the cold side of the bath met her hip. Finally he got what he was after and stood them both back up.

Ripping open the packet he was all ready to put the condom on, when Sophie beat him to it. His breath pulled from his lungs as he stroked the back of her thighs, before pulling her up and turning them around so that her legs were over his hips, and his back against the wall.

He shivered slightly at the cold tile on his back, it cooled him down just enough that he had a little more control. Sophie was grinning as the water rushed down her body her hands moving from his cock on to his arms as she stroked his muscles.

Marcus looked down and broke out in a sweat as he lowered her onto him. She was clearly impatient and angled herself so that she could take him all in one go. He nearly swallowed his tongue. He needed a moment to catch his breath and regain some control before he began moving. Her internal muscles holding onto his cock so tightly that he slammed his eyes shut and tried to count to ten. Control temporarily gathered, he opened his eyes as they started moving faster, watching as her breasts bounced and water continued to cover them both.

'Marcus, please,' Sophie cried, her muscles getting tighter and tighter, and he could feel her against his cock. She was groaning loudly now and he was enjoying watching her let go, he had always thought or hoped that she would be loud and unreserved. He adored her and wanted to adore every inch of her but that would have to wait for next time, maybe in the morning. His balls were tingling, and he knew he was seconds away from coming. He thrust into her even harder and knew from her crying out and from the scratching down his back that she was going to fly apart any second. He just hoped that he could wait a few seconds.

'Come for me, Sophie.' He was watching her face and saw her eyes open, they stared into his before her head fell back again, her eyes closing as she gasped and shook, he felt her orgasm all the way through his body and a second later he was coming too. He continued to push into her until his knees felt like jelly and he lowered them both to the bath.

'Oh God,' Marcus groaned trying to get his breath back. He could feel Sophie's slow grin against his shoulder.

'I know.'

He didn't know how long they sat like that in the bath under the shower, but it took a while simply to get their breath back. He loved the feel of Sophie on top of him, especially as she was gently stroking his neck. Unfortunately, the water was getting cold, and his bum was getting numb, and there were things that needed attending to.

'Come on, let's get cleaned up and then I'll take you to bed.' He held onto her waist to help her back into a standing position.

Chapter Twenty

Her eyes still closed, Sophie smiled. She was lovely and warm, maybe a little too warm as she woke up engulfed by a six foot two, tanned and muscular gardener god – who also happened to be a cover hog. Sophie couldn't help but imagine how luxuriously warm he would be in the winter, but as it was currently mid-summer it was a little too much. Sophie turned trying to escape the hold Marcus had on her. She was met with a grunt.

'You're too warm,' Sophie whispered.

In response Marcus kicked off the cover completely and went back to wrapping himself around her so that her back was completely pressed against his chest, nudging his thick thigh between her legs, ensuring that she was only too aware of the feel of his morning glory.

'You snore,' Marcus groaned.

'I do not!'

Marcus chuckled as Sophie hit his arm, and he nuzzled into her, his light stubble gently scratching her neck.

'What time is it?' His voice was just a little bit croaky and it sent shivers down her spine.

'Time you got up and got my garden finished.'

'You're bossy in the mornings. I've not even had a kiss yet, let alone a cup of tea.'

Moving about inch by inch, Sophie got enough space so that she could turn around, lying on her side to face him. He immediately reached forwards to kiss her. Any possibility of awkwardness that morning vanished as their lips met. She knew that their relationship had reached a new easy level. One that she hoped would mean that they got on better, and had lots of sex. Other than that she didn't have time for anything more, she just hoped he remembered that. Speaking of.

'Come on, we need to get up, now that the broadband is properly up and running I have lots to catch up on.' That's what she knew she had to do, but the way he was stroking his fingers up and down her arm meant that if she didn't hurry they would get carried away. Again.

'Yeah?'

'Yes!' she said firmly, before his fingers got any clever ideas.

'Tell me, I want to hear about what you're going to do today while I'm slaving away in your garden.'

'Well, I need to batch load some videos and schedule them for their release. I need to edit the contouring video we did and schedule that in for upload, although I think that might need to be up sooner rather than later. I have to go through my strategy and figures, and cross reference with my business plan. So there. You see, lots of fun. What about you?'

'Well, I have to do lots of manual labour in the hot sun. I might even have to take my T-shirt off. That's not going to be too distracting for you, is it?' Marcus stretched, showing her exactly how distracting his body could be.

She hummed and stroked his pecs, deliberately not going any lower. 'You know it would be, so I'm deliberately not looking.'

'OK, OK. What time is it?' Marcus groaned.

'You need to let go of me so that I can get my phone and find out.'

With a grunt, she found herself released from his grasp. With her freedom, she felt around for her phone.

'Shit. It's nine a.m. What time are Bailey and Jo—'

Sophie was interrupted by the sound of the front door opening and a 'Hello' shouted out from Bailey. 'Hey, Soph, have you seen Marcus? His van's outside but there's no sign of him. Hello?'

'I'll be down in a minute. Make yourselves a brew!' Sophie shouted back to them as she hastily got up. She looked at

Marcus, who was still in bed wearing nothing but his trademark cheeky half smile.

'You're not going to sneak through the house and then come in through the front door are you?' she asked, reaching into her drawer for clean underwear.

'Why would I do that?'

'To try and keep us secret?' She already knew the answer. He wouldn't be bothered with any messing around.

'Again, why would I do that?' He was grinning and inviting. She toyed with the idea of just getting back into bed and forgetting about real life but knew that wasn't going to solve anything. Sophie shook her head and quickly looked around for clean clothes to throw on.

'We're going to have to talk about all of this properly at some point, you know. But if you insist on letting Bailey and Joseph know you stayed over, then one of us is going to need to say something to Polly.'

Now that took the smile off his face. Sophie laughed.

'Did you really have to bring up my sister when I'm trying to lure you back to bed?'

Sophie threw a sock at him.

'Come on, get up, you have to make me a brew.' With that Sophie pulled on her T-shirt having already got the rest of her clothes on, and left the bedroom to make her way to the bathroom, before going downstairs.

She was just booting up her laptop when Bailey and Joseph walked back in through the back door, having disappeared into the garden.

'Try calling him again,' Joseph was saying.

'OK. Morning, Soph. You look good, doll.' Bailey beamed at her with his usual charming style, before picking up his phone and putting it to his ear. It took her less than a second to realise who he was calling and what was going to happen next. She didn't embarrass easy but this one was going to sting. Sure enough, Bailey was calling Marcus. The phone ringing from the stairs that Marcus was currently making his way down. Bailey and Joseph just stopped and stared, their eyes nearly falling out of their head, before they both burst into huge grins.

'Well, well, well,' Bailey said, ending the call.

'Maybe he just got here extra early.' Joseph winked.

'Yeah like last night. He's just so dedicated. Here he is. Morning, pal. Sleep OK?'

Marcus just grinned. 'Morning, lads, let's get cracking, shall we?' Marcus started shooing them out towards the kitchen before he turned around and grabbed his boots. The next thing she knew, he had kissed her. 'Have a good day at work, darling.'

Sophie was stunned.

Nowhere in the 'keeping it casual' guidebook did it mention telling all of your mates the minute after you'd had sex. All right, it wasn't the minute after, it wasn't even after the first time, but still. Surely they should have kept it quieter than this? At least at first. She was confused as to what it meant for their boundaries and the casual status of their relationship. Rather than think about all of that, she looked down at her laptop and focused on her work.

She needed to start editing the contouring video with Marcus, but first she went in and checked all her social media. Responding to questions and queries from her viewers, liking some of the comments and basically just tending to her beautiful community of supporters. One of her Facebook messages wasn't quite as nice as the others, not completely unheard of but still not exactly pleasant. Sophie recalled the first bit of hate mail she had received, just as she had started to hit the ten thousand followers mark. She'd had to develop a thick skin for keyboard warriors. She was sure that this one would be no different.

You are so fake. Why are you wasting everyone's time with this? It's not like you're saving the world. You always were self-obsessed.

Sophie shook her head and deleted the comment. Only to find it repeated on Instagram and Twitter and in the comments on YouTube. All with the exact same wording. Deleting them all, she put it to the back of her mind, deciding to go over her comments a little more carefully from now on.

She started to load up the contouring video to begin editing it. Her head was clearly not in the game, as she missed how long the video was, and just started at the beginning. First, run through would be to take out any mistakes and any of the prolonged umms and arrrs.

Editing was slightly more difficult in that it used so much brainpower. Due to its very nature, editing was usually tedious and time-consuming, especially on a video as badly prepared as the contouring video. There was a certain charm though, it had to look like it wasn't prepared in advance, so mostly the editing on this one was all about finding the balance. Keeping in some of the imperfections but not too many that people won't watch it, and also remembering that a make-up company have asked for her to review it so it really needed to be good.

Sophie's phone buzzed. It was Polly. She momentarily froze until she realised she had to answer it, after all there was no way Polly could tell over the phone that Sophie had slept with her brother. She had a quick look outside to see if Marcus was nearby, but he was at the other end of the garden, presumably telling Bailey and Joseph what they needed to be doing today. She was on her own with this one.

Try and sound like you're not sleeping with her brother, she kept repeating to herself. 'Hi, Pol, how you doing?' There. Easy breezy, in no way sleeping with your brother.

'Yeah, I'm OK. Are you in today? Can I call round? I have to chew your ear off about the date last night. It was weird.'

'Yeah, I'm working but, for you, I can spare an hour or so.'

'Thanks, Soph, see you in a bit.'

Sophie's shoulders relaxed as the call ended knowing that

she had bought herself twenty minutes at the most. She didn't know how Polly was going to react at all. She might well be furious.

'Ahhhh,' Sophie groaned. 'It's not even a serious thing to get upset over.'

Suddenly, something on the screen caught her attention. 'Wait, how long is this video?' She was skipping towards the end of it just as Marcus came in.

'Hey, Soph, you want a br— What the hell? Is that us?'

Sophie looked back at her laptop and yelped.

'Holy shit we have a sex tape. Does it look any good?' Marcus moved over to Sophie so that he was stood next to her and could see the screen. They both watched it for a minute before a noise outside made her realise that Bailey and Joseph were not far enough away. She slammed the lid shut.

'We looked hot. I want to see more.'

'No! We can't. Bailey and Joseph might see it and besides which your sister is coming over soon. I'll just have to work on it later when you've all gone and I can delete it.'

'Can you send me a copy?'

'No, get out, and yes, I want a brew.' She had to shove him away from the desk. Once he had crossed the threshold into the kitchen she gingerly lifted the lid of her laptop. There they were. She had her clearly naked back to the camera. Pleased to see that she didn't have any unsightly spots. It was the look on Marcus's face that was taking her attention. He looked enraptured, as he studied her body. She was getting hot again and she had to cross her legs to try and stop herself getting any more turned on. Contemplating playing a bit more of the video, she quickly changed her mind and turned the editing program off before anyone could see it. She was sure it would be awful watching it back, no one but the professionals made good sex tapes, but she suspected that she would be watching it later tonight. OK, she knew she would be watching it again later, without a doubt.

Marcus walked back in with a brew in his hand, placing it on the table.

'Was it that good? You look a little flushed.' Marcus's grin was particularly wide.

'No. Which one of us is speaking to Polly about this?' she said, pointing back and forth.

'About the sex tape? I don't think either of us should.'

Sophie rolled her eyes, 'About us.'

'I don't mind. I've just had a grilling from the guys so it's probably your turn.'

'What did you say to them?'

'Don't worry I said exactly what you told me – that we are keeping it casual, just having fun, and not getting in the way of each other's work. See? I can pay attention.' He put his hands on the table and leaned towards her. 'You should know though, that you're going to want me forever at some point. I just think it's only fair to give you advanced warning.'

He was so close, she was hypnotised by his eyes, his smell, even his voice. She wasn't completely tracking what he was telling her. She looked at his lips willing him to move closer an inch and kiss her. Suddenly, she remembered where they were and what she was supposed to be doing.

Sophie quickly pulled away. 'Look you're already distracting me from my work, get out.'

'Good morning to you too, sunshine, enjoy your brew.' He blew her a kiss as she watched him stroll out into the garden.

Completely distracted by knowing that he was outside; and with the knowledge of what was currently on her laptop, and with the fact that Polly was coming round, Sophie found herself messing about doing nothingy bits of work that really weren't all that important. Frustrated she covered her face with her hand.

'Casual. It's casual for exactly this reason; he's already disrupting my work. I can't think straight.'

'Who's distracting your work?'

'Shit!' Sophie jumped as Polly walked towards the table and sat down.

'Sorry, I didn't mean to make you jump but the door was unlocked, so I let myself in. Are you OK?'

Oh God, what was Polly going to say? Sophie couldn't decide what would be worse; if Polly got upset or if she got delighted and declared her a sister. The sister one definitely, that would be much worse.

'Hi, Pol, you OK?'

'Yeah, I'm going to go make a brew. You want one?'

'No, I've got one already, thanks.' Taking a sip she tried to calm down. It was casual, not a big deal. No stress.

She waited until Polly was back in the room and sat down, still not sure what she was going to say. She moved her laptop out of the way, face flaming again with the realisation that there was some graphic evidence of what she was about to admit.

'Come on then, Soph, who's the mystery man distracting you from your work?'

'Well... erm, it's...' Sophie was looking everywhere other than at Polly. 'Erm, well, it's Marcus, we're... I guess we're seeing each other.'

Polly gasped in shock, then put her hands to her face. 'I can't believe it, I mean whoever would've guessed?' Polly grinned unable to keep up the act of faux shock any longer.

'Wait... what... you knew?' That sounded like a shriek, why was she shrieking?

'Duh, anyone who watches your videos knew it was going to happen sooner or later. Besides which Paige told me the other day.'

'Oh.' Sophie wasn't really sure what to think about that. She wasn't too much of a fan of people talking about her behind her back, but then again it meant that it was easier to explain. 'You don't need to worry it's no—'

'Let me guess, it's nothing serious. Sure, Soph, whatever you need to tell yourself. Just be careful, OK. You have a history of pulling away when things get too intense. You could be pulling away from something awesome there, and I'm not just saying that because he's my brother. I mean gross. But the chemistry you two have, well, it's fun to watch in person and online.'

Sophie tried to mull that over but instead watched Polly as she became transfixed by something outside. Turning around, she saw what the problem was. It was a hot day, and even though she knew Marcus had taken his T-shirt off to torment her, Bailey had done it for no reason other than he was hot, and it was practical to do so. He didn't need to worry, he was hench too, he just saved his showing off for picking up women at the bar – or he used to.

'So how was the date last night?' Sophie asked to try and help Polly out.

'It was weird.'

'OK, how weird? Usual weird, Tinder weird or weird weird?'

Polly began playing with her hair, twisting it around her fingers and back again.

'He introduced me to his mother.'

Sophie sputtered, nearly choking on her tea. 'On the first date?'

Polly nodded.

'He seemed really lovely. When we spoke online he was really polite, really attentive and I know it shouldn't matter but the care taken with his replies was obvious and there wasn't a single aubergine or dick pic. When we met up he was in a smart outfit and really well put together. Not joggers and flip-flops like some guys do. It all seemed perfect. I hadn't noticed the woman he came in with and didn't notice her for ages as she was sat behind me. Anyway, long story short, it was his mother. It was also his mother I'd been chatting with online and she coached him through the entire date by signalling behind me.'

'What?'

'Yes, and I know all of this because afterwards she came up to me and explained who she was and would I give feedback on his performance. On the plus side, he paid for both drinks, well presumably with his pocket money.'

Sophie was speechless for a minute.

'Oh, Jesus, Pol how the hell do you find them? How did Paige and I miss it?'

'You wouldn't necessarily spot it unless you were actually on the date. Besides I was safe enough, just weirded out.'

'I'm speechless. It's like the world's worst threesome.'

Polly choked on her tea. 'Ew gross.'

Sophie grinned. 'Maybe you need a new dating app?'

'Yeah, I don't know, maybe. It's got to work out at some point though, right? Besides I'm not desperate to meet the one, I'm happy to have fun with no strings. It's just that I am not even finding anyone to have fun with.'

Sophie pondered about what to say next, and whether or not to say what was on the tip of her tongue.

'Look, Pol. I have to ask, what's going on with Bailey?'

'Nothing. Why?' Polly's head moved so fast it was a wonder she didn't pull something. Sophie finished her brew and didn't say anything else. What else was there to say? Hopefully at some point, things might actually happen for the two of them, but until then, apparently, it was going to stay as a fake kiss and a series of bad dates with creepy men.

'So tell me about your work. Your latest videos seem to be doing really well. Are your subscribers increasing?'

'It certainly looks that way, I mean I actually haven't had time to go through it all properly yet. What with the broadband issues.'

'Oh yeah.' Polly grimaced. 'Are you all caught up now?'

Sophie tried not to blush as she thought about what she

had been doing recently instead of working. 'Yes, just about. I'm going to start going through the stats next. See what's worked and what hasn't.'

'OK, well, I'll leave you to it. You at the bar tomorrow night?'

'Yeah.'

'OK see you then.' Polly glanced towards the garden again.

'OK. Pol, if ever you wanted to talk about anything... else you know you can, right?'

'Thanks, Soph, you too. Just maybe not too much detail about my brother, yeah? See you later.'

Chapter Twenty-One

Sophie put her hand to her face, she was definitely flushed. She was beyond glad that she had waited until the lads had finished for the day before editing. She was trying to edit the contouring video that she had made with Marcus but instead found herself watching the last part. The part without any make-up. Or clothes, for that matter. It was captivating, she couldn't take her eyes away. It wasn't explicit, not by any stretch, the angle of the camera and the fact that Marcus had put her on the table meant that all you could really see was her back. Maybe a little bit indecent when she was stripped but mostly you could just tell what Sophie was building up to as it got hotter and hotter. As she sat there watching the video, she felt herself responding. Her breathing increasing, her mouth drying, her stomach clenching, her body tingling in ways that were never normally involved with her usual make-up videos. It was hot to watch it, especially as she recalled not having orgasmed that hard in a long time, if forever.

'Wow, that is hot!'

'Shit! What are you doing here?' Sophie jumped out of her skin at the same time she slammed the lid of her laptop down hoping she hadn't just broken it. She'd really had enough of being snuck up on today.

Mya was smiling. 'Wowsers, seriously, Sophie, I didn't realise you were so kinky. It's not for the vlog, is it? You'll certainly get more followers with that! Am I right in guessing that that was Marcus doing all the hard work?'

Sophie groaned, her hands covering her red-hot face. 'How much did you see?'

'I'm sorry to say that I interrupted at the wrong time, it looked like you were getting close there.'

Sophie wasn't sure if she meant on the video or now, so decided to ignore it all together. Instead, she jumped up and all but ran to the kitchen to get some water. Unfortunately, Mya followed.

'So, was that Marcus's hands and head I could just about see on that video?'

'Yes, and no, you can't make a big deal out of it, and you absolutely cannot tell him what you just watched.'

Mya grinned.

'Mya! I'm serious. Not a word. It was an accident, I was doing the recording of a makeover and forgot to turn the camera off.'

'Like I said, I didn't have you pegged for such kinky stuff, but then again you never can tell, can you? They say it's usually the quiet ones but then if memory serves you were never a quiet one either.' Mya was creased over laughing.

'You're enjoying this, aren't you?'

'Yes. I really am. So how long have you been seeing each other, in the flesh, as it were?' This just set her off again.

Sophie drank her water and tried to calm her racing heart that was currently beating so fast you'd have thought someone had watched her accidental sex tape… oh wait.

'That was the first time,' she whispered mortified.

'And forever kept. It will make a wonderful story at your wedding.'

'Yeah, my mother would be thrilled. Actually she probably would. No, it's not that big a deal, we're just seeing each other casually. It's nothing serious.'

'That's a shame. Someone that can do that to you, you don't really want to be losing.'

'I've got too much on at the moment with work. I can't be sidetracked when I am so close.'

'You certainly were close.' Mya was gone again wiping the tears from her face.

Sophie just rolled her eyes and hoped that this torture

would soon be at an end, she'd never been so embarrassed and just wanted this whole thing to be over with as quickly as possible. Her face was blushing so much she wasn't sure if she hadn't completely altered her skin tone forever.

'Just be careful,' Mya said, when she finally calmed down.

Sophie raised an eyebrow. 'He's not the sort to mess me about and, like I said, it's just casual and we're both adults.'

'That's not what I meant. I am asking *you* to be careful that you don't let something fantastic disappear because it's convenient to blame work. Anyway, what are you going to do with the video? Presumably, you don't want to upload it or are you toying with the idea of being another Kardashian?'

'No! Of course not.' Although, she did let the idea filter through her head for one whole second before she realised that she would be mortified, not to mention her family would see it, and of course the impact it would have on Marcus. 'Besides my current figures are doing really well. I don't need it, I'm doing better than my business plan had predicted at this point.'

'Really, that's amazing. How come?'

Sophie coughed and looked down. 'Marcus,' she muttered.

'What?' Mya asked, a wicked smile on her face.

'My viewers are responding really well to him. He's dropped in on a couple of videos.'

'Presumably it's not hurting having his toned body in the background either. Come to think of it, I am a couple of videos behind. I really ought to catch up. Or maybe I should wait until you upload this new one and then binge.'

Sophie walked back to the table and sat down behind her laptop.

'So is Marcus's gardening business experiencing the same boost?' Mya asked, still following her around the house, like the world's most annoying shadow. Why did she keep asking awkward questions?

'Well, no, because we haven't actually mentioned his business yet.'

'Why not? Wasn't that the point?'

'He's coming over in a bit. I'm going to do another live video and he can answer some questions put to him by the viewers. I've told them that we'll be live at eight so he'll be here any minute. It's quite exciting, I think there might be a few people actually scheduling in to watch us.'

'Just make sure you keep this video PG, yeah? I'll go upstairs and make sure I'm out of your way, I need to unpack anyway.' Mya's laughter could be heard all the way up the stairs as she made her way to her bedroom, her case thudding behind her on each stair.

Sophie hid her face in her hands. She couldn't believe that she hadn't heard Mya come in. At least it wasn't Polly, she thought. Trying to forget about the last five minutes she took some deep breaths before tentatively opening up her laptop lid. Sure enough, her naked body was on the screen paused where, if memory served, she was about to climax. She quickly shut down the programme so that she wouldn't get caught again. What was she going to do about that video? In her heart of hearts, she knew she didn't want to delete it, but it certainly couldn't stay where it was. Squaring her shoulders she opened the programme again and cut the entirety of the sex scene and saved it separately. She hesitated not sure what to call it. 'Sex tape' seemed too perverse, and obvious if anyone borrowed her laptop. But if she called it anything make-up related she always ran the risk of accidentally opening it, or worse, accidentally uploading it. She simply called it 'Sophie & Marcus', and closed it again, before focusing her attention on the actual contouring video, after all the company had requested the video be uploaded no later than Monday.

Marcus pulled up outside Sophie's house and did a quick check to make sure he had the essentials; phone, keys, wallet.

He had to stop himself from running to the front door, he was so eager to see her. If he thought he had feelings for her before, it was nothing to the effect she was having on him now. He was grinning like an idiot and couldn't help it. Besides, he figured that Sophie should see how happy he was, it might rub off on her too, it certainly couldn't hurt. He rang the doorbell and listened for the sounds of Sophie approaching.

She opened the door, and his heart flipped. She wore a loose white T-shirt and leggings, her hair tied up in its usual messy bun, make-up free. If she was trying to discourage him, he had news for her, he thought she looked stunning.

'Hi, gorgeous, had a good day?'

She reluctantly smiled and pulled his hands away from her waist. 'Yes, but I need to tell you something, come on.'

As he followed her through the house he couldn't help but wonder if this was it. He hated that she wanted everything so casual, when he wanted to shout his feelings from the rooftop. She dropped down on her chair and continued to look at her hands. It was the tell that it was something serious. Please don't be about us, he hoped. He hadn't had time to completely win her over yet. Sitting down next to her, he took her hands in his and waited.

'So, the contouring video,' she started.

OK now he was confused. 'What about it?'

'Mya saw it, most of it.'

'Isn't that the point? That people watch your videos?'

'Not the end of that particular video, no.'

Marcus made a show of looking confused and casting his mind back as he studied her face. She was embarrassed, her face was blushing and she was playing with their hands.

'Oh, you mean the bit where we had sex.' Marcus grinned. 'So what did she think? Did she score my performance out of ten? What did I get? Was she kind?'

'You're not upset?'

'Nope, not really. Unless you're planning on screening to the whole street or putting it on your vlog?'

'God, no.'

'OK then. So when do I get to see it?' He watched as her face jumped up in surprise.

'What?'

'Surely I get to see it? It's the only way to make it fair. It can't be that Mya has seen it and I haven't. I'm the main star. I can't look that bad in it, surely? Or is it you, do you look awful?'

'Shut up, I do not.'

'OK, cool so I can watch it later?' He looked at her as she struggled to find a good enough reason for him not watching it. Not giving her the chance to think of one he carried on. 'So I've ordered pizza for nine, I figured we'd be done with the live video by that point?'

Sophie sputtered, clearly put out. 'Erm, yeah, that's great. Thanks.'

'Come here, Soph.' He held his arms out to her but had to meet her halfway and bring her towards him until she sat lightly on his leg. His arm rubbed her back, while his other hand rested lightly on her thigh. 'What's the matter?'

'Nothing. I'm just flustered from before. Mya walked in on me watching it...'

'And... Come on, Soph I know there's more.'

'It was hot,' she whispered.

He grinned. 'So you got all hot and bothered while watching yourself get all hot and bothered. I cannot wait to watch it. But don't worry, Mya's seen worse, I'm sure.' He reached up and gently kissed her. He wanted to try and un-rattle her as she clearly didn't like feeling so unnerved. He guessed it was because she was always in control, she was going to need to regain her confidence and find her stride before they did the live video.

As they sat quietly he felt her soften and, finally, she wound

161

her hands around his neck. He pulled away and gently placed her back on her chair. He rested his hands on her legs. 'So tell me what I need to know about tonight's live video?'

She took a deep breath and her face relaxed, the scowl gone. 'Well, for starters we both need to be at least a little bit professional, so no kissing on camera.'

'Shame.'

'I'm going to do a basic nude makeover based on the new colours that are available at the moment. It shouldn't take longer than ten minutes. I am going to talk through it, but only giving the basics. I thought that you could look at the comments and respond to any questions. Hopefully, someone will ask about your work and that way you can naturally add in about your gardening business.'

'Perfect. Sounds like a plan.'

'OK then, let's get set up.'

He smiled, knowing that she was back to her usual in control self.

'So there you have it.' Sophie finished her make-up tutorial and smiled at the camera, turning her head left and right.

'She looks gorgeous, doesn't she?' Marcus had to resist kissing her. It wasn't new, he'd had to resist for the last twenty minutes, the last few weeks really, the last twelve months – in fact, he wasn't sure for how long. The live video was only supposed to have taken ten minutes but the questions and comments kept pouring in. Marcus answered them in his usual cheeky way. He realised he enjoyed doing these videos with Sophie, not as much as the first video obviously and he wouldn't want to do them all the time – Sophie wouldn't want that either – but it was fun. Their banter was quick and funny, at least according to most of the comments. Some of the comments, however, Marcus had deliberately chosen to ignore, one in particular he would talk to Sophie about afterwards.

'OK, thanks, everyone. I'll see you again soon. Remember to subscribe to my YouTube channel for all of the latest videos, and you can follow me on all the usual places. Oh, and, of course, you can find more information about Marcus's gardening on his website and social media, I will leave the links in the comments. Bye.' Sophie blew a kiss and waved as she clicked to end the live video. Marcus was stunned.

'My website and social media?'

'Yes, I had some downtime at the bar and, well, I hope you don't mind but I had the video of the garden before, and there are some pictures since, and I used the information on your original Facebook to sort out your new social media business pages. It really will be good for your business. Oh I left your Instagram alone. You seem to be doing very well on there, you seem to have built up some followers that I'm sure has nothing to do with your topless profile picture.' Sophie laughed.

Marcus was speechless. It wasn't that he was upset about what she had done, far from it. It was more that she had taken time out of her busy schedule to think about him and his business and create something that would help. He was touched. He was also trying to not read too much into it, but would a casual couple go to such lengths? Then again it was Sophie's area of expertise, so the whole thing probably did only take her ten minutes. Still.

'Why aren't you saying anything? I can delete them if you want? I just thought...'

Marcus grabbed Sophie and kissed her.

'Thank you. I knew they needed doing and I was probably going to ask for your help with them anyway. What are the passwords?'

'Here. Change them when you can.' Sophie handed him a piece of paper.

'So was that live video good? Did I do OK?' Marcus asked, wanting to change the subject.

'Yes, you were brilliant. I'll go through the video again tomorrow. To look at all the comments, etc. It's hard to do that and give a good make-up tutorial at the same time.'

'Sophie, can we talk about the comments?'

She sighed, and her face fell. 'I know what you're going to say.'

'Who the hell is CarBeFoxy?'

'I don't know and, honestly, I don't think I want to know.'

'Is she... I'm assuming she's trolling you?'

'Yes, but it comes with the territory. It's no big deal. I don't let it get to me.'

'But some of the stuff she's saying. Can you not block her?'

'I did and then she comes back as someone else, but I can tell it's her. I'm not going to lie, it's pretty scary at times when I allow my imagination to run wild, but really I'm sure it's just some pathetic, jealous individual trying to make my life difficult for their own amusement. I actually asked a couple of people I know who have experienced the same thing, and, well, I now have someone highly recommended looking into it to see if they can find out who the person is. And the least I tell you about that the better. It's not exactly above board.'

Marcus didn't care, he was just glad she was looking into it. He'd only caught a comment or two on the last vlog, but this time he'd been able to see how often the troll was spouting abuse. It seemed to be getting worse and it also felt oddly specific.

Sophie started tidying her stuff away as Mya walked down the stairs.

'Great video, Soph.'

'Did you watch it?'

'Duh. But who the hell does that Car fox bitch think she is?' Mya walked into the kitchen and pulled a bottle of wine out of the fridge. 'You need to do something about her.'

Sophie just grunted. Marcus reached to clear away the cups and biscuit detritus.

'You were hot as always, Marcus. Shame that you kept your clothes on for this one, the one I saw earlier was much better.' Mya was laughing as she got the glasses from the cupboard.

'Thanks, Mya, I'm glad you liked it, coming from the industry's top porn queen herself, it means a lot.'

Grinning Mya replied, 'The secret's out.'

Sophie's mouth fell open in shock.

'I'm joking, you idiot. Although I have been offered a porn deal and that is true. But I won't say any more, I don't want to give the game away. What time is the pizza getting here?'

Chapter Twenty-Two

Sophie was getting dressed. Not able to believe that it was Monday once again, she pulled on her 'bar' work jeans, knowing that Mondays were usually pretty quiet, with just a few of the local business people coming in for lunch. In theory, she should have plenty of time to be able to get on with planning the videos for the next couple of weeks. The contouring video was scheduled to be up later today, and she was more than a little bit nervous. She had emailed her named product contact to tell them when it would be uploaded and on what channels. What if the make-up company hated it? Well, if they did, hopefully other make-up companies might like it. At least she had been honest about the product, and really that was the main thing.

The live video had gone really well on Friday and Marcus had finally been able to talk about his business, but not before wooing her viewers until he had them eating out of his palm – well, nearly all of them. Her mind kept going back to CarBeFoxy. There had been some more comments today, the same insults, but it was the references to how she had been 'before' that struck a nerve, as if the person had known her. But then again, Sophie guessed that internet trolls would say whatever they could to provoke a response. She just had to hope that her contact found out who it was soon.

In the meantime, she thought back to how Marcus had been in the video. He really was a natural, he should consider doing some live videos as part of his business as it would stand out as different from his competitors. Sophie reached for her phone to make a quick note.

Pulling her hair up she looked out of the window and saw Marcus, Bailey and Joseph working on the garden. It really was looking amazing now. All the brickwork had been completed, that would just need finishing, or pointing or something, she wasn't too sure what, and some of the turf had been laid. The garden space seemed huge, much bigger than before and she was seriously impressed with what they had managed to create so far. That wasn't the only part of Marcus she was impressed with.

Sure enough, they had watched the 'Sophie & Marcus' video, but not before they had eaten pizza with Mya in the front room. It was nice, just being able to hang out. Once finished, they had brought her laptop up to her room. She had been hoping to open it for him and then hide somewhere but he wouldn't let her. She had to sit next to him on the bed so that they could watch it together. They didn't actually manage to watch the whole thing before they were showing themselves how it was done. She grinned at the memory, it had been even hotter that time. More than anything though, being with Marcus was fun. The fact that he was so cool about keeping everything low-key was brilliant. They could hang out together one minute, and have sex the next if they wanted. No strings, no pressure. It was perfect. It meant that she could dedicate the time she needed to her work, keep her focus where it needed to be.

She watched as Mya walked out with a tray of hot drinks. They all put down their tools and laughed at something Mya said. Sophie shuddered, her cheeks burning as she still couldn't believe that Mya had seen the video. She turned around picking up her handbag before going downstairs.

'Hi, guys, how's it going?' Sophie asked as she finished putting her shoes on and walked out the back door into the garden.

'Morning, gorgeous,' Bailey shouted over with a wink before he was nudged sharply in the ribs by Marcus. Marcus then made his way towards her, staring at her intently the entire time. She felt her heart rate increase, his eyes really are his best feature, well that and his bum. OK, his bum was spectacular and his eyes weren't far off. He had really great arms though, getting lost in her appreciation of him, as Marcus bent down and kissed her. Someone wolf whistled. He pulled away slightly. 'Good morning, gorgeous. Did you sleep well?' He knew she had, he'd only left her bedroom a couple of hours before.

'I did, thank you. Did you?' He grinned, and Sophie smiled. 'Right I'm off to work. See you later.'

Marcus gave her a quick kiss before letting her go. 'Me too, have fun.'

She turned around and made her way through the house, smiling all the way.

Marcus watched as Bailey took his brew and made his way over to the furthest part of the garden. He was really working hard today and Marcus was impressed.

He turned back around and grabbed his brew off the tray, stopping when he realised that both Mya and Joseph were staring at him.

'What?' He grinned.

Mya started, 'So you and Sophie…'

'What about it?' he asked, wondering why they both looked so serious. Was he about to be warned off? If so it was too late for that.

'Let me guess, she's told you that it's nothing serious and she wants to keep it casual?' Mya had raised an eyebrow and her lips were pursed. She was pissed off, and he had no idea why. Deciding to play it cautiously, he said, 'Erm, yes. Why?'

Mya sighed. 'Because I love that girl, but she's an idiot sometimes.'

He shook his head. 'I'm confused.'

'In my line of work, I have had to learn to read people. Trust me, I'm really very good at it. Regardless of how much she feels for you, she will always try and keep you at arm's length, even more so if she likes you as much as I think she does. It's a protection thing, but it's going to cost her if she's not careful.' She looked over at Joseph a small sad smile on her lips. 'You know him best, but you understand what I'm saying, right?'

'I'm afraid I do.' Joseph nodded.

'Good. You take care of him. I'm going to work on her.' With that, she took the now empty tray and went back inside.

'What the hell is all this about? Am I being warned off?'

Joseph took a sip of his brew before shaking his head. 'No, not at all, quite the opposite in fact. Look I know it's none of our business but I know how much you feel for Sophie. It was the same way I felt and still feel for Harriet. All we're saying is that Sophie more than likely feels it too. She's just not going to admit to it too soon. In fact, if she senses things are getting too serious she is likely to cut you loose. For now, you need to keep playing the game, keep it casual, she'll soon see that she needs to keep you around for good.'

Marcus sighed, grateful that he wasn't being warned off, but his heart dropping at the confirmation of his fears. Deciding that there weren't many secrets left, he replied, 'I don't know what to do. Or what state I am going to be in by the end of this.'

Joseph patted his shoulder. 'I remember that feeling well. It will all work out in the end, just remember that. I have no doubt she loves you just as much as you love her.'

Marcus opened his mouth to argue, but instead found himself whispering, 'Is it that obvious?'

'I'm afraid so, son. But don't worry, it will be worth it in the end.'

'I'm glad you're confident because frankly I constantly worry that at any moment she's going to toss me aside.'

Joseph nodded. 'You're doing fine. Just keep doing what you're doing. You never know, you could both have rings on your fingers soon enough, and you'll know that you belong to each other forever.'

Marcus laughed. 'I didn't have you pegged as a romantic.' He nudged Joseph's shoulder.

'I'm not, I'm just happy and trying to share my wisdom and experience from all of my years.'

'Not that many years.'

'Enough to know. Then we need to work on him next,' Joseph said, pointing towards Bailey.

'Yeah if you have any advice about him, I would appreciate it. He's kicking ass one minute, disappearing the next.'

'Hmmm, I think that you need to wait and see on that one too.'

'Anyone ever told you you're a one-trick pony? Is everything just wait and see?'

'Usually.' Joseph chuckled before placing his cup down and getting back to work.

He wasn't surprised by what Mya and Joseph had had to say, he was simply surprised that they had said anything at all. He got the impression from Mya that she didn't really take anything too seriously. She was quite like Bailey in that respect. And Joseph, well Joseph pretty much kept himself to himself. He appreciated their support, it felt like they were on the same page, he just wondered what Mya would be saying to Sophie to win her over, or even if she could. Oh well, for now, he was having fun, and as much as he wanted Sophie to be his, he could carry on as they were, it was hardly difficult.

Chapter Twenty-Three

'Well, that's that. It's uploaded now,' Sophie said, after a quick glance at her watch as she pulled a pint.

'What are you talking about?' Paige asked, raising an eyebrow.

'The contouring video has been uploaded. I spoke to the company and they agreed it should go out tonight at nine. So that's it. It's out there. It's the first one that I've done with products sent to me by a company. It's a bit make or break. If I have done it well, then they will repost it, then I should get a few more followers and hopefully more make-up to review. If it's bad… I don't even want to think about it.'

'Hmmm,' Paige said, extraordinarily, annoyingly non-committal.

Sophie sighed, before quickly turning on the spot. She needed to keep busy and stop thinking about anything. It was a steady night and as long as it stayed steady then she wouldn't be looking at her phone every five minutes. Where was Paige going? Sophie groaned and upped her pace.

'Yes, what can I get you?'

Having worked in bars for a number of years, while she was trying to figure out what she wanted to be when she grew up, Sophie could take drink orders in her sleep. It wasn't difficult to switch her brain off, but the job had the added benefit of keeping her hands too busy to reach for her phone, which was currently secured under the bar. As she pulled pints she realised with a start that she had actually been doing bar work on and off for a lot longer than she had originally planned.

It was a while before Paige came back, and when she did she had a weird look on her face.

'What's wrong?'

'I've just watched your video.' Paige's face was giving nothing away.

'What are you talking about?'

'The contouring video.'

'OK… Why are you being so weird about it?' Starting to get agitated Sophie wiped down the bar counter with a bit more vigour than was necessary.

'Did you mean it to include you and Marcus getting it on on the table? I'm not sure that particular make-up company is going to send you any more freebies, but I have a feeling other different companies might.' Paige winked.

When they say that the blood rushed from someone's face, it happened to Sophie right then. Only she could feel every last drop, and it was all heading for her feet. She suddenly felt unbalanced, her feet suddenly too heavy, she was going to fall over, or maybe vomit. It took a few moments before her brain fully processed what Paige had said.

'Oh God. I'm ruined. Oh God, people have seen me having sex! My mum subscribes and so does my dad. Fuck!'

'Oh my God, calm down. I'm winding you up. Mya texted me and told me to say that to you. Definitely worth it. I'm just gonna Snapchat her a picture of your face. You've never been so pale.'

Paige was grinning as she snapped away on her phone and all Sophie could do was try and breathe, and even that wasn't working very well. How is it her body had forgotten how to breathe?

'Are you serious?' It came out as a croak. Sophie coughed and tried again. 'Are you serious?'

'I am one hundred per cent pulling your leg. Well, about the sex part at least. I did watch the video, and I can guarantee there is no sex scene in there. But you and Marcus made a sex tape, hey? I didn't have you down for being that kinky.'

Why did everyone keep saying that? Well, she wasn't, not really, it was an accident and she certainly would never have suggested it. The results were hot as hell though. Oh God, why did she feel the need to argue about how kinky she was? She was losing the plot, which wasn't surprising considering her heart had only just restarted and was now making up for every missed beat. Her fingers were tingling from the blood slowly returning to them. Adrenalin coursing through her body making her whole body shake.

'You've got me worried now and I checked a million times before I uploaded it. There was no sex, right?'

'No sex.'

'Can I get two—'

'Just hang on. It's just a make-up video, right?'

'Yes. Just a make-up video. Sorry, what can I get you?' Paige turned around to take the drink order.

Sophie willed her body and her head to calm down. She was going to get Mya back for this. That was so mean, and was a million times more embarrassing than the one time Sophie recorded Mya's sex moans and saved it as her ringtone.

Eventually, Sophie got her shit back together enough that she could carry on working. Paige and Sophie continued to serve customers side by side not saying much until there was a small lull.

'I wouldn't say it was *just* a make-up video though,' Paige muttered.

'What do you mean? Do not make me freak out again!'

'Calm down. I just meant that there is something special about it. I really think that this is going to be a big deal for you, Sophie. I'm proud of you. I think if you play it right, you might be out of here sooner than you think.'

Sophie stood up straight. 'Really? What makes you say that?'

'Stop fishing.'

'I'm not. I was terrified that it might be rubbish and no other company would send me make-up ever again. My reviewing wasn't exactly detailed, and they didn't say anything about whether or not I could put make-up on a man. Not that it should matter.'

'Have you finished?'

'Yes, sorry. I'm just so nervous.'

'There's something special, but I think it's between you and Marcus rather than the make-up.'

Sophie stayed silent. What could she say? There was something between them all right – amazing sex. But anything more than that, she really wasn't sure, and she didn't have time to pursue it.

'Look,' said Paige. 'Why don't you have a quick look on your phone now and see how it's doing before they come back for last orders? Where's Marcus by the way? I assumed he'd be here tonight.'

'No he's had his first garden transformation enquiry so he's working on the quote,' Sophie shouted behind her as she went towards her phone. She picked it up, first wiping off some beer, glad as always that she had a phone cover on it.

'That's weird,' muttered Sophie with the phone in her hand.

'What is?'

Sophie looked up not realising that Paige had followed her.

'I could have sworn I'd charged it before I got here.' Sophie reached forward and plugged her phone into the charger at the wall with the optics. 'I'm still not sure what you mean by special.'

'Look, just have a look and see what your regular viewers thought about it.'

Paige walked off to deal with a couple of customers. Not wanting to let her down, Sophie served a couple more patrons before it was quiet again and she could get back to her phone. She pressed the button and her phone lit up.

'What the—?'

Her screen looked as though it had measles with red

notification dots everywhere. Missed calls, texts, WhatsApps, emails, and notification after notification from *all* of her social media. Sophie just stood staring at her screen, not doing anything and didn't notice Paige walking over to her, a concerned look on her face.

'Shit,' whispered Paige. 'I wasn't quite expecting that.'

In shock, Sophie just handed her phone over to Paige. 'What do I do?' It was no wonder her phone had run out of battery.

'Look it's nearly last orders. Let's finish serving this lot then we can go through it together and see what's what.'

'You're certain there was no sex scene?'

'Promise. Come on, I'm ringing the bell now.'

Paige went over to the bell, ringing it for last orders. Sophie took a minute to take a deep breath and although she was desperate to find out what the hell was going on, she knew she wouldn't be able to tell from a quick glance if it was good or bad. Thinking that it might have been bad, she decided that it could wait, and got the drink orders sorted proficiently, but with none of her usual cheer.

It was thirty minutes later before she could glance at her phone and they hadn't even started cleaning the place yet. The glasses had been put away to wash and the others away on their shelves but the rest of the place looked like a stampede had come through.

'Come on, let's sit over here.' Paige sat down, and reached into her hood.

'Come on out, little dude, you can help Sophie figure out what's going on.'

'Ha. I knew it had been too long between kitty fixes. Come here, big guy.' Getting a quick squidgy kitten cuddle she passed him back to Paige, who held him close to her chest with one arm, as she got out her phone with the other.

'I think I know what's going on. But here, drink this first.'

Sophie did as she was told, momentarily surprised at the shot Paige had managed to place in front of her, grateful to have some instruction.

'Right, OK. Let's see what all of this is about.'

She opened her phone and didn't know where to start. She had a look at the missed calls from her mum, Mya, Polly and one from Marcus. Deciding to find out what was going on first, she left the voicemails for now and moved over to Facebook. The notifications number had got stuck at five thousand. She went over to YouTube to see how many views her contouring video had had. A small purr momentarily caught her attention as Paige stroked her cat while watching Sophie's face.

'That can't be right,' Sophie said as she tried to focus on the number on her screen. It was a ridiculously high number, and all of her other videos had seen a surge in views as well. 'There's something wrong with YouTube,' Sophie said, head burrowed down as she moved back to Facebook.

'All of these comments are about my make-up review – about the contouring video. How did they all see it? I mean my numbers have been growing but I didn't have this sort of reach. My page has got so many new likes.'

Sophie took a few minutes to try and read some of the comments, her heart fluttering wildly in her chest, but there was just so much to take in that her eyes were skimming over most of it. 'They're all really nice. They must really like the video. There's a lot of love hearts.' Sophie let out a little squeal. 'Paige, do you realise? Do you know what this means?' She jumped up, her chair falling to the floor. 'I have to capitalise on this. I half wrote a plan just in case something like this ever happened, I just never thought that it would, or at least not with a simple review video. I have to go home and make the most of this. This is my chance.'

'It's amazing, it really is, but don't you think you should sit down and figure out why?'

Sophie stood for a minute, her feet wanting to run out of the door so that she could get in front of her computer and handle all of this professionally. The other part of her still wasn't sure that the sex tape hadn't leaked.

'Yeah, you're right. I just don't know where to st— Oh, I know, I'll go to the make-up company and see what they thought about it. They must have reposted it or something.'

'Oh, they reposted it all right.' Paige had already gone to the make-up company and was waiting for Sophie to discover what she had.

A few taps on her phone later and Sophie was surprised to discover the cause of the events so quickly.

'What have they done? They can't do that.' Paige leaned over to look at Sophie's phone, even though she already knew.

'I told you that it was a special video.' Paige shrugged.

The make-up company had reposted the video, but they had given it a new title, with a new backing song, and, possibly to her professional eye, a new filter. It made the whole video feel soft and romantic and the title was, 'Make-up You Can Fall In Love With.'

'What the—? They've changed it. They can't change it, surely?' Sophie looked to Paige for help.

She just shrugged. 'I'm guessing that as they haven't changed what was actually said between the two of you, just added a song in the background, it isn't really a major change.'

Sophie looked again, it didn't help that the image they had chosen as the cover image was Sophie looking into Marcus's face. It was one of the final bits because she had a make-up remover in one hand, and was holding Marcus's face in the other. Just as she suspected you could tell her hand was shaking, the hungry look in her eyes there for the whole world to see. Why hadn't she spotted that when she was editing it? She rolled her eyes, she knew why. She was so paranoid that the sex scene would end up in there that she didn't focus as much on the rest.

'What are you going to do?' Paige asked.

Sophie quickly scanned the post that the make-up company had released. They were happy with the review calling it fair but saying that they had never anticipated the results. Sophie closed her eyes and took a deep breath.

'It doesn't change anything. If they're foolish enough to spin it that way, then I am brilliant enough to take advantage. I never thought I would have this much reach and this much presence. I have to act on it. I have to do more videos, more live feeds.' With that Sophie dashed to the bar and quickly disappeared behind the door to grab her handbag.

As she reappeared Paige asked, 'What about Marcus?'

'He knows the situation, I was very clear that work needed to come first. I need to capitalise on this before it disappears. See you later.'

With that, Sophie ran through the door and didn't hear Paige mutter, cradling her kitten, 'That wasn't what I meant, was it? We know exactly what's going on, don't we? Do you think it will end well? Yeah, me too. We need to get you upstairs and into your bed with your siblings. I know it's all going to work out, so don't worry too much, OK?'

Chapter Twenty-Four

'Dude, where were you today?' Marcus asked as he sat down on Bailey's sofa and looked around his apartment. It should've been your typical bachelor pad. In fact, it used to be.

'What have you done to the place?'

Marcus looked around trying to pinpoint what the actual changes were. Fewer video games as coasters and more actual coasters. Was that a new coffee table? He wasn't sure, but then again it had been a little while since they had been able to hang out and play FIFA. Partly his own fault because he had been spending so much time with Sophie and partly Bailey's fault, for suddenly being aloof.

'I told you, I had something else that I needed to work on. I knew it was going to be a quiet day at Sophie's house, considering it's gearing towards final touches and, yes, I have just tidied the flat up a little.' Bailey shrugged, but he avoided Marcus's eye.

'What's going on with you?'

'Nothing. I just tidied up a bit, that's all?'

'Is it for a new girl? Who is it? I haven't seen you with anyone in a long time. Actually, come to think of it, it's been a while. Come on spill, what's going on?'

'Nothing is going on. Jesus can't I just clean the place up? Anyway, I know what you're doing and it's not going to work.' With that Bailey made his way to the under counter fridge and grabbed two cans.

'What am I doing? Thanks.' Marcus took the can and opened it, taking a large gulp. Bailey was right, it was far easier to try and talk about Bailey than it was talking about himself. Marcus's head was a mess.

'Things still weird between you and Sophie?'

Marcus just shrugged, it had been a few days since the contouring video uploaded and Sophie had been nonstop busy with her work ever since. At first, Marcus had been completely understanding, after all, he knew the rules. But after a while he suspected it was more likely that she was just avoiding him and using work as an excuse.

Bailey got out his PlayStation and set them up so that they could play FIFA. Bailey was right, and he'd obviously noticed things were weird with him and Sophie and he was a little lost about how to fix it. In fact, all he could see was that the garden was nearly finished, so really it was only going to get worse.

'So her work is really picking up. Looks like it was a good idea getting you in to transform her garden, and your gardening business is picking up too, I guess, right?'

Marcus coughed. 'Yeah, we're getting loads of requests for quotes and two new jobs confirmed to start when Sophie's is finished.'

'Here.' Bailey handed him a controller. 'Kick my ass on FIFA. That always makes you feel better, and if you decide you wanna talk about it you can do.'

Marcus did as he was told, his brain not firing on all cylinders, 'Her work really has picked up. She's still getting abuse though, even worse now.'

'What is she going to do about it? Does she know who's behind it?'

'Last I spoke to her she's got someone looking into it, but I've not heard any more as I've not been able to spend any time with her properly since she uploaded the contouring video.'

'That video.' Bailey nudged him, smirking like a teenager.

'What do you mean *that* video?'

'The sex video that never was. Oh, don't look like that, Paige told me. Besides, I watched the video for myself, and, mate, you really feel for her. You can tell.'

Marcus groaned and his head dropped. 'What can I do? She made it clear work came first, but this is more than that. I think if she could, she would be completely avoiding me. She's freezing me out.' With the realisation that it was happening again, Marcus started to get agitated. 'Can't she see it? How can she not see it?' Marcus pulled at his hair at the same time Bailey paused the game and turned to face his best pal.

'We both know that you have had a crush on her for a long time. You've had a chance to take that further, but have you laid your cards on the table and told her how you really feel?'

'No.'

'Why not? Look, mate, I'm not being funny but if she is freezing you out, then actually you have nothing to lose, do you? She can only say no, that she doesn't love you back. But I honestly can't see her saying that. Your romance has been building live on social media for the world to see, and they have.'

'I don't think I can do it again. What happens to me if she shoots me down?'

'You'll be too busy working.' Bailey shrugged.

'It's so easy for you, Bailey, I wish I was as chill and carefree as you.'

'Sure.'

Marcus wasn't certain but it looked like he had managed to piss Bailey off, as if he had said the wrong thing entirely.

'Worse case,' Marcus added, 'we go back to being each other's wingmen.'

Bailey didn't say anything he just hit the start button and un-paused the game, his shoulders up and his jaw clenched. There was certainly something wrong with Bailey, and Marcus did feel guilty, but truthfully he didn't have the headspace to try and delve into that right now. He really had to figure out what he was going to do with Sophie.

'I'll talk to her in the morning. You guys don't have to come in tomorrow as we've nearly finished anyway. I'll text Joseph now.' Marcus hit pause and grabbed his phone. Bailey picked up his too. Marcus presumed he probably had girl trouble of his own. That was why he was in a sulk.

Chapter Twenty-Five

'Hey, Soph, I'm just going to tidy some stuff in the garden and prep for the final bits and pieces. Then maybe we can have a brew, yeah?'

'Sure.' She smiled and waited for Marcus to leave the room before she let out a long sigh. It wasn't that she didn't want to talk to him, it's just that she knew what was coming and wished that it wasn't. He was going to try and talk about what was going to happen next. The garden was nearly finished, maybe one or two days tops. They were having fun, he occasionally stayed over, a little less often lately sure – OK a lot less – but she needed the time to get on with her work.

She could just about make out a whisper that maybe she would miss hanging out with him and having a laugh. But like she told him from the start, work came first and it was going better than she ever could have predicted, well not really, just a lot quicker than she had predicted. This whole getting the garden done thing was genius, she would have to get Polly something to thank her. Deciding that she should say thank you while it was in her head, she picked up her phone.

'Hi, Pol. How are you?'

'Hi, I'm good. You?' There were some weird noises coming from the other end, it didn't sound like Polly was at work.

'Where are you?'

'Just at work. So what you up to?'

Sophie's brow furrowed, something wasn't right. 'It's really noisy, is that music I can hear?'

'Hang on I'll step outside... There is that better? Work is crazy busy today.'

'Hmmm, OK, well, I was just mulling over how well the last week has gone with regards to my vlogging and realised that I never actually thanked you. If you hadn't suggested getting the garden done, none of this would have happened.'

Polly sighed. 'Come on, Soph.'

'What?'

'Do you really need me to spell it out for you?' There was a definite pissed off tone to Polly, but Sophie had no idea why.

'I was just saying thank you, what do you need to spell out?'

'Exactly how much of the garden have you shown on social media?'

Sophie opened her mouth to speak and then paused. Well, not that much actually. It was a mess for a good week and a half. Very much the omelette egg breaking stage. It was looking amazing now though. It made her realise that she should really move things around so that she could have more of the garden featured in the background and optimise the natural light, after all wasn't that the entire point?

'Not that much I guess, why?'

'So if it wasn't the garden that made that big an impact, gee, I wonder what else it might be?' Yep, Polly was pissed.

'Marcus.'

'Not just Marcus. *You* and Marcus. Look, I've got to go. I'll speak to you later.'

'Wait— Nope she's already gone.'

Sophie sighed. She was still not a hundred per cent sure why Polly was so upset though. Did she think that Sophie was using her brother? Sophie wasn't a complete idiot ordinarily, she knew that her viewers had responded well to her and Marcus but, this was her work, it was her baby, and if they liked her before – which they did thank you very much – then they will like her after. Well, most people liked her. Sophie shuddered as she lent down to her handbag. The letter she had received yesterday had been a printout of the hurtful comments that CarbeFoxy and a couple of others had left on her social media. It could've been printed by anyone, but the letter, coupled with the emails she had recently received, were really starting to get to her. The fact that this person, if it was the same person, knew her address was unsettling to say the least. But there still wasn't any actual threats, not that she wanted to be threatened but she suspected that without them the police weren't exactly going to do much.

Sophie looked at the garden, her new sanctuary and felt her blood pressure drop. But once the garden was finished she really wasn't going to see Marcus all that much and he wouldn't get as much screen time. An odd brick-like feeling settled in Sophie's stomach. She wasn't sure how she felt about that, or perhaps more likely she didn't want to think about it too much and find out. Sure, they could still get together occasionally, but she knew that Marcus wanted more, he had said as much.

Sophie jumped up to stick the kettle on. She looked out of the window and watched Marcus as he moved about the garden. It was for the best, they needed to keep it low key if they could, and if they couldn't... well, that would be too bad, but he knew what he had signed up for. He knew how important her work was, and, by all accounts, his work was already picking up too, so surely he would be too busy for her as well. That was only fair.

Sophie felt a pang in her chest and knew that her body was trying to tell her something her head didn't want to hear. She realised with a sick feeling that there would be other gardens he would be working from, and more than likely other women, and men, that would want to sit and watch him work all day. Sophie looked over at her desk. She had implemented her new work scheme following the near viral success of her last make-up review. She had five more already in the pipeline, a bunch of videos edited and ready to upload, she was on it. She realised she was excited about work again. All of her videos sparkled now, especially when compared to the videos three months ago, it was no wonder she'd stopped getting any new subscribers. That had changed now though. She was nearing the crucial million mark and she'd be there any day if she played it right. She looked back at Marcus and the garden. It really did look beautiful. Walking over to the French doors she pulled them open and watched as Marcus turned towards her.

'Are you busy?' Sophie shouted.

'Nothing that can't wait, why? What did you have in mind?' Marcus asked as he wiped his hands clean on his shorts.

'Let's go and do something.'

'Really, are you not too busy with work?'

'I'm all caught up.' Sophie grinned. 'Come on.'

'OK.'

He packed his tools away, turned around and made his way towards her, his eyes never leaving hers. There was no great plan, Sophie just wanted to make the most of this time with her friend, before he was too busy working on other people's gardens.

'So what do you want to do with me?' He winked as Sophie laughed.

'Not that, well, maybe later. I thought we could go shopping?'

'Shopping?'

'Yeah.' It wasn't inspired, it wasn't even that creative and she knew that some blokes really hated it, but ultimately she could do with more make-up supplies, and she couldn't say that she enjoyed shopping all that much, but it might be fun with Marcus.

'OK, fine. On two conditions.'

'Depends what they are.'

'One, that I get to go suit shopping and two, that we go out as a couple so I can make out with you whenever I want.'

Sophie's brow furrowed. 'Why do you need a suit?'

'It's for Joseph. He and Harriet are celebrating their wedding anniversary next month, and they're going all out. Bailey and I have been invited to their party.'

'That's cute.'

'Yep, so do we have a deal? I'm going to drag you around all the suit shops and you're going to help me pick the right one.' Marcus raised an eyebrow.

Sophie sighed. 'OK, fine.'

'And when we're not doing that you get to hold my hand and drag me wherever you want to take me.'

Sophie looked at Marcus. She wanted to say no, it was a bit couple-y and they were just casual, but she also knew that it was likely to be a one-off. They wouldn't get many other chances for a day off.

'Don't worry, it's not breaking any of your work comes first rules.'

'OK then. Come on. I'm driving.'

'OK, so what sort of a suit are you after?' Sophie asked as they got out of her car and made their way towards the shops.

'Not sure. I just know that I want to look lit.'

'Lit?'

'Yeah.'

Sophie rolled her eyes, but her grin spread over her face. 'So, a three-piece, two-piece, tie?'

'Yep.'

Sophie laughed. 'You're clueless. I had no idea that you were going to be so bad at shopping.'

'I'm not bad, I just don't know what I want yet. We're going to have to try them on. But I'm not minted enough just yet to go to a tailored suit place so we're going to just have to go to a regular shop and see what we can get, and you're going to need to tell me if I look good or not.' Marcus pouted and moved his face to look moodily into the distance.

'Wow, you're going to be a brilliant model. Come on then.' Sophie pushed the door to the department store and started striding towards the men's section when a polite cough and a shoulder tap brought her attention back to Marcus. She raised an eyebrow.

'Aren't you forgetting something?'

'Huh?'

Marcus grabbed hold of Sophie's hand. 'OK, onwards.'

Sophie rolled her eyes but she couldn't stop her smile from spreading. His hand, as always, was warm and a little rough in hers, but he held onto her, their fingers entwined, grinning all the while.

The department store wasn't too busy, just a few people roaming around, and some parents with children in pushchairs, your usual Thursday traffic.

'We should take some pictures for your social media,' Marcus suggested, holding his other hand out for her phone.

'You don't have to, you know. I know it's really annoying when your girlfriend— I mean friend, wants to take pictures all the time.'

'It's OK, it's for your work, friend, and once we've done that we can crack on. OK, big cheesy smile.' Marcus held his arm out to capture a picture of them both. 'No wait, come over here, we'll get a mannequin in the shot with us.' Standing in front of a suited mannequin Marcus took a series of selfies.

'OK, now look like you're really thinking about something, like you're really concentrating. Close, now try that concentration face you pull when you're trying to be professional but you really want to rip my clothes off.'

'What? I don't have that face.'

'Yes, you do. OK, let's do a couple of model shots, where we are all looking in different directions. OK, now just pull a face.' Marcus was snapping away and Sophie was trying not to grin.

Laughing Sophie grabbed her phone to look at the pictures. 'These are great. Thank you.'

'Hang on, one more.' This time Marcus took out his own phone to take a picture of the pair of them grinning. Very quickly without any thought, Sophie leaned into Marcus and kissed his cheek as he took a picture. Moving around to face her Marcus leaned forward for a proper kiss, his arms dropping to her waist as the kiss deepened and changed from U to PG. Reluctantly Marcus pulled away. 'Let's not get too carried away. We don't want any more of those type of pictures.'

Sophie looked up at him and felt her heart go funny in her chest, it only intensified when Marcus once again made sure they were holding hands, and Sophie once again tried her hardest not to love it and become completely attached to him forever.

Trying to shake off that last thought, Sophie said, 'So colour? Charcoal, navy, black?'

'What do you think? Why don't we try one of each?'

'OK. What size are you?'

As Marcus shouted out his vital statistics, they went from row to row picking out the styles she thought would suit him best. There was a formal black two-piece with a grey shirt and black tie, there was a charcoal grey that had black piping on the edges teamed up with a black shirt, and, finally, a navy three-piece with a white shirt and blue and silver tie. Every time Sophie picked up a suit, Marcus reached over and took it from her so that he was carrying them around.

'Are you sure you want to try these on? Have you seen any others that you like?' Sophie asked.

'Let's go with your judgement first, and if you have hideous taste, then I'll have a go.'

'I do not have hideous taste, thank you very much.' Sophie slapped his arm.

Marcus led them towards the changing rooms. 'Sit here and we will find out.'

As Marcus made his way into the cubicle Sophie sat on the sofa in the waiting area. He was in the first cubicle and even though she couldn't see anything, she could hear him as he undressed, and she could see in her head quite clearly what he would look like as he did it. His arm muscles flexing, his strong thighs bulging from his tight underpants as he pulled his trousers down. Taking a quick breath Sophie tried to regain a little composure, but ultimately she was a little breathless at the weird intimacy their little shopping spree had exposed her too. Marcus walked out in the black suit. He was gorgeous. He strutted out towards her, rocking the model mode he was currently in. He flipped up the collar and pouted. Took his jacket off and swung it over his shoulder. Sophie was laughing so hard, but not hard enough that she didn't see the appreciative glances both the female staff were giving him as he twirled.

Marcus looked at Sophie, his eyes asking for her thoughts.

'Hmm, it's nice. I like the black and grey it's, yeah, it's nice.'

'Nice? Is that the best you can do?' Marcus looked down at himself and back up at her.

Sophie just shrugged, but she could feel her face getting hotter.

'Hmmm.' With that Marcus strutted off and went back to the changing room. Once again Sophie found herself transfixed on the curtain as if she could see through it. Hearing the zip and the soft thud of the suit trousers landing on the floor. Sophie recrossed her legs and got her phone out to try and distract herself, but she couldn't avoid looking up again and again.

This time Marcus came out in the grey suit with the black piping. He did his model strut towards the mirror and back, before coming to stand in front of Sophie.

'What do you think? Do I look a little gameshow-y, or is it just me?'

Sophie burst out laughing, she hadn't thought he did until

he said it. Marcus walked over to the shop assistant, who was only too keen to assist. 'Excuse me, can you tell me how much this suit is?'

'Sure.' The sales assistant blushed as she reached around him to look at the tags. 'The full suit would cost one hundred and seventy-five pounds.'

'The price is right!' Marcus cried.

Sophie laughed and rolled her eyes as he made his way back towards her.

'What do you think? Higher or lower?'

'I know what you're doing!'

'What do you think? Our survey says?'

'Oh God, you're ridiculous. Just go and try the last one on.'

'No likey no lightey?'

'Just go!' Sophie gently shoved Marcus to get him back into the changing room. The sales assistant came over to her.

'You two are such a cute couple.'

'Oh no, we're not really a… erm… well, it's… erm.'

'Sorry, I didn't mean anything by it.'

'No it's fine, it's just… erm, you know a casual thing—'

'Oh God, why? I would snap him up so— I mean, sorry it's totally none of my business. I'm going over there now.' The sales assistant ran off to stand next to her colleague and pretended to look busy. Sophie definitely heard the other one say, 'So can I give him my number then?'

Just then Marcus walked out in suit number three. The one that Sophie thought would be a bit plain and nondescript. It wasn't. By a long shot. It was the navy blue suit with waistcoat, trousers and white shirt. But the fit was extraordinary and the colour did amazing things to his already slightly tanned skin tone. Sophie was a little breathless and the sales assistants both whispered, 'Wow.'

After accidentally shooting them both a dirty look, Sophie watched on as Marcus did his strut. He took his jacket off and casually draped it over one arm. He undid each shirt cuff and laying the jacket carefully down, he slowly began rolling his sleeves up his forearms, displaying his slightly dusted with hair and tanned forearms. Sophie forgot where she was for a moment as she watched engrossed at what felt like her own male burlesque show, staring, and perhaps drooling as more of his arms were revealed inch by tantalising inch. When he'd finished with the sleeves Sophie had only a moment to return to Earth before she looked at Marcus as a whole. The effect was equally as devastating, he turned and the damned waistcoat was sculpted onto his back, drawing the eye inevitably down to his perfectly encased bum. Sophie was staring, her eyes refusing to blink. As was everyone else.

'So what do we think? I like this one. The navy is a little less formal, less funereal and gameshow— Soph? Are you OK?'

Sophie coughed. 'Yes, yes, I think that's the one, yeah. It's really nice.'

'You sure you're OK, you look a little warm?' Marcus's cheeky grin made it clear he knew what he was doing to her in that suit.

'It's a nice suit. I don't think we need to look for any more unless you're not sure.'

'No, I like this one. It has a great effect.' Marcus winked and walked back to his changing cubicle, drawing the curtain.

Sophie finally found that she could breathe normally again and the sales assistants were fanning each other dramatically. Sophie found herself throwing more dirty looks in their direction and realised that she was feeling a touch possessive. She rolled her eyes at herself, way to keep casual Sophie, she thought to herself, getting worked up about sales assistants is not the way to do it. She looked back at the cubicle to see that the curtain wasn't closed all the way around and there was just a small gap of a couple of inches. The sales assistants were still talking to each other about how great

Marcus looked. Sophie glanced at the curtain again, her eyes stuck watching as Marcus undressed. If he was sexy as hell in the suit, he was even sexier getting out of it. Sophie tried to look away feeling more than a little pervy and, if she was completely honest with herself, a little bit – OK, a lot – turned on. Trying to get her mind onto other, calmer non-sexy things, she glanced down at her phone selecting the pictures they had taken earlier deciding what to publish. She wasn't doing all that well because her eyes kept looking up to see what the gap in the curtain was displaying. One of the sales assistants moved, and Sophie realised that she might also catch sight of Marcus. Without a second thought Sophie stood up and walked to the curtain pulling it completely closed, before turning around and sitting back down again, eyeing daggers at the sales assistant.

'Let me just go and chuck this suit in the car and then we can do the rest of the shopping. Where do you need to go?'

'Debenhams and Boots.'

'OK then, come on. Then we'll get lunch. My treat as a thank you for helping me pick out an awesome suit. It's a good suit, isn't it?' Marcus suddenly had a small doubt that he'd misread Sophie's reaction to the suit. Maybe it was hideous, but she hadn't said that much.

'It really is a gorgeous suit, even the sales assistants thought so.'

'Did they? I didn't notice.' Marcus opened the boot and put the suit in. 'Right then take me to your temple.'

Instinctively he put his arm around Sophie's shoulders and leaned in for a kiss. Too late he thought that maybe it was a little too much PDA, but she didn't seem to care, and if she didn't then neither did he. When they pulled apart he knew he had a huge goofy look on his face. How could he not? He was having a fantastic day. He left his arm draped over her shoulders so that he could stroke her skin. Sophie moved until her hand held onto his side just over his hips, and Marcus could feel the heat from her fingertips through his T-shirt.

'Right, OK, in here. I need to look at the make-up and see what I need to get and do some research, that type of thing. It might take a while, is that OK?'

'Sure. If it gets really bad, then I'll find something else to do. Like try on different lipsticks or something.'

Sophie laughed. He loved that sound. Yes, it was soppy, no he didn't care, because it was such a contrast to where they were just a few weeks ago. It was where they started at the house party last year. He'd said something ridiculous and it made her laugh, they'd chatted for ages, and then kissed and then bam. Game over. He tried not to grimace as he remembered what it was like being shut down by her. She moved his arm off her shoulder so that she could look at the make-up but not before she kissed his hand.

He watched as she flitted from one make-up counter to the next. Looking at the new products, occasionally taking pictures, or making notes on her phone. Every now and again she looked up at him and smiled. He could do this all day. OK not all day because it would definitely get boring at some point, but he was certainly happy to play guard, and to reach for the higher things she couldn't and when she ran out of arm space to try samples of who knew what, he offered her his arm without a second thought. They'd been there for a good thirty minutes and Sophie had a basket of supplies that she was more than happy with.

'OK, come on, I have more than enough. Let's pay for these and get some lu—'

'Oh my God, it is you. I thought I recognised you. You're Sophie, right?'

Marcus watched as Sophie smiled awkwardly.

'Erm... yes.'

'I love your make-up videos and ahh!' Marcus covered

his ears as she literally screamed. 'It's you as well. Oh my God I can't believe I've seen you both in real life. I'm a huge fan. So you two must be a couple, why else would you wait around while she shops. Ahhh you're just so cute. I have to get a selfie with you both. My friends aren't going to believe this. In fact, Karen... Karen look who it is. Oh my God, we were just talking about you two and here you are.' Karen – presumably – made her way over.

'Oh my God, it's actually Sophie and Marcus. I can't believe this. Chanelle we were just talking about these two.'

Marcus looked at Chanelle and Karen. They both wore identikit black T-shirts and trousers with little make-up aprons on. Their make-up was thick and they were clearly in the biz. Marcus looked down at Sophie wanting to make sure she was comfortable with this. He hadn't really thought of her as a celebrity but he supposed she was nowadays, and, by association, so was he.

The girls both squealed. 'We really are huge fans. I've been watching since before Marcus, by the way, but I do love both of you together. It's too cute. Oh, I really loved the video where you did the crown style eyeshadow with the jewels. That one was brilliant. Karen's a more recent subscriber. Aren't you?'

'Yes, but I love it and so do my friends. Can we have a picture, please? Would that be OK?'

'Thank you, that's so sweet. Erm... of course you can have a picture.'

Karen and Chanelle stood either side of Sophie and took a selfie.

'Do you want me to take a picture?' Marcus asked.

'Oh yes, please, but then can we get one of all of us?'

Marcus looked at Sophie who just shrugged and smiled. Marcus dutifully took a picture of the three of them and then stepped into the picture and held out the camera to take a group selfie.

'Say eyeliner,' Marcus called.

'Eyeliner!' screamed the girls.

'Thank you so much. You two are just the cutest.'

'No problem, thank you, Karen, thanks, Chanelle.'

'Oh, maybe you can give us a mention on your next video.'

'Erm... OK, I'll try to.'

With that, they both threw their arms around Sophie in a group hug before they squealed again and ran back to their make-up station.

Sophie made her way to the till and Marcus kept his hand on her back. If he was honest, he was a little shook up. He knew that Karen and Chanelle were harmless, but this was going to become more and more common as Sophie got more and more popular, and she would, he had no doubt about that. Marcus couldn't help but think about the more sinister ones, the trolls and the haters. While most of them were undoubtedly keyboard warriors, the problem, of course, was not knowing if any of them were more serious. Especially with that one that really disliked her and commented regularly saying as much. He needed to speak to Sophie again about it.

Sophie paid for her goods and they quickly made their way out of the store.

'So that was weird. Has that ever happened before?' Marcus asked.

'Not really, not like that. I can't quite believe it. They were really lovely though, weren't they? I can't believe I... I mean we... were actually recognised.'

Sophie was laughing as they walked into the coffee shop, but Marcus couldn't shake his concerns.

Chapter Twenty-Six

'OK and finally a shout out to Chanelle and Karen for being so super lovely when we went shopping the other day. OK, everyone, let me know how you get on, and as always if you have any questions or comments just throw them below and I'll get back to you as soon as I can. OK thanks, everyone. Byeeeee.'

There was a soft knock, knock on the wall. 'Are you finished?' Marcus whispered.

'Yep all done. Just got to do the usual editing and titling etc. but I'll do all that tomorrow. What are you doing here?'

'I brought food. I thought we could hang out?'

'Sure. Let me tidy my stuff away, then I have something really awesome to show you.'

Sophie's heart did that weird extra beat thing it did whenever Marcus appeared. He was definitely looking hotter these days too, but maybe that had more to do with how much more of him she was seeing, rather than any actual changes. Even in T-shirt and jeans, as he was wearing now, she loved how the T-shirt was just that little bit tight on his arms, and if he reached up his jeans were just a little low, so she could just about make out his gorgeous v lines or maybe a hint of his six-pack. He really was stunning. Sophie shook her head as she questioned how it had taken her so long to really appreciate the gorgeous package she'd had right under her nose.

'What's this?' Marcus was waving a piece of paper and a gold token.

'Oh my God it's the awesome thing I was going to tell you about. You have to read it!'

'Why does this look like a gold digestive?'

'Read it!' Sophie shouted.

'"Dear Sophie,"' he read. '"We're delighted to make you the newest member of the exclusive McVitie's Biscuit Club as we've heard about how much you love our biscuits." What?! This is amazing.'

'Carry on it gets better!'

'"Please enjoy the gold-plated digestive biscuit we have sent you, exclusive to each Biscuit Club member." Oh, my... "Being part of the Biscuit Club means that you will receive unlimited free products for one year to satisfy all those McVitie's biscuit cravings! We hope you enjoy being part blah blah blah." Oh my God. Free biscuits. Is that because you always have a brew and a biscuit when you're filming?'

'Yes, I guess so!'

'Wow, and free products for a year! That's better than money. What are you going to pick?'

'No idea, there's too many to choose from. I know what you'd pick though.'

'Yeah?'

'Ginger Nuts, without a doubt.'

She watched as he thought about it, but then grinned. 'Yeah, you're right. They are the best though to be fair. Wow, amazing, well done, Soph!'

It was ridiculous she knew but a sudden tremble went down her spine. She wasn't sure if it was a good tremble or a bad tremble but the fact that she suddenly knew Marcus well enough to know his favourite biscuit made her feel... nervous? Excited? Of course, the immediate thought that went through her head, as always, was if he was a real boyfriend, then, of course, she would know his favourite biscuit, but this was casual.

Inside her head Sophie groaned, and then reasoned that she knew Mya's favourite biscuit was those weird waffle ones that go on top of your cup of coffee. Paige's, well, she wasn't sure she'd have to ask. Polly liked a Jammie Dodger. Maybe it wasn't such a big deal that she happened to know Marcus's favourite biscuit. Wanting to slap herself in the face for being ridiculous, but also knowing that would make her look even more ridiculous, Sophie finished tidying her stuff away.

Chapter Twenty-Seven

Sophie could hear the chatter and knew that in a matter of seconds her brand new sanctuary was about to be overrun. She looked around at the garden. It was a work of art. The white Indian stone paving, the dark grey of the decking, the sumptuous cushions adding a splash of colour, the green of the new turf, the red acer bold and magnificent, expertly lit up from underneath with some hidden lighting. All of which made Sophie's belly do a little turn that she had difficulty properly understanding. She watched as Marcus dashed out of the French doors and ran towards her.

'It is absolutely gorgeous. You should be really proud, it's fantastic,' Sophie whispered as she wrapped her arm around his waist and stared into his eyes.

'Well, there's just one or two finishing touches to do, and a little bit of the lighting to finish but, thank you. That means a lot.' She saw something in his expression that she wasn't sure she'd ever seen before. His eyes were sparkling, and it gave her the impression that he knew something she didn't.

Sophie didn't have long to think about that look, as the noise and chatter from inside began spilling out into the garden.

Sophie led the way towards the sunken seating area and fire pit located towards the rear of the garden. There was a neat little stone path in the grass that split off the stepped sunken area and the solid grey decking. The stone path continued running through the lawn towards the house until it reached the smaller decking behind the French doors of the kitchen area, on which stood a small collection of plants including the red acer to the left.

'God bless this garden, and all those who sail in her,' Mya announced, brandishing a bottle of Prosecco.

'Mya no!' Sophie just managed to grab the bottle that

Mya was about to smash into the side of the concrete fire pit. 'Why don't we just drink it?' Sophie suggested removing the bottle from Mya's hands.

Polly took the bottle and began the process of opening and eventually pouring Prosecco into the champagne flutes.

Mya shrugged before grabbing Marcus and kissing him on the lips. 'This is gorgeous. Thank you.'

If Marcus was in anyway perturbed by Mya's kissing it certainly didn't show.

'Do I get one of those?' Bailey asked, his eyebrows raised.

Sophie watched as Mya stepped towards Bailey, and pulled him into a huge hug. She couldn't hear what Mya whispered into his ear, but whatever it was, it made him grin and very furtively glance at Polly.

'Come on, everyone, sit down let's have a toast,' Polly suggested, as one by one, Sophie, Marcus, Bailey, Mya, Joseph and Harriet sat in the new seating area around the fire pit, that Joseph had lit earlier. Paige was there too but on FaceTime as she had been unable to leave the bar – but more likely not wanting to leave the kittens alone. Considering that they had recently taken quite an interest in anything electrical, Sophie couldn't blame her. Polly had just placed a glass of Prosecco next to her anyway.

'Sophie do you want to do the toast, or should I?' Mya answered her own question, not waiting for Sophie to answer. 'You know what, I've got this, babe. Thank you to Marcus, for his incredible vision, for Polly for thinking of Marcus's incredible vision and to Sophie, for securing us mates' rates for the foreseeable future. To me for paying for all this. To Bailey for showing up and working here occasionally, and for giving the neighbours something interesting to talk about, and finally to Joseph for keeping everyone in check, and providing us with a gorgeous bod to ogle at – Harriet you are one lucky lady. So please raise your glasses, as we toast The Prosecco Paradise.'

'The Prosecco Paradise,' everyone repeated as glasses were raised and clinked together.

'Mya that was a fantastic toast – is that what you do for a living? Do you travel around the world as a professional toastmaster?' Polly asked half joking but still trying to wrangle the truth from Mya.

'Hmmm. I do travel the world, but then you already know that. I don't usually have to give toasts, in fact it's usually more the opposite.' With that Mya grinned and sat herself down next to Harriet and struck up a conversation as if they had been friends forever, despite having met only ten minutes earlier.

'But what the hell does that mean? Is she professionally silent? Is she gagged?' Polly asked.

'Give it up, Pol, she's never going to tell us,' Marcus reasoned.

As the Prosecco was shared, and everyone took it in turns to congratulate him on the garden, Marcus looked around and felt a wonderful feeling of warmth at seeing his close friends all gathered and happy in a setting that he had created for exactly that purpose. He also felt a strange feeling of fulfilment, everything in his garden was rosy. Except for one thing. Now the garden was finished he did not have an excuse to see Sophie every day and he wanted to – oh how he wanted her to be the first person he saw every morning and the last one he kissed goodnight. He loved her – yeah, he loved her – of that he had no doubt at all. But did she love him?

Harriet and Joseph had been the first to leave, closely followed by Polly who claimed she had somewhere else to be. Bailey left not long after, leaving Marcus, Sophie and Mya to order a takeaway. Once the pizza arrived, Mya shot off explaining that there had been an unexpected development in her work that she needed to take care of. Muttering something about 'newbies, and the tables being turned' as she studied her phone.

Marcus grinned at Sophie. 'Why don't we eat this upstairs?'

She happily agreed and within minutes they were snuggled up together.

'I love eating pizza in your bed.'

'Yeah, I just wish you wouldn't get crumbs everywhere.' Sophie rolled her eyes at him.

Marcus leaned over and took a clumsy bite of his pizza crust dropping crumbs all over her stomach.

'Whoops, sorry, I'd best clean that up.' He was grinning as she watched his head lower, a lazy smile on her lips as he bent down and licked up all of the crumbs.

'So another busy day for you, how did it go?' she asked to distract him so that she could eat her pizza.

'Another two quotes, one of them accepted and the other I am waiting to hear back on,' he said, sitting up again and biting into his pizza again. 'What they want is quite ambitious and it will cost a fair bit but it's exciting. I hope they can afford it as it would be an awesome project. I need to work out some bits and pieces though, like what the hell I'm going to do with my dad's old clients, but I can think about that another day. For now, it's just starting to take off, but it's really early days. What about you? Now that you're part of the Biscuit Club does that mean you've made it? Or do you need to give me another makeover?'

He grinned and his eyes lit up, and it made her heart sink. It was time to really admit it, to face it head-on. She was going to miss him. The sex, she would miss as well, he really knew what he was doing there, but it was the fun, the chatter, the catching up on each other's day, the ribbing each other. It was the stuff she didn't really have time for. Even now part of her brain was thinking about what she needed to do next for her work.

'Yes, it's going really well, thanks to you.' She coughed. 'The garden is amazing.'

'Yeah, well that's pretty much finished and when it is, look, I think— hang on, that's my mum's ringtone, I need to get it, I won't be a second.'

Marcus lent over to the floor to grab his phone out of his jeans pocket, flashing his gorgeously defined bum as he did so. She gave it a little slap so that he yelped just as he pressed the button to answer. She grinned at him as he sat back down.

'Hey, Mum, are you— Oh. OK. Is it—' Sophie watched as the colour drained from his face. 'Yes, I'll get there right away. I'll find her and bring her too. OK, Mum, see you soon. Love you.'

'What's wrong?' Sophie asked, holding onto his arm.

Marcus just stared at his phone, his face pale. 'It's my dad, he's had another heart attack. He's in hospital.'

'Polly isn't picking up her phone and I've called Paige and she says she's not at the bar. Do you know where she might be?' Sophie asked as she pulled on her jeans.

'No, I don't. We can keep trying, the main thing is that we get to the hospital.' Marcus was tying up his shoes as he spoke.

'Erm, are you sure you want me there?' Sophie didn't look up as she shoved her flip-flops on and grabbed her hoody.

'Yes, I need you there. Besides you can keep trying Polly.' Sophie impulsively hugged Marcus.

'OK then, let's go, and before you say anything, I'm driving. You're in shock.'

She grabbed the keys, her phone, her phone charger and her handbag and they were out the door in record time. Sophie cast a glance at Marcus as she set off. His leg was bobbing up and down and he was chewing on his nails as he looked out the window.

'How bad is it?'

'They don't know yet, but he wasn't responding, so it sounds pretty bad.'

Sophie was at a loss. She didn't really believe in false hope, and as they didn't know what was in store she was struggling to think of what to say. Her stomach was in knots as she hated to see him like this, and she prayed that his dad would be OK. She decided to focus on what she could do, so she got Polly's number up and called her over the speaker in the car. It continued to ring out until it got to voicemail.

'Polly please can you ring me when you get this. It's urgent.' She hung up. 'I can't believe we've lost her. How is it that none of us knows where she is?'

Sophie immediately clamped her lips together, aware that she was only making the situation worse. Oh God, she needed to just focus on driving, it was the only thing she could do right now, get them safely to the hospital so that they could find out more. The hospital was about forty minutes away, but the way she was driving Sophie reckoned that they would probably get there in thirty, especially considering it was only nine in the evening and the traffic was very light.

'Wait, I can use "Find My Friends".'

Sophie jumped, having not really expected Marcus to say anything. He started pressing buttons on his phone. 'Come on, come on.' Sophie was trying to look over but needed to keep her eyes on the road.

'Got it! She's in a club somewhere in town.'

'OK do you want us to go and get her?'

'No, it's in the opposite direction. I'll call Bailey.'

'OK hang on.' Sophie pressed the buttons on the steering wheel until they could hear the dial tone on the speakers.

'Hello, gorgeous, have you had enough of Marcus now?' Bailey was laughing.

Marcus cut in. 'Bailey, listen my dad's in hospital—'

'What do you need?'

Marcus took a deep breath. 'Thanks, man, I need you to go and get Polly and tell her because she's not answering her phone. She's at some bar in town. I'll text you the address. I don't know why she's not looking at her phone.'

'Sure, no problem. I'll set off straight away, but listen, how bad is it?'

'It's another heart attack. He's been rushed in, I don't know.' Marcus sighed.

'OK. I'll tell her and bring her straight to the hospital. We'll be there as soon as. If there's anything else I can do just shout. Text me the address, I'll see you soon.'

Marcus typed some stuff on his phone and then sat back and continued to look out of the window.

'I should've been more focused on his clients.'

'What?'

'I know it's stupid, but I feel like I've let him down. I haven't been focused on his customers. I've let it slip.'

'I don't know why you think that. What has that got to do with anything?' She took a deep breath, why was she shouting at him? Why couldn't she help more, like Bailey? She bit her tongue, why was she making this worse?

Marcus just sighed again and shook his head, and went back to looking out of the window.

They spent the rest of the drive in silence. There was nothing to say. They just had to wait and see what the doctors were going to tell them. But all the while, Sophie just kept wondering how she was going to help when all she seemed to be doing was making it worse.

Finally, as they approached the hospital in what felt like both ten seconds and ten hours simultaneously, Sophie was worried that they wouldn't find a parking space. When she found a space close by, she really wasn't sure if it was a good sign or not.

'I'll get a ticket and meet you in there.'

'OK,' he mumbled.

Sophie was happy to finally feel like she had been productive and dug around in her purse for loose change. Walking over to the machine she paid in what she had and got a ticket. She wasn't sure if she had enough time, but really, did it matter? She took the ticket and put it in the car. Taking a minute, she stood and took a deep breath. She needed to pull herself together for Marcus's sake, at least until he saw his mum. If they had some news, then he probably wouldn't need her after that point. There was a small part of her that hoped it would be that simple. She had to admit, she was way out of her comfort zone, and she really didn't know what she was doing here.

Chapter Twenty-Eight

Sophie watched on as Marcus grabbed his mum in a huge hug. Feeling awkward she hung back a little so as not to interfere. Instead she looked around at the row of chairs as was standard in hospital waiting areas. The colour scheme, the smell, there would never be any confusion, never able to forget for even a minute where they were.

'How is he?' Marcus asked, holding his mum's arms and studying her face.

'I don't know. They're still running tests. I don't know.' Sophie watched as his mum rubbed his back. She stopped. 'Where's Polly?'

'She's on her way. Bailey is bringing her.'

'Is he? He's such a good boy. He should be here too, he's family.'

Sophie tried to swallow the lump in her throat, at the same time shifting her weight moving from one foot to the other, talk about awkward. She ought to leave them to it. She wasn't family. She reached forward to grab Marcus's sleeve.

'Listen, I'll just—'

'Hello, Sophie love. Thank you for bringing Marcus. I've watched your videos. You're really doing very well.'

'Erm... thanks, Brenda. I... erm... Can I get you anything?'

She watched as his mum looked from Marcus to Sophie and back again.

'No, but thank you. I'm just going to go and ask if there's any more news.'

Marcus came and stood next to her, the pair of them watching as his mum made her way to the reception desk.

Marcus reached down and held her hand. 'Thank you so much for being here. It really means a lot.'

What could she say? What was there to say? *'It was a pleasure?'* *'You invite me to the nicest places?'*

'Why don't we sit down?' It was the best she could come up with. They sat down in the row of chairs facing the vending machine and watched as his mum finished chatting to the receptionist and made her way back.

'She said that there's a possibility he might need surgery but it's too soon to say. They're trying to stabilise him and run some tests. It might be a long night.'

'Mum!' Polly ran over and threw herself into her mother's arms as she burst into tears. Bailey made his way over to Marcus and sat down next to him throwing his hand on Marcus's back.

'You OK, pal?'

'Not really.' Marcus sighed, looking over at his mum and sister.

'Shh, come on now, Pol. Your dad's a fighter. He's going to pull through, I'm sure of it. Besides, we were mid-argument and you know he likes to get the last word.'

'Oh, Mum.' Polly sighed as she disentangled and took a step back.

Bailey stood up and took Brenda into a hug kissing her on the cheek. 'So what happened, Mrs B?' At the same time, Polly walked over towards Sophie as she jumped up and wrapped Polly up in a quick hug.

'Hello, Bailey my love. Come on, let's sit down.'

Polly took the adjacent seat and her mum sat next to her on one side with Bailey on the other. 'We were just having a discussion, I can't even remember what about. He'd been complaining of being a bit under the weather for a few days, I should've known. I kept asking him to go to the doctors... Anyway, he... well, he collapsed, and I called the ambulance and here we are.' She sighed and stood up pacing the space in front of the chairs.

Bailey was studying Polly as she turned and gave him a

lopsided smile. Polly's eyes were red and Bailey held her hand tightly in both of his, offering up his strength.

Sophie looked at Marcus to check his reaction at Bailey and Polly's interaction. He hadn't noticed, or if he had, he didn't care. Sophie shook her head. Trust her to focus on something as trivial as hand-holding when lives were at stake. Although she really hoped they weren't.

She looked at her phone. It was ten p.m. She couldn't help but wonder when they might hear more.

As the hours passed Sophie watched as everyone in the family took it in turns to get up and move about, occasionally jokes were made to try and lighten the atmosphere.

As Bailey was stretching his legs, he said, 'He's going to want to be better before next month. The footie season starts again.' Everyone politely smiled or chuckled.

Sophie just felt worse. It wasn't that she wasn't sympathetic, she knew that if it was her dad in there she would be in bits, barely able to keep it together. She knew that she could hold Marcus's hand, or hug Polly, but it all felt so futile. She was out of her depth and she knew that part of it was because she felt like a fraud. Things with Marcus weren't serious enough to warrant her being here. This was for family. She was just, at best, a 'friend with benefits'.

They all looked up as a woman in a white coat appeared.

'Mrs Bowman?' She looked up from the folder she was carrying as Marcus's mum stepped forward.

'How is he?'

'I'm Dr Huang, we've stabilised your husband and the tests show that he's had a heart attack. We will need to perform surgery due to some old scarring, but it's a routine procedure. He's going to be fine.'

'Oh thank God!' Everyone's shoulders dropped and deep breaths were taken as the doctor just politely smiled.

Brenda looked back at the doctor. 'Is he really going to be OK? I mean, can you be sure? Can we go and see him?'

The doctor patted Brenda's arm. 'He's fine. We are preparing him for surgery, but you can go in and see him now for a few minutes.'

Marcus and Polly jumped up. Marcus turned around to Sophie and gave her a quick kiss. Sophie looked up to see Bailey pulling away from Polly having just given her a hug. As Polly, Marcus and his mum followed the doctor, Bailey came and sat next to her.

'Phew. I'm so glad he's going to be all right.'

'Don't you want to be going in there with them?' she asked, moving from side to side in the plastic seat.

'No, they need to see him, make sure he's OK. I'll mither him later. Are you OK though? You look a little weird.' Bailey was staring at her, his gaze making Sophie even more uncomfortable.

'Yes, it's just been a bit tense, hasn't it. I'm fine. I'm tired though.'

'Are you sure that's just it?'

'Yeah, in fact, I really am tired, and now that I know his dad's going to be OK, Marcus isn't going to need me here.' She jumped up and grabbed her bag. 'Erm... besides Mya will no doubt be wondering where I am. My parking is about to run out too. I'll get going. Just get in touch if anyone needs anything, yeah?' She raced towards the exit, feeling like shit, but not knowing what else to do.

Sophie gently shut the front door. She felt awful. Worse than awful. Her insides were tossing and turning and so was her head. She knew she couldn't have stayed but she also felt wretched for leaving.

'What's going on? How's George?'

Sophie looked up at Mya as all the energy, all the worry, just bottomed out. Her limbs suddenly felt heavy, as she realised she hadn't been this exhausted in a long time, if ever.

'He's going to be OK. He's got to have surgery but it's routine.' Sophie dragged her feet towards the sofa and collapsed.

'It must have been quite a night, huh?' Mya asked, leaning on the doorframe.

'What? Oh yeah.'

'What's going on?' Mya asked, casting a quizzical eye over her friend. 'You're not telling me the whole story.'

Sophie sat up on the sofa and groaned. 'I just left.'

'What do you mean?'

'Marcus needed me, he said so. But as soon as I found out that his dad was going to be OK I just... I ran out of there as fast as my legs could carry me.' Sophie covered her face with her hands. She felt the sofa dip and a gentle arm stroking her back.

'Why, Soph?'

'Because it was so serious. I was so worried. I didn't know what to do for the best and it's all so serious. It was never supposed to be serious.'

'OK, so it's actually about yours and Marcus's relationship?'

'What am I going to do? What kind of a person just walks away?'

Mya sighed. 'You, Sophie. You walk away and you consistently walk away from Marcus. You need to figure out why once and for all.'

'I don't have time for anything serious. I told him that. I told him that right from the start. He knew. He knew I needed to focus.'

'I know,' Mya continued to rub her back, 'but you knew he wanted more. He was as clear with you as you were with him.'

Sophie's throat was tight and her stomach was in knots. She tried to breathe slowly and clearly so as to not cry, but a tear escaped.

'I'm not a horrible person. I just can't help him right now. But I know I shouldn't have left when I did. But I just had to get out of there.'

'You're not a horrible person. You know what I think?' Sophie looked at her friend and raised an eyebrow. 'I think that you are overwhelmed. With everything. The changes in work, the increased popularity, this stuff with this weird online stalker, your relationship with Marcus. Can I be honest with you?' Sophie just nodded. 'You're in over your head.'

'No, I can handle the work, it's all going to—'

'I'm not just talking about work. I'm talking about Marcus. For the final time, you need to think about what you want. I think that you have found yourself in the beginnings of a serious relationship. A relationship you claim you didn't want, but that I think would be wonderful for you. Marcus is amazing and he clearly adores you. From what I've seen, you adore him too. That's why you feel so guilty right now, and why you hate not being able to fix it for him. You just don't like the idea of being tied down, of losing ambition, of having it all. But they aren't mutually exclusive. You could be losing something even more important if you're not careful.'

'It's so easy for you to say. You don't know what it's like. My work is finally paying off. It's going places. It's taken years to get to this point. I've already given up so much. I should've been doing my video editing this evening but I wasn't. I was hanging out with Marcus and then in the hospital with Marcus. Marcus, Marcus, Marcus! It's not that easy to have it all, and maybe it's just not possible. I need to focus on me, on my work, or forever be wondering what if!' Sophie was shouting and she never shouted. She took a deep breath to try and calm down but her blood was boiling.

'You listen to me, and you listen good. I love you, Marcus loves you, your friends and your family love you. If I needed to go to the hospital tonight, you wouldn't have thought twice. You would just be there. This is life. Life gets in the way. You cannot work all of the time. And I'll tell you something else. Life can be fun. You could be having fun with a partner like Marcus, someone who has your back and has been more than willing to give you the time you need to work. You're using your work as an excuse not to have a relationship and guess what? Marcus doesn't deserve that!' Mya stood up from the sofa. Her eyes blazing as she stared down at Sophie. 'And neither do you.'

Mya walked off and Sophie listened as she stomped her way back upstairs. Suddenly, and without warning, Sophie let go. The tears streaming down her face, her throat tight as she took in deep breaths. She tried to figure out why she felt so horrible but just couldn't get to it. Instead, she just rode out the tears and the shakes and the nails biting into her own skin as she gripped her arms, until finally, it passed and she felt hollow, and, if possible, even more exhausted.

She moved like a zombie into the kitchen where she grabbed a glass of water. Shuffling upstairs she placed the water on her bedside table before she fell onto her bed, landing face first on the pillows. All she could smell was Marcus and it set her off again until the crying eventually slowed and sleep took over.

Chapter Twenty-Nine

Sophie looked down at the note on the table. 'Gone out. See you later.'

'It's not very detailed, Mya, but I get the message loud and clear.' Sophie almost sympathised, she didn't really want to be around herself either so she couldn't blame Mya for avoiding her.

It had been a terrible night. After passing out cold, Sophie awoke three hours later, fully dressed and with a dead phone. The charger was downstairs in her bag and she didn't have the energy to go and get it. From that point on she just tossed and turned all night.

Reaching into her bag now, she got her charger out and plugged it in next to the kettle. If she was being honest – which was not her forte at the moment – she was a little scared to see what her phone might say once recharged. It was as she was putting the kettle on she heard the start of the wrestling match her postman had every day with the old letterbox. She took a deep breath glancing towards her phone. What if there was a message from Marcus saying that his dad had died? Yes, the doctor seemed pretty convinced he was going to be OK, but these things happened. What if he messaged saying how upset he was that she had left and that he wanted to call things off? She shrugged, it was what she deserved. She heard the little buzzing sound indicating her phone was switching back on. She slowly walked over to her phone, studying it as she made a brew. Nothing, there was nothing. Shouldn't there be something? Now even more confused she went to get the post, taking it back into the kitchen.

Immediately discarding the usual bills, the thick purple envelope addressed to herself stood out like a golden ticket.

She racked her brain to think who she knew that was getting married. With nobody springing to mind she moved her cup out of the way clearing the surface as she ripped into the envelope. Half a dozen bits of paper all fell out and one was a thick card, she read it.

'Holy... Oh my God I can't believe it. No freaking way!' Trying to not scream too loud so as to wake the neighbours, Sophie whisper screamed and jumped up and down. This was it. The sign that she had made it. That it had all been worth it. She'd been nominated for a Social Media Award, with a reception dinner and celebrities and everything. Sophie immediately loaded the webpage on her phone to get the information on the award itself, and also to see which of her fellow Media Personalities had been nominated. She looked at the invitation again; she had been nominated for a 'Rising Star' award.

She was so excited she was reading the bumpf and scoping out information on her phone at the same time. She had half written a text message to send out to everyone when she suddenly stopped and realised that actually, as of this moment in time, she only had one person she could tell that would understand and that was Paige. She couldn't send it to Polly or Marcus, they had enough going on with their dad. She couldn't send it to Mya because she was clearly mad at her. Her excitement bubble burst slightly, she could call her mum or her sisters but they wouldn't get it. Not really. They wouldn't understand all the work that had been put in, or what a huge achievement it was.

Sophie clutched the paperwork as she moved towards the table her mood dropping with each step until she fell into the chair. Slouched over the table Sophie got all of the paperwork together and looked at the nomination in more detail.

'Congratulations Sophie (& Marcus), you're vlog series has been nominated in the category of Rising Star. The award ceremony will be held at the Midland Hotel in Manchester.

It is black tie and takes place on the...' and on it went. She looked at the next page. 'Please confirm if you: 'Sophie (& Marcus)' will be attending or if you would like to prepare a video that can be played in the event that you are awarded the prize.' Then there was the usual admin details about any dietary requirements, etc. It spoke of Sophie's state of mind that it was a good ten minutes before she violently stood up, her chair flying backwards.

'What do they mean Sophie & Marcus? It's not a Sophie & Marcus's vlog series. It's mine. I did all the hard work, all the research, all the hours.' She straightened her chair. 'How the hell can this be? He's only been in one or two.'

She opened up her spreadsheet that detailed all her videos and live feeds and began to count them. Expecting the number to be no higher than three she was quite surprised to discover that over the last month he had appeared, in some way or other, in over half. No wonder they thought it was a collaboration.

Sophie began chewing her lip as she thought it through. There must have been some kind of mistake, they must be inviting Marcus as a joke. Maybe they just assumed he would be the plus one. That would seem like a fair, if not a possibly incorrect, assumption. She had a look at the paperwork to see if there was a number she could call to set them straight and let them know, in a nice way, that the nomination should be for herself and that Marcus wasn't really supposed to be a part of it, and if it was just that they had assumed he was her plus one, well then they really shouldn't assume anything. She was firing bits of paper all over when she heard the door.

'Who the hell...' Clutching her dressing gown tighter she made her way slowly to the front door, still fuming at the audacity of the awards people to assume she was officially collaborating with Marcus.

She opened it and shook her head. Speak of the devil. 'What are you doing here? Shouldn't you be at the hospital? How's your dad?' She felt her face get hot as she was embarrassed anew at running out last night.

'He's had his surgery. He's come round so I've been home to get showered and dressed. I thought that I would come in and see you before going back in. How are you, are you OK?'

Sophie coughed. 'Yes I am fine, I'm glad your dad's all right.' She was desperately trying to keep it civil but her insides were squirming and she had a bad taste in her mouth from the awards invite.

'About last night—' They both spoke at the same time.

'Sorry, what were you going to say?' Sophie asked.

'I'm sorry about last night. I know it was a lot of pressure to put on you, but I am really glad you were there. I know that you probably had work or something.'

'Wait, aren't you upset that I ran off?'

'What do you mean ran off? Bailey just said that you had to get going. I was a little surprised to see that you had gone but you had waited with my family for ages. I probably would've suggested you leave then anyway. I don't understand.'

How the hell did he not get it? Sophie threw her arms down.

'How can you be so reasonable? I legged it out of there as fast as I could. Don't you want to know why?'

Marcus's brow furrowed and his arms folded across his chest. 'Sure, why?'

'Because that's where a partner or wife should be, not some girl that you are sleeping with when she has the time to let you. We're not that serious. And while we're on the subject, I don't want you taking over in my work life as well. I feel like you are everywhere at the moment. You're everywhere I look, I can't get a break. There's no room. It's too much.'

When she had finished her little speech, Sophie watched as Marcus's eyes changed in front of her. He was frowning until she finished, then quickly his face just went blank. Her stomach was churning, originally with anger but now with something she couldn't find a name for. She hadn't meant to say all of that, it just poured out. Maybe Mya was right, she certainly sounded overwhelmed at this point. She had to look back up at him, he still hadn't said anything.

'OK,' Marcus said, his face still blank.

'What do you mean OK?'

'OK, fine. If I am too much in your life, then I can make that change really easy. See you around.' She watched as he started to walk away. 'And don't worry, I already know how to get over you, so I should be able to bounce back really quick.'

He spun around and walked back to his van. Sophie closed the front door and slowly made her way back to her computer, hoping that her heart rate might start to slow down. As she sat at the table she reflected on what had just happened. That didn't help, she felt even worse now. She sank back into her deflated little bubble. If she wasn't bad enough for leaving the hospital when she did, she was a monster now. What kind of a person breaks up with someone like that?

'I shouldn't have had to break up with him, it was supposed to be a fling and that's the whole point.' Trying but failing to cling to the anger that had propelled her not seconds before, she looked down to see the awards invitation shining up at her. She threw it all on the floor and dropped her head between her knees. She felt sick and was fairly certain she was about to throw up. She took some deep breaths but nothing helped, her stomach hurting as it turned at a million miles per hour. She kept playing back the conversation over and over, feeling as though it had happened to someone else, that she had been someone else. She slowly raised her head and looked at all the work she had scheduled for today. Making an executive decision she decided that she wouldn't be in a fit state to work right now. She slowly stood up and looked down. Good, she was in her pjs and dressing gown already. In that case, she was definitely going back to bed.

A few hours had passed, Sophie wasn't entirely sure how long. She'd dozed, tried to watch Netflix but nothing was really holding her attention. Her brain was in a whirl unable to stay on any one train of thought. There was a knock on her bedroom door and Mya's head poked in. 'So Polly has texted me. Apparently you broke it off with Marcus. Want to talk about it?'

'Are you going to have another go at me?'

'That depends. Why did you break it off?'

'Because it was supposed to be a fling. Not a great romance.'

'Sophie, if you use the phrase, "I don't have time" then, yes, I probably will have another go at you.'

Sophie didn't say anything for a little while. 'I got nominated for a social media award.'

'Wow that's amazing news, but what does that have to do with Marcus?'

'Marcus was nominated too or he was automatically invited, I'm not sure which. It was for Sophie & Marcus.'

'I see.'

'Do you, because I am having trouble getting my head around it.'

'I'm going to close this door and go downstairs now,' Mya said, her caring tone disappearing.

'Why?'

'Because I am likely to have another go at you.'

With that Mya closed the door and Sophie just groaned, before pulling the duvet cover back over her head.

Chapter Thirty

Marcus stared at the new app on his iPad, and studied the graphics clearly displaying where all of the features in this new garden were going. His fingers moving confidently around the screen, looking at his virtual plans from all angles. Glad to be busy. Glad to keep his mind focused.

'Hey, boss, I bought you a drink. How are you? How's Mr B doing?' Marcus looked up as Bailey walked through the garden holding two coffee cups.

'Wow, this is a surprise you never bring me coffee. I should tell my dad to have a heart attack more often.'

'That's not funny.' But they were both laughing.

'He's doing really well. He's grumpy and argumentative, so he should be home tomorrow. They've changed his medication and just want to make sure that he is settled on them, then he will be back to bothering Mum in no time.'

'Listen, pal, I need to have a serious conversation with you. Can you spare five minutes?' Bailey asked perching on the wall and nodding at Marcus to do the same.

'You? Serious? I'm worried now, but sure.'

Marcus studied Bailey's face trying to get a clue as to what was coming. Whatever it was, it was definitely important. Bailey took a drink and Marcus took pity on him.

'Look, does this have something to do with your disappearing? Because, frankly, I really need to talk to you about it, but I keep putting it off. What are you up to, Bailey? Are you in trouble?'

'God, no. But yes it is about the disappearing. So... I love working for you, man, I love being a gardener. I have great ideas of my own that maybe one day I could throw at you but for now, well, let's put it this way, how many requests for quotes have you had this week?'

'I've had five. I don't know what I'm going to do. I want the business to be a success but at this rate we're going to have to turn work away, not to mention the pressure I am getting from my dad about making sure to look after his loyal customers. I really have to figure this out.'

'I already have done.'

'What do you mean?'

Bailey took a deep breath before he continued, 'I've been looking after your regular clients. It's where I've been disappearing off to. You spoke to me about the work plan for Sophie's garden. I saw the days where you were able to manage without me, and I made sure to add your regular customers into my work pattern. I have the invoices and payment details in the van before you think I was trying to rob you or anything. I want to be more than a labourer. I want to be a partner. This business is going to be huge. If you'd have me I could really help. I've really buckled down this last couple of months, I've been dedicated and if you're not sure you could go and see the work I've done. I'm guessing you've not received any complaints so I can't be that bad, right?'

Marcus was stunned, and took a sip of his coffee as he processed everything he had just heard. He had noticed a difference in Bailey, but it had been masked with his concern over what Bailey had been up to. Marcus had no idea that Bailey had been working so damn hard.

'Really? You've been looking after the old clients?'

'Look.' Bailey bit his lip. 'Cards on the table. I'm getting really pissed off at people telling me I'm not serious. I know I deserve it; I've pulled some crazy stunts over the years. People think I'm a player, and I just rock up but that's not me any more. I guess I've changed or something, but that's not me.'

Marcus couldn't help but wonder what had led to this drastic change. Now that he thought about it the flat had been properly kitted out and tidy, and he realised that Bailey had dropped the dating and bar pick-ups, plus he'd been working hard. Maybe there was a girl? Marcus glanced down at his iPad, the details of all his work, all the quotes still to do. Holding in his hands the signs of his own transformation.

'Sure,' Marcus said.

'Sure, what?'

'Bailey. You've certainly been different, I just hadn't noticed it until you pointed it out. And if you've done what you say you've done with the old clients, then I am forever in your debt. Two heads are better than one. We can both manage and have labourers work for both of us. I reckon we can make it work. You more than deserve to be a partner. Let's do it.'

'Are you— I mean, don't you want to check that your customers are happy?'

'No, man, I trust you. Just tell me next time! This is going to be so good, I can tell. Bowman and Johnson are ready to take the gardening world by storm.' Marcus had a huge grin on his face as he slapped his best mate's arm.

'Well, we will be once we have all the branding, marketing and contracts in place.'

'My God you really are serious,' Marcus said.

Bailey shrugged. 'Yep.'

'In that case, cheers.'

'Cheers, pal. I won't make you regret this.' Bailey was blushing a little and Marcus felt himself relax. Not realising how worried he had been about accommodating it all.

'So just to check, you haven't been sleeping with the clients then, have you?'

'Well, Mrs Isherwood on Bluebell Drive keeps giving me the eye and suggesting it's too hot for me to work with my T-shirt on, but so far I have managed to keep away.'

'Glad to see that serious you still has a sense of humour.'

'Well, come on it's not a complete personality transplant.' Bailey grinned, and Marcus was pleased to see the devilish look back in his best mate's eye, and hoped he'd be just as happy as that again soon, once his heart had mended again.

Chapter Thirty-One

'Are you sure?' Sophie asked, chewing on her finger, the other hand holding her phone out on speaker for everyone to hear.

'Absolutely. I've sent you over all the details. Check your emails.'

'OK, thank you again, I owe you.'

'No problem.'

'Bye.' Sophie hung up the phone and put it back on the coffee table in Paige's front room.

'So?' Polly asked eagerly, the tuxedo-marked kitten nudging her hand for more strokes.

'The details are in my inbox.' Sophie wasn't sure how she felt. What was she going to do with the information? How would she explain to the police where she got the information from anyway? She couldn't think straight, but then what else was new?

'OK, well fire it up, let's see what we're dealing with,' Mya said, her nostrils flaring in anger, the little black kitten playing with her Mulberry handbag as usual, trying to get inside.

'Come on, Sophie,' Paige said, gently nudging her hand. 'Take a look while I open the wine and we can come up with a plan of attack. We need to know what we're dealing with.'

'What if it's just some random troll sitting in the middle of who knows where?' Mya asked.

'Then we know not to worry. Come on, Soph, or do you want me to do it?' Paige reached out her hand and Sophie felt herself pass her phone over, as if it was happening to someone else.

Paige pressed the phone and got to the bit she was looking for. Sophie scratched the ears of the kitten next to her. Looking down she realised how big they'd gotten over the last few weeks. Their purrs and meows louder and more confident. Paige's hood was now being forcibly lowered with the weight of the black kitten, who was far too used to being carried. Sophie smiled to herself. Paige was a terrible foster mum. Sophie just knew Paige would end up keeping that one, if not all of them.

'OK, so who the hell is Clara Devonshire?'

'What!' Polly straightened and the poor kitten jumped a little. 'Oops, sorry, little one. Paige are you serious?'

'Do you know her?' Mya asked.

'Sophie and I both know her,' Polly cried out.

Sophie felt all eyes turn her way, her own brain sluggish like poor Wi-Fi. She did know that name but where from?

'I know a Clara Baxter, but not Devonshire.'

'It's the same person. Devonshire is her married, or should I say divorced name.' Polly was practically bouncing with rage.

'Wait, do you mean Clara? Clara from school Clara?' Sophie asked her brain suddenly rebooting and coming to life. She snatched the phone back from Paige and began typing furiously. 'I think I have an address. But let me make sure, hang on.' She pressed call and pushed the phone to her ear.

'Mum, hi, sorry really quick. I've arranged to meet up with Debbie's daughter Clara, only I'm a little early. Have you got her address so I can swing by and pick her up...? Oh she's back at her mum's again, is she...? Well, that's just too bad... Yes these things do happen... Yes divorce is very common these days. OK, Mum I have to go, but I'll call you later, OK?... Yes, I'll let you know how we get on... You're right, I'm sure we'll have a lovely catch up. Bye.' Sophie nodded, her brain spinning. 'I have an address. What should we do next?'

'You've got an address. Right, that's it. Come on. I'm going to give her a piece of my mind, and she'll be lucky if that's all I give her. Hold my kitten.' Mya passed the kitten to Paige as she quickly stood up, her movements jerky as she gathered her things and Paige's car keys. 'Come on, let's go. We'll take Paige's car. What are you all waiting for?' Mya was not messing around as she tapped her foot impatiently as everyone else gathered up the kittens making sure that they were safe, until finally they were ready. Mya led the way as all four of them marched out of Paige's apartment.

'OK so what now?' Polly asked leaning forward in the back seat.

Sophie sighed, that was the question wasn't it. 'I'm going to go in and talk to her. You guys are going to wait here.'

'What! That's not fair,' Mya cried out.

'Calm yourself down, Uma Thurman. It's Sophie's call,' Paige explained.

'I'm going in. I'll call you if I need you, OK?' Sophie unclipped her seat belt and opened the car door, bracing herself with every step as she got closer and closer to the front door. Braced she might have been, but she didn't have the first clue how she was actually going to deal with the situation with Clara. Sophie reached forward to press the doorbell her hand surprisingly steady.

After a moment the door opened and Sophie watched as Clara's face went from neutral, to worried, until it settled into petulant. With that one expression Sophie was reminded of how this girl had been nothing but a cow to Sophie and Polly in school.

'What do you want?' Clara asked, giving Sophie a quick up and down look. Sophie returned the gesture, taking in what she could. For starters, Clara, despite all her posturing, looked a little broken to Sophie. A little frayed around the edges. Maybe it was something she recognised in herself. Moving back home after the break-up of a marriage must be difficult, although Sophie didn't presume to know the

226

circumstances. What Sophie did know was that this was absolutely a keyboard warrior, a virtual bully and nothing more.

'You know precisely why I am here. I have all the evidence of what you have been doing to me and about me online. I have the proof that it is you. Not only that, but I have enough evidence to hand over to the police. However, I thought I would do the decent thing and tell you to your face. Stop it now, or face the consequences.'

'I don't know what you're—'

Sophie took a step closer and Clara shrunk backwards, before she could stop herself.

'I don't know why you and I have never got on. I don't know why you're wasting your time trolling my account, but whatever reason you had, it ends today. Are we clear?'

'Or what? You'll give my details over to the police? And what exactly are they going to do?' Clara was finding strength in her words and began standing straighter, slowly inching her way towards Sophie, her confidence growing with every passing second.

Sophie stood her ground. 'I could add an "or else" here if you prefer?'

'Oh, please, what can you do to me. You're pathetic.'

Sophie smiled warmly. 'I warned you. Debbie! Mrs Baxter, are you there?' Sophie called out sweetly as she smiled at Clara.

'What are you doing?' Clara spat out.

'I'm doing that age-old thing. I'm telling your mum.'

'Oh my God, you're snitching on me?'

'Yeah she might even ground you and take your Wi-Fi away. Or she might see the severity of it and insist that we all go down to the police station. Alternatively you can give me your word that you'll pack it in and we can all play nice?'

'Oh my Lord, Sophie, is that you? I can't believe we have an actual celebrity on our doorstep and you haven't even invited her in. Sophie you look just as gorgeous as you do in your videos.'

'Oh, Mrs Baxter, you're so sweet. I'll be sure to give you a mention in my next one.'

'It's Debbie to you, dear and oh my God, would you? That would be incredible. What brings you here?'

Sophie looked back at Clara. The two of them locked in a stare off.

'Well actually, Mrs B—' Sophie began.

'She came to see me, Mum. She was just in the area and knew I was here and wanted to say hi.'

'That's right, but I do have to dash now. I'm sorry I couldn't stay longer, maybe next time?' Sophie looked pointedly at Clara who nodded once.

Message received.

Sophie ran back to the car. That was one problem in her life solved. If only the others were so easily handled. The immediate one being who to take to the awards ceremony now that she had pushed Marcus from her life completely.

Chapter Thirty-Two

'He might not do it,' whispered Polly to Mya.

'Yeah, and who could blame him. Let's just hope three is the magic number. Just make sure that you are in position. If this doesn't do it, then it really is game over. On the plus side if this does work then they will have their happily ever after.'

'I didn't take you as the type to believe in happily ever after.' Polly looked shocked.

'You'd normally be right, but frankly she's doing my head in. If this doesn't work, then nothing will,' Mya grimaced 'and she'll be a real pain in the arse then.'

'Shh, she's coming back.' Polly nudged Mya, and the pair of them tried to look innocent. They failed.

'What are you guys whispering about?'

'Nothing important. We just didn't want to distract you when you were doing your make-up for the big night.' Mya's eyes were wide open with over-exaggerated trustfulness. Sophie looked at them suspiciously, clearly not buying it for a second.

'Well, whatever you're up to it's going to have to wait. Right, come on then, Polly, we need to do a quick Facebook Live before we go. Come here, let me look at you.' She picked up her powder brush and gently brushed over Polly's face and tweaked her hair. 'There. You look amazing.'

'You shouldn't be worried about me, I'm not the one picking up the award.'

'I won't be either, it's just nice to be nominated. Right, sit here next to me.'

'It's not going to turn into one of your famous sex tapes, is it? Isn't that how the last one started?'

Mya and Polly were doubled over laughing. Sophie joined in but it was all show. She was faking. If she was honest that was all she had been doing for the last few weeks. Smiling for the camera, smiling for the customers at the bar, smiling at her friends. She was putting on a show twenty-four seven and she was exhausted and, if she was honest, she was scared. It was too easy to put on a front, the mask too easy to slip on, as easy as applying make-up. She was scared that she had broken in some way and wondered when she would next have any real feelings. Hopefully the award ceremony tonight would sort it out. If she didn't get excited about reaching a huge milestone in her career then what exactly would do it?

Getting back to business, Sophie asked, 'OK, are you ready?'

Polly nodded. 'I've not done one of these before.'

'You'll be fine it's easy, and it will have to be quick because the limo will be here in ten minutes. OK here goes.' Sophie reached forward to press the button to get it started.

'Hi, everyone, it's Sophie here and I am with my gorgeous friend Polly who is accompanying me to the awards tonight.' Sophie stopped to take a breath and a quick glance at the comments, everyone was already asking the question that she was hoping she would be able to avoid, 'Where's Marcus? Why aren't you taking Marcus?'

'Let me get closer to the camera. I asked you to choose my "look" for the evening and this is the one that got the most votes in all its unfiltered glory on me. Polly is sporting the "look" that got the second most votes. Polly, do you want to show them?'

'Hi, everyone, look how wonderful Sophie is, hasn't she done a great job? I'm sure that you will all join me in wishing Sophie good luck for tonight. I'm going to try and take over her phone, and do some more live videos at the actual event.'

Sophie smiled, or as close to one as she was able to fake. 'That's if we don't get too carried away on the free wine. So stay tuned, you'll either get live videos of the awards event or end up with two drunk ladies with Facebook Live regrets in the morning.'

Sophie looked at her image on screen and saw that her eyes were giving her away. No sparkle, no shine, even with all the best make-up on her face. The eyes were really the giveaway. Hopefully, she would be the only one that would notice. Mya had magic'd up some Prosecco and she took a glass. She waved it at the camera. 'See you soon, wish me luck. Love you lots. Bye.' Sophie blew a kiss took a drink and then clicked the button to end her live video.

There was a polite knock on the front door. Mya squealed. 'That will be the limo, you guys are going to love it.'

Polly stopped. 'When were you last in a limo?'

Mya smiled and winked. 'What if I told you I am in them all the time for work?'

'When will you tell us what you do?' Polly moaned.

'Never! Go on you two have fun. Good luck. Keep me posted.' Mya was practically shoving them outside. Sophie could only stare at the limo as she went out of the door. She was trying so hard to take it all in. This was what she had dreamed of, this level of success. Only it wasn't sinking in, she was going through the motions and she was numb.

Polly grabbed her hand. 'Come on, Sophie, this is going to be amazing.' They got into the limo with their drinks still in hand. Sophie couldn't tell if Polly was nervous or if she knew Sophie needed an anchor but she glanced down, grateful that Polly never let go of her hand.

Walking through the grand hotel they were led towards the banquet hall that had been set up especially for the awards that were being live streamed on the sponsors' websites. Sophie mulled over the publicity implications for her work. Just her name being mentioned as a nominee was going to be enough to catapult her career enough that maybe she could give up bartending. She was shown to a table with other social media presenters. Some of them she knew, some of them she subscribed to. She was a little star-struck and suddenly felt that maybe she didn't belong here at all. Polly kept pointing out the people that she knew.

'Sophie, look isn't that Sven from Sven and Steve? Over there that's the woman from *Coronation Street*, isn't it?' And on she went. Sophie looked around at all of the opulence. It was lush and dark velvet covered every possible surface. The lights were all candle and fairy lights with cleverly hidden spotlights. Under some of the spotlights were exotic flower arrangements that must have been three feet tall, and they added a burst of tropical colour. The tables were all circular and there was a menu and a goody bag in front of each seat. It was a lot to take in. At the front was a huge stage with a podium and a massive screen at the back that wouldn't have been out of place at the cinema. It was currently advertising the event sponsors as people took their seats waiting for the dinner and award ceremony to begin.

Polly squeezed her arm and whispered excitedly, 'Ohhh a goody bag. I wonder if it's like the Oscars. Do you reckon they'll all have free iPads in them?'

Sophie smiled at her dear friend's eagerness, wishing that it would rub off on her.

'Thank you for coming, Polly. I really appreciate it.'

'That's OK. This is incredible. I really feel like we're at the Oscars.' They sat down and got another glass of fizz. 'Let's take a picture and send it to Mya.'

Sophie smiled as Polly snapped a couple of selfies, then they settled down to enjoy the most delicious dinner. It was as Sophie was taking a last spoonful of dessert that her phone went off.

'Why the hell is my mum FaceTiming right now?'

Polly grinned. 'You have to answer it, she has a surprise for you.'

Sophie looked puzzled but quickly clicked 'Accept'

and answered her phone. 'Mum, I'm at the Social Media Awards!' Honestly, she was a little upset that her mum hadn't remembered what tonight meant to her.

'I know, sweetheart. Look.' Suddenly the camera moved around and Sophie realised that she was at Paige's bar. Then the camera turned back round to where Mum, Paige and Mya stood together with Pornstar Martini's in their hands. In the background she could see her Dad chatting with some of the regulars.

Holding Polly's hand Sophie grinned into the phone. She couldn't quite believe it. She studied the scene on her phone, her joy short-lived. Bailey and Marcus weren't there. She hadn't seen or heard from Marcus since that morning on her doorstep after his dad's heart attack. The morning that she wished had never happened. It was painful to compare how she felt at this moment, against how she felt before she had 'made it'.

Her eyes filled with tears at the thought that he was not around to celebrate this big night for her – a night, she had finally admitted to herself, that he had been a big part of making possible.

'We've got the awards ready to stream, they're going to be projected onto the screen here at the bar and all of your friends and family are here ready to cheer you on! Come on everybody.'

Suddenly the whole place erupted in cheerful shouts of, 'GOOD LUCK, SOPHIE!'

'Oh my God, you guys. When did you plan this and, Mum, no offence but how did you manage to keep this a secret?'

'Paige, Mya and Polly did all the hard work, I just avoided you a little for the last few days, so as to not let the cat out of the bag. Speaking of cats out of bags, Paige has just filled me in all about the troll. I cannot believe that Clara would be so horrible. You just let me know if she does it again, and I'll get right on to Debbie.'

'Mum, we're not ten any more.'

'I know that, sweetheart, but... oh my, did the lights just dim? OK, we'd better go. Whatever happens, well done, darling. I'm so proud of you and I love you so much.'

'And me!' Paige and Mya shouted.

'Good luck, sweetheart. Go knock their socks off.'

'Thanks, Mum, love you.'

Sophie put her phone down her eyes wet as she looked at Polly. Polly was grinning and clapping her hands. 'Are you surprised?'

'Are you kidding? I had no idea. How did you sort that out?'

'It was your mum's idea. She messaged me, Mya and Paige and there we are.'

'Yeah... I didn't see Marcus there though. Or Bailey.'

'No, I think they said something about working.'

Sophie tried not to feel deflated, but it was hard. Instead, she recalled what she had just seen, all her friends and family at the bar cheering her on. It meant so much, the support and well wishes taking second place to the knowledge that everyone knew the work she had put into it all. She grabbed a tissue and dabbed at her eyes. Polly lent over her chair and gave her a small hug.

The lights dimmed a couple more times. 'Ohhh it must be about to start. When's your award?'

'Near the end, I think? I'm pretty sure there's an interval.'

Polly just nodded. Sure enough, a celebrity from one of the reality TV shows came to the stage and introduced themselves and ran through the plan for the evening. Sophie tried to listen, she just kept zoning out, looking absently at the twinkling lights and sipping her drink. Smiling and laughing and clapping as appropriate. The first few awards were very specialist, and Sophie hated to admit it but her mind was somewhere else entirely. It wasn't that she wanted to get to her own nomination, more that in her current state it was the same thing: names, clips, winner, speech, applaud, repeat. She looked around at the lights and the tables and was reminded of the time Marcus took her to the garden centre. That's not to say the garden centre looked as done up as the Banquet Hall but the way the lights moved around, and the smell of the flowers. She felt a tear escape and try to make its way down her cheek. She brushed it away quickly and whispered to Polly, 'I just need to nip to the bathroom before the intermission. I won't be a minute.'

'OK, if they pass round more wine I'll grab you some.'

'Sure, thanks, Pol, back in a minute.'

Sophie walked to the bathroom careful to avoid her heels catching on the small train of her dress as she navigated around the tables. Finally making it to an open area she dashed towards the toilets and ran straight to the cubicle. She put the seat down and sat down, taking some breaths to try and compose herself. It was no use, the tears silently fell down her face. This was what she wanted, what she had always wanted, what she had given up so much for. She would ask herself why it wasn't enough, but her friends had been far from subtle. She knew it, and finally recognised that the gap wasn't her work, it was her partner in crime. It was the man that made her chuckle, made her mad, made her scream and at this moment was making her cry. It wasn't his fault, not even a little. This was all her fault. She had driven him away twice, why in hell would he come back a third time? He wouldn't. Why would he?

The tears fell a little faster with that realisation. Suddenly she heard someone enter the bathroom and remembered where she was. Taking some deep breaths and getting some toilet paper to try and do some damage limitation to her skin she was thankful to the gods that the event planners had made the banquet hall as dark as they had. She came out of the cubicle and spent a good five minutes trying to make it look like her heart hadn't broken, or at least to make it look like she hadn't spent the last five minutes crying. There was only so much she could do, but hopefully her face would be less blotchy by the time her nomination was announced.

Opening the door once again she waited a moment letting her eyes adjust. Carefully making her way over to Polly she wondered about whether or not to let on about her revelation. It was too late, all of her friends had warned her over and over, knowing her better than she knew herself. Polly was having a good night, she didn't want to ruin it. Taking her seat, she saw that Polly was happily flirting with the guy next to her, drinking the free fizz as if it was, well, free. Good on her. Sophie would've joined her if she didn't already feel sick to her stomach, instead she went through the motions clapping as each award was handed out.

'OK, ladies and gentlemen we are halfway through, so we're going to have a break in a minute. Give you all a chance to stretch your legs before we announce some more winners. But first, we are going to show you a quick overview of the presenters up for the Rising Star Award.'

Sophie's eyes widened and her heart raced, she hadn't known they were doing this. Polly squealed and grabbed her arm, cutting off the blood. The first one-minute clip was for Patrick Handley, he was a make-up artist from Australia. His work was flawless and he used the most exquisite filters, everything always looked so soft and romantic, he was one of her favourites. She applauded when the clip finished. In her opinion, Patrick was likely to win it, if not him then, yes, Gina Del Savio. Again she watched in wonder. Gina's work was based on her years of theatre make-up. It wasn't to Sophie's taste but it was unquestionably fascinating to watch. Gina had real talent.

Suddenly she saw her own face, Sophie Timney written across the bottom of the screen. Polly screamed and more than a few people turned around to stare. Sophie watched in wonder as her face – which frankly had never been bigger given that it was cinema screen sized – appeared and she saw the way her eyes sparkled, they hadn't done that lately. They had chosen a few clips, most of them with Marcus, or to her trained eye, the clips where she remembered Marcus was in the background making a brew, or doing the garden and just generally being by her side in some way or other. She could see clearly now that it was shown to her so vividly, the love that shone out of her eyes and that she had crushed out of his. Butterflies suddenly escaped and she felt jittery. Love. She loved him. She absolutely loved him. What the hell had she done? What on earth could she do now? She had kicked him out twice. She looked at Polly knowing her eyes were filled with desperation. Polly looked at her with expectation, an eyebrow raised.

'Polly, I—'

'Say it, Sophie. Say it.'

'I love Marcus.'

'Finally!'

'What the hell do I do now? How can I tell him? What if he doesn't want me? I think that's safe to assume.' Sophie shot up. 'I have to go and see him right now.'

'What about the award?'

Sophie shrugged, before gathering her bag and taking off.

Chapter Thirty-Three

Polly waited for just a second as Sophie jumped up from her chair and ran out of the hall. Then she grabbed her phone and sent a text.

Hope he's in position as she's on her way.

Then making a rash decision she picked up Sophie's phone – which she had left on the table in her haste to leave – and started a Facebook Live.

There were people milling around, the intermission well underway, meaning that it was quiet at their table. She opened up Facebook and facing the camera, pressed to go live.

'Ladies and gentlemen, I need to let you in on a secret. Sophie and Marcus had split up, but wait, before you disappear, yes, I can confirm that they were together off-screen as it were but through nobody's fault, it didn't work out. OK let me be even more honest, Sophie messed it up big time. She's been a mess ever since. You probably wouldn't have noticed because it's easy to hide away the uglier side of life on social media and just show you the pretty filtered elements. Anyway, the reason I have hijacked her Facebook Live is because one day she is going to look back at this moment, as the greatest moment of her life. God I hope so. Anyway we were halfway through the awards ceremony when Sophie had a revelation that Marcus was more important than any award. Right! So here we are in a love story. She kicked him to the kerb and now she's determined to win him back. She's making her way out of the venue. Let's go and see what's going to happen next. Stay with me a minute, guys.'

Polly got up and continued commentating into the phone as she dashed towards the exit. 'You see, Sophie is truly an awesome lady and she is a very talented make-up artist, but sometimes her friends know her better than she knows herself.'

Polly burst through the doors and when she got outside she stopped in her tracks, but quickly changed the camera focus so that it was recording what was happening in front of her. Sophie was stood still like a statue, she wasn't going anywhere, and she wasn't going anywhere because Marcus was stood there in a stunning navy blue suit. Yes, he was her brother, but even Polly had to admit that he cleaned up well. Polly moved to the side keeping the camera on the both of them. It was quiet on the street everyone else having stayed inside.

Marcus coughed. 'I really don't know why I am here. Joseph said that they had to change the date for the wedding anniversary party and Bailey just dropped me off and told me to wait for him. I guess I've been set up.' Marcus muttered something about seriousness at that point. Taking a deep breath he said, 'Did you win your award at least?'

Polly grinned, glad that Bailey had spoken to Joseph, it had been a huge gamble, but she was glad that Bailey had managed to get him here. Polly felt a little bad to be spying on this private moment with, a quick glance at the phone, hundreds of other people, but she had to believe it would all work out, and that she would be forgiven tomorrow. She looked again at the phone, made sure that the camera was covering what it needed to – holy shit a lot of people were watching this. Polly's hand shook slightly. Please God, let this work. She focused back on Sophie who still hadn't said anything.

Marcus was starting to look annoyed. 'I thought Bailey had turned over a new leaf, I guess I was wrong. See you.' Marcus put his hand up and turned on his heel.

Polly quietly gasped and whispered, 'Come on, Sophie. Make it right, you can do it.' Sophie couldn't see it but the comments were going through the roof.

Suddenly Sophie leapt forward and grabbed Marcus's arm.

She looked like she was in pain, the doubt and the fear clear to see. Marcus looked at her grudgingly.

'I... erm, I don't know if I've won. I don't think they've announced it yet.'

'Why are you out here then?'

'I... I... I realised that I don't care about the award.'

'How could you not care about the award? This is the sign that you're on your way. What could be more important?'

'You.' Sophie dropped her hold on Marcus's arm and looked down at her hands. 'You're more important. I'm sorry that it's taken so long for me to realise. I know that I've messed everything up. I know that I've hurt you twice now, both times without really meaning too, but that's no excuse. I don't know if you will ever be able to but I am hoping that one day you might forgive me. I kept thinking about all the what-if's, the opportunities I might miss in my work with you in my life. But I was wrong. I see that we work better together. I'm stronger, more confident, more daring, with you in my life. The only what-if worries I have now are what-if I've really messed this up forever. What if you'll never forgive me? What if you'll never trust me again? I want you taking over in my life and my work life. I want you everywhere I am. I want you everywhere I look. I don't want any room between us. I want you. I... I...'

'Come on, Sophie just say it already!' Polly whispered into the phone.

Sophie straightened and looked directly into Marcus's eyes. 'I love you, Marcus, and I am so sor—' before she could finish her apology Marcus had pulled her to him and kissed her, and didn't stop. The pair of them in their own little bubble of happiness, broadcast live to, Polly looked down, well, a hell of a lot of people.

Sophie pulled away slightly. 'I'm really sorry, Marcus.'

'I know,' he said, before pulling her face back towards his.

He pulled away again. 'Oh and I love you too. But listen you can't toss me aside again. If you feel like there's too much pressure then at least talk to me about it. OK?'

'Marcus I promise I will talk to you, but now that I know, now that I appreciate how wonderful you are, you're the one likely to feel pressured by me. You've seen how focused I can be.'

They kissed again. Polly squealed. Sophie and Marcus both moved, their bodies still touching as they looked over at Polly.

'What are you doing, Pol?' Marcus asked.

'Erm.' Polly just pointed at the phone.

Marcus looked at Sophie. 'Sophie the award, come on we have to see if you won.'

'I already did.' Sophie smiled.

'OK, that was too much. I want the real Sophie back.' Marcus grinned holding onto her waist as they all ran back up the stairs and raced into the banquet hall.

Chapter Thirty-Four

'Hi, everyone it's Sophie here as always—'

'Hi, everyone, I'm just making a brew.'

'And Marcus, of course. It's just a quick video today to say thank you so much for everything. I know it's not quite the morning after the night before.' She grinned. It wasn't, it was the morning after the morning after the night before, but she had been a little busy until now. Sophie smiled wider, it was unbelievable how different she felt now compared to two days ago. She marvelled at how quickly things could change. She was beyond elated.

'Thank you for your support with the awards and huge congratulations to Patrick. It was so well deserved. I will add a link to his YouTube page in the comments if you haven't checked him out already, you really should.'

Sophie genuinely wasn't upset about not winning. She was too happy with the way everything had worked out. It also didn't hurt that Polly's Facebook Live prank had pulled in the highest number of live viewers on her Facebook history to date.

Marcus pulled up the chair next to Sophie, placed the cup on the table, and dropped a kiss on her cheek. 'Here you are, love.'

'Thanks. I promise that from now on the videos will be back to their usual make-up craziness but again, I just wanted to say thank you. It's been one heck of a journey and I'm sure it will continue to be a crazy ride, but thank you for being such a huge part of it. Which reminds me, you guys, I never properly walked you through the garden, or The Prosecco Paradise as we're now calling it.' Sophie reached forward and picked up the camera that she had been recording onto. 'Come with me, guys, you have to see it, it's stunning.'

Marcus watched as Sophie gave a virtual tour of the garden, her face lit up with excitement as she explained every little detail. He supposed he should've been out there, but frankly he had that much work lined up now, he didn't need the online exposure. Eating his biscuits he watched as she spoke so animatedly about the garden, slowly making her way back into the house. 'Well, that's it. I'll do a video tomorrow about what was in my goody bag at the awards, because I know a lot of you have been asking. That's right, Karen and Chanelle, I'm talking about you. Well thank you again, guys, none of this would have happened without you, lots of love, bye.'

'Bye,' Marcus said as he waved and Sophie pressed the button to end the recording.

'So I've had another idea for another live video,' Marcus said quietly.

'Oh yeah?' Sophie asked, looking intrigued as she grabbed her mug.

'I was going to ask Polly if she thinks we should live feed our wedding.'

Sophie spat out her drink and looked up in shock at Marcus.

'Did you just propose?'

'No, not yet, but I'm giving you time to get used to the idea. Will I have to ask you three times before you say yes?'

Marcus chuckled and Sophie scowled. 'Too soon.' Besides Sophie had already thought that when the time was right, she'd be asking him.

'Thanks for the brew. Did you get the Hobnobs?'

Marcus scoffed. 'Of course. It's like you think I don't know you at all. Love you.'

'Thank you. Love you too.'

Thank You

Dear Reader,

We need Happily Ever After's now more than ever. If this book has given you even a second of light relief, then please do consider telling your friends, or doing a quick review over on an eBook retail site. The more people that get to experience the sheer delight of a good romance the better (in my opinion).

Now I know what you're thinking. What on earth happened with Polly and Bailey, well you'll have to read book two to find that out. However if you go to my website www.lucykeeling.com you *may find a scene between them that was cut from this book. * Ohhh, it's delicious.

But yes, I hear you shouting, what about Mya? Well again, you'll have to stay tuned for that, but if you think you know what her secret career is please feel free to contact me. Anybody that guesses right gets an acknowledgement in her book. So do get in touch you can find me in the usual places, Twitter: @Lucy_K_Author | Facebook:@lucykeelingbooks | Instagram: @lucy_k_author.

A big thank you too.

Thank you dear readers, you are the best and you have excellent taste.

Lucy

x

About the Author

Lucy Keeling is an author writing fun, sexy, stories with all of the happily ever afters. When she's not typing at the kitchen table, she's arranging and then re-arranging to see her friends for the occasional spot of day drinking. Lucy is currently writing the third book in a contemporary romance series, the first of which was runner-up in Choc Lit's 'Search for a Star' competition which was sponsored by *Your Cat* magazine.

Lucy lives in Greater Manchester with her family.

For more information on Lucy:
www.twitter.com/Lucy_K_Author
www.facebook.com/lucykeelingbooks/
https://www.instagram.com/lucy_k_author/

More Choc Lit

From Lucy Keeling

Just Friends

Book 2 – Friends

**Friends do nice things
for each other, right?**

That's what Polly Bowman tells
herself when she agrees to be her
friend Bailey's 'fake girlfriend'
to help him keep a promise to
his family. After all, Bailey has
always supported her through
difficult times – he even knows
about her secret singing sessions
at the local speakeasy bar.

But maintaining a fake relationship isn't easy, and when
Polly's meddling but well-meaning group of friends throw her
and Bailey together as best man and maid-of-honour for an
upcoming wedding, Polly soon realises she's going to have to
confront a few long-kept secrets head on …

Just Friends in Vegas

Book 3 – Friends

Is love always a losing game?

When Mya is with Smithy, it feels like her eyes are constantly rolling. His wheeling and dealing charisma charms everyone but her. Well, that's not strictly true – Mya is only human after all, and there's no doubt the man is hot with his suits and swagger. It's just that Smithy knows Mya's secret, and she's not sure she can trust him to keep it from their group of friends.

As they immerse themselves in the glamorous and mysterious world of 'The Suits', growing closer as a result, Smithy has to question whether his time with Mya is destined to become a case of 'what happens in Vegas stays in Vegas' …

Visit www.choc-lit.com for details.

Introducing Choc Lit

We're an independent publisher creating
a delicious selection of fiction.
Where heroes are like chocolate – irresistible!
Quality stories with a romance at the heart.

See our selection here:
www.choc-lit.com

We'd love to hear how you enjoyed *Just a Boy Friend*.
Please visit **www.choc-lit.com** and give your feedback
or leave a review where you purchased this novel.

Choc Lit novels are selected by genuine readers like yourself.
We only publish stories our Choc Lit Tasting Panel want to
see in print. Our reviews and awards speak for themselves.

Could you be a Star Selector and join our Tasting Panel?
Would you like to play a role in choosing which novels
we decide to publish? Do you enjoy reading women's
fiction? Then you could be perfect for our Tasting Panel.

Visit here for more details…
www.choc-lit.com/join-the-choc-lit-tasting-panel

Keep in touch:
Sign up for our monthly newsletter Spread for all the latest
news and offers: www.spread.choc-lit.com. Follow us
on Twitter: @ChocLituk and Facebook: Choc Lit.

Where heroes are like chocolate – irresistible!